THE TIME TRAVE'

SECRETS
OF THE
NILE

Here today, erased tomorrow

PAULENE TURNER

SECRETS OF THE NILE

PAULENE TURNER

First published 2023 by Salty Dog Press
Copyright © Paulene Turner 2023
The moral right of the author has been asserted.

ISBN: 978-0-6457308-0-7
e-book: 978-0-6457308-1-4

Salty Dog Press acknowledges the traditional owners of the country on which we live and work. We pay our respects to all Aboriginal and Torres Strait Islander Elders, past and present.

To Andy, Alex and Tash, my first readers.

Chapter 1

If you're reading this, it may mean I'm in trouble. Or that I don't exist anymore. Time travel's like that. Here today, erased tomorrow.

My name is Madison Bryant. I'm seventeen now but I'd just turned sixteen when my friend Riley Sinclair built his first time machine. This is my account of events that followed. When I'm done, I'll leave sealed copies with people I trust, instructing them to break the seal if I disappear suddenly or if my name no longer seems familiar. That way, my story might survive—even if I don't—and serve as a warning to others.

On time travel and its risks, there's a lot to say. But a couple of points are worth making up front. First, the consequences of our actions—no matter how minor or well-intentioned—can be devastating on an epic scale.

And, second, if time were a person, it would be a mugger, waiting in an alley. And you'd never see it coming.

Thinking back through all that's happened in the past fourteen months—the places I've been, the people I've met and the events that cascaded through the time continuum to bring us to a dark place—my thoughts pull up outside Crows Nest High School, one Wednesday in September. And I marvel at how the beginning of the end seemed just like any ordinary, boring school day.

I was late, as usual. As I sprinted to school that morning, the only thing on my mind was late notes—how I didn't want a second one that week and the detention that went with it—when I ran into Riley at the front gate.

He was wearing his Crows Nest High uniform—grey pants, white shirt, bottle-green tie and coat. But instead of white socks, his were the colour of a newborn chick and about as fluffy. Clearly, the boy needed rescuing. Though my margins were slim. Still, when it came to time, back then, I liked to play the odds and stretch it as far as I could—never imagining one day it might snap right back at me.

I stepped in front of my friend, looked down and shook my head. "Yellow socks? Seriously?"

"Oh!" His eyes were moon big as he regarded his feet. "I just grabbed some out of the wash. They must be my sister's."

So much for scientific powers of observation! "Quick! Hide!"

We ducked behind the pink flowering hedge as a pack of guys from our year went by. They were the alphas, not a drop of humility among them and yet so much to be humble about. If they saw Riley in these socks, he was a dead man.

Taking the back way to the Lost Property office, we lurched through the doorway as the first bell rang. *Great! Now we're officially late!* Mrs Hurley, the secretary, took her time unlocking the door to a storeroom containing two plastic bins overflowing with uniform bits. I was glad it was Riley, not me, burrowing into that mucky pile of battered green hats, suspiciously soiled blazers and manky shirts before emerging with two socks the colour of dead fish.

PAULENE TURNER

As he pulled them on, a sour scent wafted up, though he didn't seem to notice.

"I was working late last night," he said. "Guess I wasn't too focused this morning."

"Ya think?"

"I had a breakthrough."

The breakthrough, I knew, related to his project for the NSW School Science Fair. He'd won first prize the previous three years and everyone expected even bigger things from him this time. News reporters had already contacted the school to line up interviews with him. And once, I walked in on the Head of Science, Mr Johnson, rehearsing his acceptance speech. ("I'd like to think I had some part to play in the development of this extraordinary boy." *Yeah, bet you would, Johnno!*)

I'd have hated all that pressure on me. Riley didn't say much, but for the past few weeks he'd been turning up to school with unfocused eyes and wild, wild hair clueing me in to the long hours spent in the lab.

"You can't work all the time, Riley," I said. "You need to get some sleep."

"But I'm so close."

"Yeah, you were *close* this morning," I said, "to getting seen in those socks and being labelled the biggest loser in the history of school losers. It's all very well to be Mr Super Science but you have your image to think of. And mine." Since I was his closest friend.

"Sorry, Maddy," he said.

We cut through the Humanities block, zipped past the canteen and began crossing the main playground—an expanse of grey concrete with a splash of well-worn grass—when a shrill voice called from behind. "Madison! Wait up!"

I stopped, squeezed my eyes shut and gritted my teeth. By the time I turned back around, I was smiling sweetly.

"Morning, Ms Braithwaite," I said.

"Are you late for class again?" Our Year Adviser, in grey pencil skirt and crisp white blouse, did not look happy. "When I gave you that note on Monday, Maddy, you promised you'd be on time the rest of the week. I should write you up for afternoon detention. Both of you." She took out a notebook and flipped to a blank page.

"We would have been on time, Miss," I said, "except we had to do an errand for Mr Johnson."

"Is that true, Riley?"

Riley opened his mouth to speak, then froze, his eyeballs the only part of him moving as they swivelled from her to me and back again.

"Check with Mr Johnson if you don't believe us," I said, smiling-not-smiling.

She gave me the Laser Stare for several long seconds then the notepad snapped shut, like a croc's jaws. "Just be on time the rest of the week."

She walked away, high heels clip-clopping on the concrete, and we took off.

"What was that goldfish impression back there, Riley?"

"Sorry, I didn't know what to say. I'm not as good at—"

"At what?"

"At...err..."

"Lying?" I suggested.

"I was going to say improvising," said Riley.

"It wasn't really a lie. We were late because of the socks, which you only had on because you were dazed after a long night working on your project for the young scientist competition, which, if you win, will benefit Mr Johnson. So it was kind of a favour for him."

It took him a few seconds to make all the connections. "What will you do if she checks with Mr Johnson?" he said.

"That won't happen. The two of them don't get along."

"How do you know?"

"I've watched them at assembly. One time, there was a seat free next to her. Johnno walked past that, across the stage to a chair on the end. And I saw the look back he gave her."

"You worked all that out from a single encounter?"

"Well, yeah. People don't tend to make neon signs about what they're thinking. You have to do some detective work to figure it out."

"Like Sherlock Holmes?"

"Plus, I knew Johnno would go along with almost anything we said to keep you off detention so you can carry on working on the science project, for the school's glory and his own. Not necessarily in that order."

Riley shook his head, jaw loose. He was great at lots of things—science, maths, music, gymnastics—basically anything involving patterns. He read heaps, knew all sorts of facts about stuff. But he didn't do sub-text. He wasn't much good at lying either. Luckily, I could help with both those things. They were my areas of expertise.

We passed a tall girl with a super-short dress. "Hi, Riley," she said, smiling coyly.

"Hey, Riley," said another, with dark-red lipstick like a gash of blood.

He glanced their way with little recognition, though, this close to the fair, they'd have to have been see-through and shaped like a test tube to get his attention.

When a third girl swerved onto his path, I stepped forward and shouldered her aside. "Later, Olivia."

"Who made you his keeper?" she shouted.

A fair question. The answer was, I did. All the drooling over Riley was getting to me. It was better before when he was the skinny, geeky guy with a fringe that never sat right and people left us alone. However, sometime in the past nine months he'd grown taller and more muscular. I'd heard girls and a guy or two describe him as "surfer hot"—I suppose because of his white-tipped blond curls and eyes as blue as the waters of the Barrier Reef. Though, being my buddy, I didn't see him that way.

Riley had no idea what to do with all that attention. It fell to me, as his closest friend, to head off these romantic assaults so he could keep his mind on science for the benefit of all humankind (and mine—he was my go-to guy for science and maths assignments). You could say I was a bimbo bouncer and a pretty good one, too, though some were harder to deflect than others.

Like my best friend, Lauren, who had lately had the hots for him.

"Hi, guys," she said, catching up to us as we swept through the corridors. "Riley, I didn't see you in maths yesterday. I saved you a seat."

"I...err...was busy in the lab," said Riley.

"He's working on his project for the science fair," I said.

"Oh. What's the project?"

"I...err...can't say yet," said Riley.

I could see Lauren wasn't happy with that answer. But she was no quitter. "Well, if you need a break at recess, you're welcome to sit with us. I know you're busy but even scientific geniuses have to eat. Right, Maddy?"

Leave me out of this. "Right," I said.

"Thanks, I...err..." He took off at speed.

I shrugged and hared after him.

As we entered the science block, a foul stench arose from an experiment in one of the labs. *What is it with science teachers and rotten egg gas?*

"Yuck," I said, pinching my nose.

"What?" Riley was clueless as usual.

We walked along the corridor, lined with chemical elements posters, constellation charts and portraits of Albert Einstein. Outside Johnno's office was a glass case with animal parts and insects in jars. On the top shelf were the three *Young Scientist of the Year* trophies Riley had won. They'd been shifted slightly to the left of their usual spot, as if to make space for a new arrival. I think Riley noticed at the same time as me because he licked his lips like they were super-dry.

"You know if it's not working out this year, you could tell them you don't want to do it," I said.

"But I do."

"What is your project anyway?"

I didn't usually ask questions like this—Riley's techno-explanations were so boring they made me lose the will to live. But given the hype around this year's entry, it seemed rude not to ask.

"I can't say yet." His eyes slid from side to side, checking no-one could hear. "But it's something big, something amazing."

"So tell me," I said.

"Tell *you*?"

"Yeah, tell *me*. Your closest friend."

Riley pressed his lips together so hard they turned white.

"Unless you think I can't keep a secret?" I added.

"No, it's not that. It's just..." He swallowed, like he was trying to slide a rock past his larynx.

"Just, what?"

Tiny pink specks like fairy footprints appeared along his cheeks. "Well, sometimes you say things you don't mean to, in the heat of the moment and—"

"You think I've got verbal diarrhoea?!"

"No! You just get excited and...blurt things out."

"Well, excuse me for having some actual human emotions. Just because I'm not as buttoned up as you and say what I feel occasionally, you think I can't control my mouth?"

"No, no. You have perfect control. I see that now."

With a muttered farewell, he escaped through the lab door. It locked shut behind him.

CHAPTER 2

I felt a little guilty in class later, for saying Riley had no emotions. I mean, he must have had some. Not that I'd seen much evidence of it. Even when his mum and dad split up the year before, he didn't seem that bothered. If anything he was more focused on science than ever, as if the family stuff hadn't affected his concentration one bit. But though he didn't show much, I knew that deep down he probably did feel something.

And if I was mean, it was his fault for not trusting me to keep a secret. *What an insult!* The worst part was that now he wouldn't tell me what his project was, I *really* wanted to know. I hated secrets. They gave me actual physical pain. Riley had never kept anything from me before, which made it even more mysterious. And annoying.

So when Mr Johnson announced that the science and history classes were going to an exhibition of Egyptian artefacts at the Australian Museum, I knew who I wanted as my study buddy—Riley, (a) because I wanted unlimited access to badger him and learn the truth, and, (b) what he didn't know about Egyptology wasn't worth knowing. We could have the excursion worksheet filled out before we'd even got off the bus.

I was about to put my hand up and request him as my partner when Jamie Fletcher came in and I got distracted.

He had these misty green eyes, like a lake in a fantasy world, and super-long lashes. I tried not to look too hard.

"Who would you like to be partnered with?" Mr Johnson asked Jamie.

"Can I go with Hannah?"

"I'm afraid Hannah won't be joining us," said Mr Johnson. "She's had a dental emergency. Let's see. Who still needs a partner?" He ran his finger down the list. "Err...Maddy, you don't seem to be paired up. You and Jamie can go together."

"What? But what about Riley?"

"Lauren has asked to work with him."

Jamie wasn't impressed. He shot me an angry glare, like I'd done something to Hannah's teeth just to get close to him, then dumped his bag on the ground hard in protest.

Riley turned up to class just after that and Lauren rushed over to tell him the "good news" that they would be excursion partners. His face turned a shade of watermelon, his eyes trawling the room till he found mine. For a few seconds, we regarded each other with mutual distress, then he smiled tightly at Lauren.

At lunchtime, Lauren fizzed over with excitement.

"Riley is sooo gorgeous," she said. "Have you noticed the way his divine blond hair always seems wild? Like he just got out of bed."

"He probably couldn't find his comb this morning."

My friends Courtney and Chi bit their lips, trying not to laugh.

"He's so smart, too," Lauren continued. "He really is the full package, not some pretty boy with an ego the size of a continent and a brain the size of a pea. How come I never noticed him before?" She turned to study me. "Were you trying to keep him to yourself, Maddy?"

"No."

"So you really don't *like*-like him?" Lauren asked.

"We're just friends."

When I got home, she bombarded me online with questions about what she should wear to the excursion—besides her school uniform. She wanted to discuss earrings and lipstick and sent me links to hair styles and shades of leg tan.

"Will this style make my head look big?" she wrote, sending an image of a ponytail fanning out at the crown.

"No," I typed. *Only as if your brain is erupting inside your skull.*

"What about this tan? Isn't it a lovely colour?"

"Yes." *If you were born in Jamaica.*

As if that wasn't bad enough, she then started doing a quiz: *IS HE MR RIGHT?*

"What are his best points? A. His lips, B. His eyes, C. His legs, D. All of the above?" To my horror, my intelligent best friend seemed to be taking it seriously, ticking D. It wasn't long ago, we laughed at lame quizzes like these. I still did.

"I have to go," I typed. "Gran's lost her teeth and I have to help her find them."

"I have not," said Gran, who'd snuck up behind me and was reading over my shoulder. "What's she doing? A quiz? *Is He Mr Right?* Who's she got in her sights?"

"I don't know."

"Not Riley is it? You have to tell her: 'Hands off! He's mine!'"

"He isn't, Gran. We're just good friends." *How many times do I have to say it?*

Gran gave me one of her interrogatory stares, which I looked away from as fast as I could. Mum, I could fool most of the time. Dad was too easy. Gran, though, was a walking lie detector. It was as if she had a map to every muscle and twitch on the human face. It was from her years playing poker. Not a great person to have around for a teen who wanted to keep secrets occasionally. Although when it came to Riley, I had nothing to hide.

Gran had been living with us for about two years now. She used to have this fantastic apartment on the harbour, one whole wall of glass right across from the Sydney Opera House. We watched the fireworks there every New Year's Eve. All that ended one night at the High Rollers table at a Las Vegas casino just after Grandpa died. She lost the apartment on one hand of poker, the contents of her bank account on the next.

"There's good news and bad news," she told my mum in a reverse charge call.

"What's the good news?" said Mum.

"I'm not going to be gambling for the foreseeable future," she said.

"And the bad?"

"I'm not going to be gambling for the foreseeable future."

Gran had no choice but to move to Crows Nest with us. But I didn't mind. There was plenty of room and she was home most of the time, so I had company while Mum worked long hours in advertising and Dad travelled the world, designing boats for rich people.

"What's for dinner?" I said.

"Some vegetable strudel thing I bought at the supermarket. I've put it in the oven to warm," she said.

Sitting down at our kitchen bench, I watched as evening sunlight reflected on Sydney's skyline, painting the buildings gold. The lights of the city began to twinkle on, like a fairy playground, as the sweet smell of pastry perfumed the room.

Gran picked at her food but I was starving and devoured chunks of the delicious hot vegetables and crispy pastry.

"How was school today?" said Gran.

"Same as usual. Boring lessons, stupid rules, pointless homework."

"You know, a few years from now, when it's all behind you, you might see it a bit differently," said Gran. "You might even miss some things about it."

"Yeah right!" I snorted. School was interminable. Like a life sentence. And when you thought about it, people got less time for murder.

"So tell me something about your day," said Gran.

"Well, I got stuck with this guy Jamie Fletcher as my excursion partner," I said.

"What's he like?"

"He's good at sports but he thinks a lot of himself and he's not very friendly."

"If he gives you any trouble," said Gran, "give him a broomstick and tell him where to shove it."

I couldn't help grinning. This was Gran's suggestion for all tricky people and situations. She meant well, I knew.

"Who's Riley going with?" she asked.

"Oh...err...Lauren, actually."

"Uh-huh," she said. "And is that all right with you?"

"Why wouldn't it be? Riley's my friend, nothing more."

"And you're making confetti because...?"

Without realising it, I had torn my paper serviette to shreds. I scooped the pieces up quickly, tossed them in the bin, then rinsed my plate and thrust it into the dishwasher.

"I've got to go to choir. See you later."

CHAPTER 3

I jogged down the street past the terraces, semis and quaint cottage-style houses that made up the suburb of Crows Nest. Then cut across the plaza to the community centre where my choir rehearsed.

Every week I was determined not to be late but somehow I always ended up squeezing into place midway through the first song. The choir master, Mr Franklin, would nod at me in this stiff way like he was annoyed.

This evening, as I raced past the tiled fountain, I thought I might actually be on time. But then I noticed a man eating food from the bin—gross chunks of leftover burger and chips—that he washed down with slurps of soft drink from a squished can. The guy looked to be in his thirties or maybe forties—old, anyway. He had sandy blond hair, a wispy beard and wore jeans and a black T-shirt with a large clock face on it, the hands set at one minute to midnight.

I groaned inwardly. If I helped him, I'd be really late. Mr Franklin wouldn't be impressed. But could I really run past the guy?

"Hello," I said, braking suddenly.

As he turned his startling blue eyes my way, I saw he was slim, tall and tanned, though not weathered in the way of most homeless guys. And he had perfect teeth. He must have had money at some stage to be able to afford that dental care.

"My name's Madison," I said. "Would you like a real meal?"

"Sounds good."

"Then follow me."

The soup kitchen where Riley and I worked every second Tuesday was only a couple of streets away. I moved quickly, still hoping to make practice by the second song. The guy kept pace easily as we passed the boutique shops that lined the main street and turned into an alley at the rear of a church. As I opened the big wooden door to the soup kitchen, a pleasant aroma of stew wafted out. I introduced him to the supervisor on shift and went to leave.

"Thanks, Madison," said the man. "My name's Peterson."

I hurried off. At the end of the alley, for some reason I turned back to look. Peterson was standing in the doorway, smiling wryly like something was funny but only he knew what. I didn't have time to ask, though, as now I was later than usual. I legged it for the last couple of blocks and crept quietly into the hall, hoping Mr Franklin wouldn't notice.

"Good of you to join us, Maddy," he said drily when the song had finished.

Lauren was in the front row of our group, the North Shore Nightingales. The top layer of her hair was gathered into a pony tail, fanning out at the crown, like a stylish two-year-old. *What was wrong with her old hair style?*

I squeezed in next to her and got lost in the music for the next hour and a half. We went through all the songs we'd be doing at a concert at the Sydney Opera House with a bunch of other choirs. It was a really big deal.

The last song of the night was an a cappella version of *Lean On Me*. I sang lead vocals with backing vocals by Lauren and two guys from a local Catholic school. We started off slowly and transitioned to a funky jazzy number. When we got all the harmonies right, it was awesome.

"Very good tonight, girls," said Mr Franklin at the end of rehearsal. "But try to be on time in future, Maddy. We don't have long before the big night, you know."

Lauren and I walked back to my place, where her dad had arranged to pick her up later.

"I can't wait till the excursion," she said, ponytail bobbing. "Me and Riley together all day. Just the two of us."

And a whole heap of mummies and broken pottery bits in glass cases, I almost added. The rest of the class might give the old stuff on display no more than a cursory glance, but for Riley it was the main event. Alongside those chipped bits of clay, Lauren wouldn't stand a chance.

Back at my house, she could hardly wait to show me the "awesome" hairstyles she'd seen online.

"Oh, look at this one, it's to die for." She pointed to some two-toned, fussy style that would take hours to do.

"Yes, when I look at that, death does seem a good option," I said.

She frowned, then knocked me off my stool. And it was on! Pushing and shoving. We ended up giggling, on our backs on the rug, looking up at the ceiling fan as it *thunk-thunk-thunk*-ed around.

"What will you do if Jamie Fletcher asks you out after the excursion?"

"That's not going to happen."

"But if he did, would you go?"

An image of Jamie's intense eyes and shapely arms popped into my head, quickly eclipsed by a memory of the stink-eye he'd given me when we were paired up in class.

"I'm not his type," I said. "He only dates the popular girls who get him the most grunt points from his caveman mates."

"I see the way you look at him," said Lauren. "You fancy him."

"Not half as much as he fancies himself," I said. "Look, nothing's going to happen between Jamie and me. We'll fill out the excursion worksheet together, or more likely I'll do it and he'll copy my answers, then go our separate ways. End of story."

Lauren rolled onto her side and gave me a stupid grin. "It doesn't have to be. You're his study buddy. You have a chance to get close to him—a chance that, by the way, half the girls in the class would kill for."

"The half he hasn't already dumped, you mean."

The guy seemed to be out to set a new record for dating the most girls from one grade. But if he wasn't content with the popular girls with their perfect hair and skin and ability to laugh non-stop at the lamest of jokes, why would he want me? I was medium height, average brown hair, blue eyes. Sort of sporty, though not like Jamie, who was into ball sports in a big way and captain of a couple of teams. A pretty good talker, except on dates when I tended to nervous babble. Not bad at the subjects I liked—mainly English and drama. Jamie was into science and maths.

"Maybe, if you played nice?" said Lauren.

"Nice?" I said. "You mean flatter him? 'Oh Jamie, what strong arms you have! Oh Jamie, you're so smart. Do you think you'll be a rocket scientist or brain surgeon when you graduate?'"

Thunk, thunk, thunk.

Lauren grabbed a soft toy dog off my bed and combed its coat with her fingers. "I hear he's a good kisser," she trilled. *Bad girl, putting ideas in my head.* "And when it's just the two of you and he's not showing off to his mates, who knows, you might actually like him."

And then I might actually care when he dumps me.

"Pass."

"Seriously?" said Lauren. "Maddy the Brave, too scared to go on a date?"

"I've been on dates before." (A total of two totally awkward evenings, where the guys barely talked and I couldn't seem to stop.)

"But you haven't been out with a hot guy," said Lauren. "One who can hold a conversation."

"Favourite topics include sport and himself. And him playing sport."

"A guy you might actually *like*-like? I'm talking about a *real* date. Your first *real* date."

I snatched the dog back from Lauren. Coco had been my favourite soft toy in primary school. Even now, I could smell my old strawberry shampoo on her fur.

"Would I have to wear my hair like *that*?" I frowned at her 'do.

"Not exactly like this. But you might have to put a bit of effort into your appearance, yes."

I groaned and rolled over on my tummy. *Kill me now!*

"Don't worry, I can help you." She sat up, warming to the idea. "We'll find a hairstyle that suits your face shape and a really cute outfit to highlight your best features."

"My best features? What are they?"

"When I'm done, Maddy, they'll all be best. You'll hardly recognise yourself."

As if that was a good thing!

What style would Lauren choose for me, I wondered? Lost poodle? Try-hard street-walker? Library hoe? Lips blood red, eyebrows arched in permanent surprise?

"And it would help if you could be a bit less..." Lauren struggled to find the words.

"Charming?"

"Sharp-tongued and argumentative."

"I'm not argumentative."

"Yes, you are."

"No, I'm not."

She huffed. "A bit less like yourself, just for the first few dates."

"So, I have to look like someone else and act like them, too, to have a chance with Jamie?"

Lauren nodded, dead serious, as if this was just common sense.

"And if I was my usual self?"

"Some guys might still be keen," Lauren conceded. "But not the interesting ones, like Jamie. They have a *lot* of girls to choose from. You'd have to put in more effort."

To think, Lauren and I used to play pirates, sailing the seas, making our enemies walk the plank! We never wanted to be princesses, dressing up to attract some shallow prince who fancied himself more than the girls he romanced!

"Oh, well," I said, "I guess the upside is that when Jamie dumps me, I won't have to take it personally or be humiliated in front of the whole grade because it wasn't really me he was dating in the first place."

"Maybe he won't dump you," Lauren said. "Maybe you'll dump him?"

Something to look forward to, then?

"No thanks," I said.

Lauren tilted her head, unconvinced. "You're not curious about a thing called love? Whether it really exists and is out there somewhere, waiting for you?"

"I'm not looking for love, especially not with Jamie Fletcher. I've barely spoken to the guy. The only thing I want from him is to fill out the excursion worksheet quickly so we don't have to spend too long together."

"What are you scared of?"

Apart from seeing myself in the mirror after her makeover?

"Nothing."

She tilted her head, not buying it.

"All right, I am scared," I said, "that I'll be bored going out with him."

"Really? Or, are you scared you won't be? That tough-talking nothing-sticks-to-me Maddy might actually like him and have to admit she has a soft side like the rest of us."

And afterwards, marshmallow Maddy could join the ranks of the rejects, sniffling in the corridors, watching Mr Right hitting on his next love fool.

"Yeah, nah," I said. "All that smiling on first dates makes my face ache."

Lauren scoffed and shook her head. "Well, you may have to find someone else to spend Saturday nights with because after Riley and I get together on the excursion, I might be busy."

"You know going out with Riley would be super-awkward, don't you?" I said.

Lauren nodded.

"So would you go, if he asked?"

"Try stopping me."

CHAPTER 4

"Is Riley home, Mr Sinclair?" I got straight on the phone when Lauren left. "I've tried his mobile but he's not picking up."

"He's in the lab at the moment," said Riley's dad. "I've heard some strange noises coming from inside. I don't like to go in."

"By the way, do you know what his project for the science fair is?" I asked. Low, I know, trying to get the scoop from a parent, but desperate times and all.

"He's keeping that pretty hush-hush."

I thought I'd better go round and check on the boy. To make sure he was okay. Oh, and while I was there, I might just happen to catch a glimpse of the mystery project.

I pulled on my trainers, told Gran I was going for a jog and that I'd be home within the hour. "Say hi to Riley for me," she called as I shut the door. She didn't miss much.

When I got to Riley's place, I slipped down the side of the house and went straight for the red door at the back of the garage, which had been converted into a lab for him.

I knocked. "Riley, it's me!"

Silence. I knocked harder. Still nothing. I creaked the door open a bit. No sign of him. So I went inside.

The room smelt of chemicals with a hint of burnt sugar. On the far side was the daybed where he dozed while waiting for brainwaves. The quilt had dogs and cats on it from when he was little. A few books were on the floor. I picked up H.G. Wells' *The Time Machine*—one of his favourites. Another one was called *The Mysteries and Secrets of Time*.

There was a sink, covered in scorch marks, and a long lab bench with a rack of test tubes filled with various coloured liquids, a miner's light with a head-strap, and strips of torn rags. A small notebook nearby was open at a page with some scribbled words: *Close to success now. Re-entry glitches fixed. Clock override req. Need safeguard to avoid theft and misuse.*

"Misuse of what, Riley?"

At school the next day, I asked Riley where he'd been.

"Err, out in the back garden collecting herbs for an experiment," he said.

But he couldn't meet my eye and his hand kept hovering around his mouth—the classic liar's tell.

"Riley, you're lying," I said.

"No, I'm not." His face turned as red as sunset.

"You are," I said. "Where were you? Tell me now and save yourself a world of pain."

"I've got to go to the library." And he took off. Just like that. So I followed.

"I saw your notes at the lab," I told his back. "I saw what you were reading. Books on time. Your project has got something to do with time, hasn't it?"

Riley turned back, eyes wide. Then sped up. I had to jog to keep up.

"Is it something to slow down time? Turn it back altogether? The fountain of youth?" I asked. No answer.

"Is it a new kind of clock? A way to speed up the school day, to make assignment dates never arrive?" (That one got my vote.)

He sped up even more and pulled ahead at a full run so I couldn't catch him.

Diabolical!

Now I'd have to wait to find out. And waiting was NOT something I was good at!

CHAPTER 5

By the time excursion day came round, I was really sorry Riley wasn't my study buddy. But he was sitting next to Lauren, who had swept all her hair into a ponytail at the side, except a few well-crafted strands to "soften her jaw line", and I was stuck with Jamie Fletcher.

Although *stuck* wasn't exactly the right word. Like magnets of the same pole, constantly repelling, we hadn't spoken a word or even glanced each other's way since being paired up. On the bus to the museum, he was at the back, I was at the front. And we stayed well clear of each other as our class milled around the museum's entrance.

The Australian Museum was an imposing building of dark stone, but someone running it had a sense of humour. As part of its exhibition on dinosaurs, there was a T-Rex head protruding from one second-storey window and, a few windows further along, the tip of a tail.

We crossed the marble foyer beneath the giant skeleton of a sperm whale, then filed past a life-size brachiosaurus model to the entry of the *Treasures of Ancient Egypt* exhibition.

When I was younger, I had been obsessed with Egypt for a while—well, mainly with dressing up as Cleopatra. In my mind some of that old fascination still lingered for a culture full of exotic dark-haired women, artistically decorated coffins and creepy mummies. I felt a tingle of excitement as I approached the entrance, which was designed to look like an ancient tomb.

And that was when Jamie and I had our first real contact. We both stepped into the doorway at the same time, wedging shoulder to shoulder before, flamingo pink with embarrassment, I lurched through.

"After you, Madison," Jamie said with a mock bow and a cascade of jeery laughs from his not-a-brain-cell-between-them mates. I gave him a couldn't-care-less head shake in reply.

The exhibition spanned three rooms. Pottery and jewellery thousands of years old featured in the first. It was dimly lit with Egyptian art and hieroglyphs on the walls.

As I stared into the first display case, Jamie sidled up to me and grunted something about "filling out the stupid worksheet quickly" so we could each return to our own friends. Suited me. The quicker I got shot of him, the better. The problem was, though, the worksheet had questions from each room in the exhibition so we'd have to hang out together for at least one full tour.

"Sorry you got me as your partner," I said, trying to ease the tension between us and "play nice" as Lauren had suggested. His reply was a stinky scowl.

The guy was a pig, I decided. Especially, when I saw him rolling his eyes to his friends. One of them even made the L sign for "loser" with his left thumb and index finger. *A loser? For being with me?* Even so, as we looked down into the first glass case, I couldn't resist checking him out, just a bit. The light from the case gave his skin a bronze sheen and made his eyes seem luminous. He must have felt me looking—his head snapped my way. I just managed to shift my gaze in time.

The case contained several bits of broken pottery and a few clay models of Egyptian gods.

"Bor-ing," said Jamie.

"Perhaps if they bounced, you'd find them more interesting," I said. Couldn't help myself.

I waited for the standard reply: "P**s off" or something like it. But...nothing. And when I looked up, I saw the left corner of Jamie's mouth curl into a smirk. Like he was amused. That was weird.

The second case had more jewellery and a green goblet with a golden snake around the belly. I smiled.

"What's funny?" asked Jamie.

"Nothing," I said.

"Tell me. What?"

"I just think that goblet's cool, that's all," I said. "I suppose you think it's bor-ing too."

"No." He grinned. "It is kind of interesting. To think someone might've drunk out of it thousands of years ago at a party. Maybe someone like us."

Us? The word hung in the air, like perfume. Or a noxious gas. For no reason, my cheeks heated up like the rocks in Dad's barbecue. To cover up, I became all business as we answered the first questions on the sheet. I began writing a sentence and, when I struggled over a word, Jamie came up with it. This was not as hard as I thought it would be.

"This is not as hard as I thought it would be," he said, giving me a small smile.

What the—? Are we actually getting along?

"Freak alert, freak alert!" A couple of Jamie's mates held their index fingers diagonally from the top of their head, like antennae. Did they mean *me*? That *I* was a freak? But, no, they were looking at Riley, staring wide-eyed and open-mouthed into one of the cases. Beside him, Lauren leaned against the glass, catching the eye of several boys in the process. But not Riley's. He was totally focused on the pottery in the case.

When Jamie stopped laughing, or, rather, braying like a donkey, he said: "Sorry about those guys. But you have to admit, Sinclair is a freak."

"If by freak you mean incredibly smart and well-read, someone who actually thinks before he speaks, then, yes, he is one," I replied. "And I'm glad he is. Oh, and by the way, in any sport, or track event, he would totally kick your butt."

Jamie was floored by that—stuck to where he stood, as if he had superglue on his feet. I drifted away, like an ocean liner freed from its mooring, Jamie growing smaller with each step away. *Good riddance.* The guy was a jerk, one hundred per cent. Well, maybe ninety-nine. I'd complete the worksheet on my own; he could copy my answers later. Anything was better than his moronic company.

I headed over to my friends Courtney and Chi, detouring past Riley on the way. "Will you stop geeking out at the exhibits?" I said. "You're embarrassing me!"

"What? Sorry, Maddy."

The second room had statues of Egyptian gods, like Anubis, the jackal god; Horus, a human with a falcon head; and Sobek, the crocodile. Plus Isis and Osiris. They were kind of awesome. I was just beginning to relax when Chi muttered: "Don't look now, but someone's following you."

Jamie was a few steps behind me, looking intense. "You think I'm not smart," he said. "But you're wrong."

"Whatever," I replied.

"I know the story of Isis and Osiris. Would you like to hear it?"

I'd rather hear the sound of your footsteps walking away, I wanted to say. Before I could, Chi jumped in: "We'd love to hear it, Jamie!" She winked, trying to take some of the pressure off.

"Well, Isis and Osiris were brother and sister," he began pompously. "But they had another brother called Seth. He was jealous of Osiris, so he killed him and cut him into fourteen parts, which he scattered all over the land."

"I'd like to do that to my brother," said one of the girls listening. Many of my classmates drifted closer, hoping to hear a gory story.

"Anyway," continued Jamie, with a glance to check I was paying attention (I was, but I stared intently at a statue as if I wasn't), "Isis loved her brother very much, so she travelled the land and collected all the parts—all except one."

"Which one?" asked Chi.

"Guess," said Jamie, arching one eyebrow.

The girls giggled, the guys screwed up their faces.

"You mean...?" Chi winced.

"Yes. The man part," Jamie replied in this exaggerated way. A gush of laughter and groans followed. "Which, get this, was eaten by a fish with a strange-looking snout."

"Cool," said the girls.

"Ooh," said the boys.

"So Isis made a golden whatsit for Osiris and sang until he came back to life. And he became God of the Underworld."

I was impressed that Jamie Fletcher knew anything about Ancient Egypt—that he knew anything about any subject apart from sports, balls or brands of trainers. Until, in the reflection of a glass case, I spotted a mobile phone in his right hand. He was getting his info from some Ancient Egyptian website.

"Did you enjoy that story?" he asked, swaggering over to me.

"It proves one thing," I said.

"What?"

"That you can read."

I braced myself for the abuse that would surely follow but, again, there was the grin. The guy was hostile and rude when you were nice to him and friendly and interested when you weren't. *Strange.*

At that point, Mr Johnson appeared and snatched the phone out of Jamie's hand. "Okay, Fletcher," he said, "you can stop scaring your classmates now. I'll hang on to this till the end of the day."

Caught out, Jamie blushed as red as the trim on his ASICS trainers.

As I moved towards the third room, Mr Johnson caught up with me. "I don't suppose you know what this mystery project of Riley's is?"

"No. Unfortunately not."

"If you find out, would you let me know? The suspense is killing me."

"You and me both, Mr Johnson."

The third room in the exhibition was the coolest, as it contained real mummies. There were three of them in their original coffins or sarcophaguses, and they had each been given a CAT scan, which was like an X-ray only better, so the doctors could make a guess at the likely cause of death. It was a bit like being an ancient homicide detective.

The first mummy was a male, aged around thirty, a museum plaque said. The scan revealed dents on the skull and cheekbones, consistent with a violent attack.

The second case contained the skeleton of a female. It looked really small to me. Apparently, she'd been found in a tomb with a second body, more elaborately wrapped. Scientists speculated that she was a servant who'd been buried with her master to attend him in the Underworld. But was she buried before or after she died? That was the question.

"They eventually stopped the practice of burying live servants." Riley was beside me and he was alone. "Instead, they put little statues of servants called shabtis in the tomb, which they thought would spring to life to help the dead person navigate their way through the Underworld."

"How's it going with Lauren?" I asked.

"Who?" Riley was genuinely confused. "Oh yeah, fine."

"Where is she?"

"I don't know. I went to the restroom. She was there when I went in, but not when I came out."

It was unlike Lauren to let the prey out of her sight. Then I remembered the girls' restrooms had two exits.

"Did the boys' toilets have one exit? Or two?"

Riley looked confused for a moment. "One. No, wait! I did come out a completely different way, now I think about it!"

Mystery solved. Riley had escaped—whether accidentally or on purpose, it was hard to say. Should I find Lauren and tell her? *Naaah.* She'd figure it out.

We sauntered over to the third display case together. It was a girl, about nineteen, someone high born, the scientists assumed, from the elaborate wrapping and pictures on the sarcophagus. And the cause of death? I frowned at the written explanation.

"Wait. She died because of a dental abscess? Tooth problems?" I asked.

Riley nodded. "There was a lot of fine sand in Egypt. It got into everything—their homes, their food. They all had problems with their teeth."

"You mean if only she'd had toothpaste...?"

He nodded. "She might have lived a normal life."

That was a crazy thought. I hated the dentist, but I'd never thought of dental hygiene as a life-and-death thing.

Lauren turned up then, her expression pinched with irritation. When Riley turned towards her, though, it morphed into a dazzling smile.

"So, partner," she said, "what are we looking at?" She draped herself around the mummy's glass case, like models do around cars.

As the tide of students flowed in, Jamie drifted in with them.

"Not trying to ditch me, are you?" he asked.

"Perhaps you are smarter than you look?" That might have been pushing it a bit. But it didn't put him off.

"Did you know that the Ancient Egyptians thought the brain of a mummy was useless," he said. "So they threw it away. How do you think they got it out of the skull?"

"I don't know," I said.

"They hooked it out...through the nose."

I winced. "You got another phone hidden somewhere, feeding you info?"

"I have read a couple of books, you know," he said. "Sinclair's not the only one with a brain."

"You're seriously comparing your brain with Riley's?" I asked. "That's like comparing Einstein's brain with Scooby Doo's. I'm sure you're smart enough to know which one of those you'd be."

This time, there was no curled lip nor hint of amusement. The look he shot me was anger, pure and simple. *Well, he deserves it.* I didn't like the cracks his friends made about Riley. Nor the way he'd treated me when we were paired up at first.

Though half a dozen paces later, when I turned back to glare again, I was surprised to see his eyes downcast and shoulders sag. Like he was more hurt than angry. *Whatever.*

I watched Riley taking notes on the third mummy and looked down at the worksheet. There were no questions on mummy number three. So what was he doing? When I tried to peek over his shoulder, he quickly closed his notebook.

"Hi," he said, blushing. "How's it going?"

How's it going? I'd been friends with Riley a long time but he'd never asked me that before.

"Is this something to do with your science project for the fair?" I asked.

"No," he said. *Way too fast.* Then he went over to Lauren—deliberately! When all day he'd been fleeing, taking cover, avoiding her. Lauren was super-pleased, but I was suspicious.

And that made me wonder—what was Riley even doing on the excursion? He could easily have missed it to keep working on his project. Johnno would have backed that, one hundred per cent. Yet here he was, wasting half a day of potential project time and taking more notes than all the other students put together. *Why is that?*

"Riley, look! A walking mummy!" I said, pointing to the right.

As his head whipped around, I snatched the notebook from his hand and took off. I ran into the second room and hid behind a cluster of kids near the Egyptian jewellery. I only got about half a minute alone with the notebook before he found me and took it back.

"Maddy, please!"

I saw he'd scribbled: *Sand BIG problem. Toothpaste recipe to incl coating agent. Floss!!!??? Cover over prep area poss?*

It was one of those moments. An epiphany. If it was a movie, a drumbeat would have started with a choir singing in high tones and harmonies. For in that instant, I knew exactly what Riley's time-related project for the science fair was going to be.

CHAPTER 6

I didn't get a chance to speak to Riley alone for the rest of the day—Lauren was stuck to him like chewing gum on a shoe. So, after dinner that night, I told Gran I was going for a run and sprinted over to his place.

Again, he was nowhere to be seen, but there was a new addition to the mess in his lab—a large empty box with a toothpaste brand printed on it. There was also a docket from Fancy Pants Costume Rentals for *One Egyptian costume*. Interesting.

I crept through the garden, up onto the back deck of the house and pressed my face to the window. Mr Sinclair was hunched over his laptop, as usual, but there was no sign of Riley. My eyes scanned the backyard, squinting through the dark. All was still and quiet. Last time I'd visited, Riley said he had been in the herb garden behind the garage. I turned towards the dark space and, just for a second, saw a flicker of gold in the blackness. So I went over.

There was Riley, dressed like an Egyptian prince in white linen sarong with shiny gold collar, sitting on a cool motorcycle with a sidecar. The bike was a dazzling creation of polished chrome with black and bronze metal trim. It had huge bullhorn handlebars, a black leather seat and a morass of cogs and pipes that twisted back and forth like human intestines.

In the centre of the machine was a thin, black computer panel with colourful lights blinking and graphics twitching.

For a few seconds I watched him on that bike, in that outfit, with his blond, wavy hair blowing back in the breeze. He rammed his foot down hard on the pedal ignition and a high-pitched whirring began.

I leapt in front of the machine. "Stop the bike! We need to talk!"

"Get back, Maddy," he shouted. "You could get hurt!"

"I know what you're doing, Riley. At least I've got a pretty good idea!" The machine's screechy pitch hurt my ears.

"What about a deer?" Riley leaned forward to hear.

"Not a deer! I have an i-dea what you're doing? A pretty good one."

"Thank you, I hope I have a good run too."

Now I was annoyed. Could he really not hear me? Or was he playing dumb to avoid answering?

"I'm leaving now. Stand back, Maddy!"

"No, wait! We have to talk."

"Get back!"

Diabolical! I'd finally got Riley alone, the project was right here in front of me, and I was STILL not going to get any answers. I couldn't wait any longer.

So I did something I shouldn't have. I leapt into the machine's side car. Not cool, I know, but I couldn't help myself. Riley watched, mouth open, his head following my progress. I had just got into the seat when—*whoosh*—the bike flew up into the air like it had been launched from a slingshot. So high it hurt my ears and gave me instant vertigo.

"What the—?"

Then we got swept up by a gust of wind and sailed fast across the clouds. It was a bumpy, sick-making kind of ride. I don't know what I was expecting, but this wasn't it. Nor what came next.

I looked down—a long, long way down—at the city of Sydney and saw it change before my eyes. The newer apartment blocks crowding the edge of Sydney Harbour grew fuzzy at the edges, then morphed into smaller houses. The Sydney Opera House was there one minute, it went see-through, then it was gone. As were the cars on the busy Harbour Bridge, then the bridge itself. *Poof!* The city skyline seemed to quiver, then crumble mid-air and vanish, like the last firework on New Year's Eve. The houses and roads in the outlying suburbs all fizzed out until there was nothing but bush as far as I could see. Then we shot even further up.

It takes a lot to make me speechless. Even this didn't manage it.

"Riley, what's happening?" I asked.

"This is my project for the Science Fair. It's a time machine," he said, fiddling with the control panel. "And we are on our way to Ancient Egypt. Welcome aboard, Maddy."

CHAPTER 7

"You almost had me there," I said when my breath returned. "For a moment, I believed we were actually flying. But of course, no-one can fly a motorbike. So what is this? Some kind of illusion? A time travel simulator or something?"

I'd come over to Riley's place tonight, ready to gloat about how I'd figured out what his project was.

"You have built some kind of time machine," I'd planned to say, my tone triumphant, perhaps a tad smug. I might even have gone on to predict that he was planning to visit Ancient Egypt in his new creation because of the notes he'd taken at the museum. I felt so Sherlock smart.

But suspecting he was building a time machine, and sailing around the sky in one as your whole world, literally, disintegrated, were two different things. *It can't be real.*

I shook my head and waggled my index finger at him. "Oh, this is really good, Riley. What is it? A 4D time travel simulator? You are going to clean up at the Science Fair with this. It feels totally like you're somewhere in the stratosphere."

I reached out and touched something solid like a wall around us. It must have been glass, but it was not like any glass I'd seen. So clear it was invisible, except for a fuzziness now and again at the corner of your eye. It had a gentle pulse like a heartbeat. Whatever the surface was, Riley must have been projecting images onto it to create the illusion we were travelling.

Riley looked up from the controls, casually. "There's no trick here, Maddy. We are travelling—through time and space too."

What

the—

?

My self-composure went the way of Sydney's skyline. There one minute, then wobbly and fuzzy, then history! *This can't be happening.*

My head swept left and right. We were who-knew-how-many thousands of feet in the air but I'd never felt heavier. All the clouds around us reshaped themselves into images of my family: Mum in her pink apron serving TV dinners on fine crockery; Dad smiling at me on Skype, his face too close to the camera, making his nose seem huge; Gran shuffling cards incessantly to keep the arthritis in her fingers at bay—that was her excuse anyway. As families went, they weren't much. But they were all I had. If anything went wrong now, I might never see them again. Or Lauren. Or Courtney and Chi.

Or Jamie.

OMGOMGOMG.

I'd always been proud of my impulsiveness. *Look before you leap* was a saying for the deadly dull, the terminally unadventurous. But how much did I wish I'd paused to think before taking that last jump?

I'm sorry to say I got a bit choked up at this point. My throat ached, tears stung the back of my eyes. I took deep, slow breaths till I felt I could hold it all together. I didn't want

Riley to see what a mess I was. Not when he was so calm about it. Ice cool. Though he had as much to lose if our craft burnt up re-entering Earth's atmosphere or if we couldn't find our way back to our own time. I began shivering wildly and not just because of the cold. I think Riley noticed.

"In the box at your feet. There's a blanket," he said.

The blue square of material was so flimsy I thought it would be little better than a sheet for warmth. To my surprise, it was quite toasty.

"Is this one of your inventions?" I asked.

"No, I bought it at a camping shop."

I sat for a while, stunned, watching the blue-black velvet sky. Clouds writhed across it like restless spirits. Stars hung dizzyingly bright. Lights flashed and pulsed on the horizon. It was a neurotic, twitching panorama full of beauty and terror. A piece of space flotsam hurtled towards my head. I squealed and ducked but it veered off at the last second.

"Don't worry," said Riley. "I've reversed the polarity of electrons surrounding the time machine and recalibrated the osmosis density ratio to prevent incursion of external gases and substances."

"In English!" I was NOT in the mood for his techno-babble.

"I've created something like a force field around the bike," he said. "You can't see it, but it's there and dense enough to allow us to breathe freely in here without an oxygen suit. Plus, it should keep us safe from most space debris."

"Should? Most?"

Terror settled on me, like a spider web with threads of ice. I tried telling myself I'd be okay. If I had to be in space,

Riley was the best person to be with. He might be clueless in the playground, but out here (wherever *here* was) he was the cool kid. At least I hoped he was. Still, I jumped every time some object flashed past, or *boing*-ed off the invisible wall. I'd never felt more out of control, more lost and afraid.

"How long do you think it'll take to get to Ancient Egypt?" I sort of shouted it though I didn't need to. The force field kept the roar of the wind outside to a background hum, like we were on a plane.

"Last time, it took approximately 14.6 minutes," said Riley.

"Last time? So you've been there before?" This was great news. The best I'd had. *In my life!* He'd already time travelled once and got home safely. Which meant we could do it again.

"I just went to have a look at the place, but I didn't get out of the machine," he said.

"We can do the same this time, can't we?" I said. "Just look. Take it all in, chill for a while, make notes. There's no need to get off the bike, is there?"

"I thought I would this time. Though not for long. There's something I want to do on the ground," said Riley. "What do you think, Maddy? Are you up for an adventure?"

He turned to me with this big confident smile like he so knew what my answer would be. But, once again, he'd got it hopelessly wrong. The guy was a genius in so many ways but he understood nothing about human emotions in general or mine in particular.

"No, I'm not up for an adventure. I want to go home. Put on my PJs and fluffy slippers, have a hot chocolate and watch a show with Mum and Gran. Turn the time machine around and take me back!"

That's what I wanted to say. But how could I? When Riley, the explorer, was totally up for it, venturing fearlessly to places and times no-one from our world had ever seen.

In this relationship, I was supposed to be the "out there" one. On top, in control. If I admitted I was scared? Well, I couldn't do it without a serious loss of cred in his eyes.

Come on, Maddy. What's more important? Your life, or your image? I wanted to live, that was for sure. But I knew there was no way I would ask him to turn back. My mouth couldn't form the words. I really, *really* hated looking like a wuss. Or a fool.

Okay, so I was clear on my priorities. Image first, survival second. *Interesting.*

I took a deep breath, held it and released it slowly. I was here now. I would hold my nerve. Stay cool. Let Riley have a brief amount of time on the ground to do whatever it was he'd planned—one day, two tops. But, at the earliest possible moment, I would "encourage" him in the strongest terms to return to Sydney.

Could I manage that? Sure I could! I'd survived Year 10 bush camp without flush toilets for four days. How much worse could this be?

O-kay.

Plan in place, I felt a tad more able to continue. Just a tad.

"Wow, Riley!" I said, trying to put some *wow* into it. "How did you manage it? How did you discover time travel?"

"It was by accident, really," he said.

He explained the process to me. It had something to do with molecule tremor velocity. I zoned in and out as he went into detail, my feelings swinging wildly between the melt-your-bones terror of our situation and the freeze-your-brain boredom of his explanation.

The gist of it, as far as I could tell, was that when atoms within a force field vibrated rapidly enough, they became elastic and divided like spaghetti. We were now moving between the strands around the bike. Like creating our own hole through time. Simple really. If you're a scientific genius.

"Get ready, we're about to land," said Riley.

I nodded, but there was nothing to get ready. Except my brain, which was set to blow into a million pieces as it tried to wrap itself around the fact that we were about to land in Ancient Egypt. THE Ancient Egypt. With animal gods and Cleopatra haircuts, giant pyramids and mysterious tombs.

And people who hooked your brain out through your nose when you were dead. That ghoulish fact popped into my head, unbidden.

Thanks for nothing, Jamie Fletcher!

CHAPTER 8

I was scared but a little excited too. And then nauseated, as the time machine plummeted from the sky like a rock hurled off a cliff.

Behind me, I heard someone scream "We're going to die!" in a voice not unlike my own. *Hang on, that was my own.* We were going so fast, the sound hadn't caught up.

"No, we won't!" Riley replied. "I've built in air-cushioning."

I'd heard of air conditioning but what was air-cushioning? The craft stopped with a jolt but, to my surprise, not a thump. I peered over the sidecar's edge. We were inches from the ground as the wind whirled and the sand swirled furiously beneath the bike's wheels.

Riley tapped the screen and—*boof*—we hit the ground. The "air-cushioning", as Riley put it—localised tornado seemed more accurate to me—had saved our butts. But it had also whipped up quite the sandstorm. For a few moments, I could see no further than my hands. I had to shut my eyes against the flying grains.

I glimpsed a lot of blue-grey, with patches of light brown and some dark stripes. The blue-grey turned out to be a river, heavy with boat traffic, the brown patches were rocks dotting the sand around us, and the stripes were palm trees lining the bank in clusters.

"Is that river what I think it is?" I asked excitedly.

"If my calculations are correct, it should be the Nile," Riley said, as he got off the bike. I climbed out of the side car after him.

It felt like we were watching a film about Ancient Egypt. And we were in it! The Nile was wide and busy with boats of a kind I'd only ever seen in kids' books. They looked like they were made of bundles of reeds, with rectangular white sails, and giant oars that dipped gently and rhythmically into the water. Bare-chested men in white linen sarongs tied at the waist crewed the vessels or tended cargoes or animals, such as geese and goats, aboard.

A small craft cut so close to the bank, I heard it scrape the shallow sand. The man operating it jumped out and pushed off again without missing a beat. He had no hair at all and his smooth caramel pate gleamed beneath the fierce sun.

A trickle of sweat zigzagged down my back. In fleecy-lined track pants and T-shirt, I was seriously overdressed. The air was desert dry and, as I inhaled, my nose felt as if it was on fire. A spicy scent peppered the air but there was something unpleasant beneath it. Baked mud, and...*waste*, if I wasn't mistaken.

Across the river, I could see farmers' fields and, on top of a hill in the distance, a collection of mud-coloured square-ish buildings. A small town, I supposed. It was difficult to pick out details as everything wobbled in a heat haze.

"Wow, Riley," I said. "You really got us here. You are truly amazing."

He blushed at that. Then squatted down to study the soil, rubbing it between his thumb and two fingers. Most boys his age did little that was remarkable and showed off heaps about it. My friend was the opposite. Mind you, I wasn't too sure at the moment which I preferred—an under-achieving show-off or an over-achieving take-off. At least with one, I'd still be safe at home.

A large boat sailed by and a thin man fishing from the side glanced at us, then looked back again in surprise. So gobsmacked was he by what he saw, he didn't notice his line snag on a rock. The rod was wrenched out of his hand as the boat sailed on. Distraught, the guy shouted and pointed at us, his face crinkled in fury. While I didn't understand the words, I got the tone clearly enough.

"Riley," I said, "maybe we should get going to wherever it was you planned to go. You did have a plan for when you got here, didn't you?" Apart from just rocking up and blowing everyone's minds. For, if these people seemed alien to us, imagine how we looked to them with our strange hair and totally weird clothing. The track pants and T-shirt I wore wouldn't even be imagined for thousands of years. And Riley's Egyptian costume—well, it might have looked just the thing in the Sydney costume shop, but I couldn't help noticing no one else had gleaming gold fabric on their collars.

"Oh!" I heard Riley say.

"What—*oh*?" I asked.

"The rocks," he said. "They're...not rocks."

The rocks around us had short legs and sharp teeth. They were actually crocodiles—young and small, but mean looking. And now I saw that there was water behind us as well as in front of us. We were on an islet in the middle of the river—one where crocs came to sunbathe, evidently.

"Riley!" I said. "Is this where you'd planned to land?"

"No, err...this is a miscalculation," said Riley.

"A miscalculation?"

I'd often wished Mr Perfect would make a mistake so he would know how the rest of us felt. But this was NOT the time or the place to start.

"Get back in the time machine, Maddy," said Riley, edging backwards, eyes fixed on the crocs.

"O-kay." My voice was high-pitched and small.

We crept backwards. After a dozen steps, I felt the sidecar touch the back of my thigh and hurled myself into the seat, hitting my arm in the process but barely registering the pain. Riley straddled the bike and pressed the control panel furiously. The crocs were moving towards us when, as one, they altered course and swished back to the water's edge.

I let out a breath of relief. "I thought they were coming to get us." Though something about this scene still bothered me.

Riley jammed his foot on the pedal ignition. Once, twice. It didn't start first or second time. Or fifth. Or ninth time.

"I hope sand hasn't got into the engine," he said, way too casually.

All the baby crocs lined up like statues at the water's edge, looking outwards.

"Riley, why do you think the crocs are waiting at the water's edge like that?"

There was a soft splash as a huge crocodile—over two feet long—surged onto the bank, water dripping off its ridged hide. That's why they were waiting. For Mama Croc to come home.

Several men in boats nearby saw what was happening and started shouting at us. I couldn't understand the words, but I'd bet it was something like: "Watch out! Crocs!"

By the time Riley notched up twelve failed starts, Mama Croc had all her limbs on land. I expected him to keep trying, again and again, but he just sat there, as still as mashed potato.

"What are you doing? Keep going!" I hissed.

"I'm giving the system a chance to reboot."

I wanted to reboot him at that moment. Mama Croc was creeping closer, her stubby legs moving so smoothly she practically glided, her yellow slitted eyes fixed on us. If it had been a cold grey day, I might not have been as worried. But I'd been to enough Australian zoos to know that here, in this blazing heat, she would be like a battery, fully charged. A race car ready to zoom.

There was nothing I could do, so I focused on controlling my breathing as I stared the croc down. It was creepy the way she didn't need to blink. My own eyes were irritated from tiny sand particles stuck in the rims. I struggled not to blink twice as much as usual.

When she began a sharp wiggly movement, tail swishing side to side, pudgy legs pumping forward, the shouts around us grew louder. A second crowd, of about a dozen people, had gathered on the bank.

"Riley, don't just sit there."

"It's almost charged. Any second."

I couldn't wait. I reached into the plastic box at my feet, grabbed the first thing that came to hand—a bandage roll— and hurled it as far as I could towards the water.

"Go fetch!" I shouted.

Mama Croc turned to a U-shape to check it out. But she didn't retreat. About half a minute later, she unfurled again. Panicking, I flung out anything and everything I could find from Riley's supplies, hoping something might catch her eye. I didn't look too carefully at what I threw, but I think it included a six pack of Band-Aids, a pair of scissors, a leather satchel with basic tools, another blanket—blue, wrapped in plastic—and a pack of astronaut's dehydrated strawberry ice cream. *Is that right? Astronaut ice cream?* I'd have to ask Riley where he got that later. I was just about to hurl out a length of rope when Riley grabbed my arm.

"We might need that!" he said.

I might have thrown it anyway, if Mama Croc hadn't shimmied about and scuttled to the edge of the bank to check out the booty (it was the ice cream that did it, I'm sure), her offspring sashaying after her.

That's when Riley hit the pedal again. The bike purred to life. Then roared like a hungry lion. A dozen Egyptian faces and as many crocs gawped at us in disbelief. And then we were off. Flying into the air again. Up, up, with alarming speed. My hair blew back so hard it hurt. I gripped the sidecar and braced myself. Up, up, we went, till we were level with the clouds.

It took a minute to stop hyperventilating and get my breathing back to merely twice its normal speed. By then we were already dropping again, super-fast.

We touched down a few minutes later. As the sand settled, we found ourselves once more on the river bank, but this time on the correct side, near some fields. The islet we'd been on was a hundred feet further along. And I fancied I saw Mama Croc's head swivel side to side wondering where dinner went!

"Quick, let's hide the machine," said Riley. We wheeled the bike into a dense patch of reeds nearby.

Riley pulled out a piece of shiny silver material from a compartment beneath his seat and placed it over the bike. And the weirdest thing happened—the bike disappeared.

"What the—?"

"It's a reflecting material," Riley said. "It reflects the light around it to make things appear invisible. But, of course, the bike's still there!"

"Did you buy that from a camp shop?"

"No, that's mine."

"Riley, those poor people back there. They saw us there one minute, then watched us fly up into the air and disappear. They must have thought they were losing their minds."

"I activated the screening shield, so they didn't actually see us go up."

"So it would have been like we'd just vanished and reappeared here. What will they make of that?"

"I guess we're about to find out," he said, looking past me. I turned to see a crowd of Egyptians moving our way, faces pinched, mouths open.

Leading the group was a tall man with thin lips and a birthmark on his cheek, like a map of Australia. He stopped a few feet from us, put his left arm out to the side as a barrier that all the others should stay behind. He didn't want to risk them getting too close.

The women looked surprisingly fresh in white linen dresses. Most of the men had sarongs tied at the waist and bare, hairless chests. One boy, aged about ten, squeezed between two women at the front and looked up at me. His brown eyes were like chocolate Rollos and his whole head was shaved except for a long thick plait on the side. Gradually, some of his friends peeked out—boys and girls, with the same hairdo.

"Riley, you did have a plan for what you would do when you landed?"

"Don't worry," he said. "Ancient Egyptians are supposed to be very hospitable to visitors from other countries."

The tall man stepped forward and shouted at us, flecks of his spittle wetting my cheek.

"Only problem with that," I said, "is no-one told him about the hospitable part."

Birthmark guy yelled a command to the crowd and two men came forward and grabbed us. The one who held me was quite ancient, with bony fingers and swollen knuckles, though his grip on my arm was strong. As they led us away, the crowd followed, intrigued to see what would happen.

I tried to stay cool, but my legs trembled, making me stumble on rocks and uneven ground.

"Don't worry, Maddy," said Riley, looking back at me. "We'll be okay."

We passed fields, where men tended crops or drove ploughs pulled by oxen. I saw wheat, corn and grape vines among others and trenches of river water running alongside the crops, presumably for irrigation. In one field, several black birds dive-bombed the crops and two boys fired rocks at them from slingshots. Half a dozen of their rock missiles soared through the air harmlessly, before—*crack*—one hit its target. The bird dropped like a stone.

We were headed for the mud brick town on the hill. Up ahead, Riley swivelled around to look back at the river. I guess he was taking a bearing on where the time machine was from here. Good idea. I did the same, noting the particular field nearest the machine and the shape of the reeds in which we'd hidden the bike. What would happen if we couldn't find it again? It didn't bear thinking about.

Unexpectedly, Riley broke away from his captor and ran over to embrace me. This sudden affection was more surprising than anything—the time travel, the landing on crocodile isle or being held captive by an angry mob of people who had been dead for thousands of years. But he had a reason. Pressing a white pill into my hand, he whispered: "Take this."

As the men surged after him, I slipped the pill into my mouth and chewed. It was only after I'd swallowed it that I wondered exactly what I'd taken. Would I grow till I was twice as big as a house? Or shrink to the size of an insect, my only worry being the Egyptian version of an anteater, if there was such a thing? When nothing about me physically changed, I began to think it might just be a headache pill which was not so bad as, by now, my head throbbed, big time.

Our captors led us through a rabbit warren of alleys between the mud houses. Some of the buildings were small and single-storeyed while others were two or three storeys high. They all looked alike—same earth-brown colour, high square windows with no glass or screens. Outside one house was a pottery dome, a bit like a beehive, smoke billowing out of the top. It was an oven, I guessed. The delicious smell of baking bread perfumed the air as a tall, elegant woman used a long paddle to remove steaming flat bread from inside.

We stopped at an open square in the town's centre. By this time, there were at least thirty people around us, staring and whispering. My captor let go of me as he talked to the birthmark guy and a third man.

"What are we going to do?" I whispered to Riley. *And what are they going to do, more to the point?*

"Well, the Egyptians are people who like singing and dancing. You're a singer, aren't you? In that choir?"

"The Nightingales. Yes, what about it?"

"It might not be a bad idea to give the people a song to show them we mean no harm."

"The oldest music I know is from the sixties and seventies! I'm not sure they'll like it."

"Well, there's only one way to find out."

I wanted to argue, but something about the way the head guy kept miming a slit throat as he looked over at us made me keen to try any distraction. So, I closed my eyes, took a deep breath, tried to imagine I was back in the Crows Nest rehearsal hall, then let rip with *Lean On Me*.

It wasn't my best effort. It was hard to sing when your throat was taut with terror. But I managed to get through it, more or less tunefully. At the end of the song...nothing. No-one clapped or spoke. They just gawped. It was totally unnerving.

"Keep going," said Riley. So I sang the next verse. I even tried to jig about and snap my fingers in time. I felt the tension ease a bit, which was good. Though I caught a few people raising eyebrows in that "How embarrassing!" kind of way.

"Poor woman. Do you think she's in pain?" one watcher said.

"I know I am," said another.

"Quick, do something before she starts again," a third speaker urged.

I frowned at the woman, who had the grace to look a little ashamed.

"Riley," I whispered, "how come I can understand them?"

"It's the pill I gave you."

"But how? And give me the short version."

"Well, basically, it alters the brain's neurotransmitting pathway and speed, redirecting it to the areas which recognise language patterns. First it stimulates the cells and speeds up neurological response, then it creates—"

"Shorter!" I said.

"It lets you speak any language in about ten minutes."

"What?" I said. "You mean I can speak a language I've never learned?"

"Yes. Though, technically, your brain has learned to identify and translate the new sound patterns rapidly. You may not even realise you're speaking a new language. It will sound like English to your ears."

I stared at Riley. His eyes were watery, his blond hair chaotic, like a surfer who'd emerged from a giant swell. *Is he really the great brain of our time?*

"And look at the way the woman is dressed," came a husky

female voice. "Like her family has disowned her and sent her out to the desert to die in shame." A lot of the girls around her found that funny.

"The only shame is upon you," I said. "For being so rude to a visitor in your country."

It just popped out. Maybe Riley's brain-stimulating pill had stimulated my mouth as well.

All heads turned to see how the girl would react. I followed their eye-line to a striking beauty, about sixteen, with fine features and delicately-chiselled cheekbones. Head held aloft, she had a touch of Cleopatra about her. She reckoned she was Queen of this village anyway.

"Perhaps it is you who is rude for subjecting our ears to that wailing," she said. Her friends giggled.

I should have let it go. But I was hot and frazzled and Riley's pill had my brain buzzing. "If I was wailing," I said, "it was because I got a look at your head."

Where did that come from? That mean, mean remark. Not that she didn't deserve it. The girl's friends stopped laughing, though someone at the back of the crowd—a lone female—seemed to find it hysterical. Her chuckles peppered the air as the girl who'd been the target of my attack gave me a final death stare, then left, her white linen dress billowing behind her.

I caught Riley watching me then, a slight crease on his forehead, like he was seeing me for the first time. I gave him a "So what?" scowl back. The two of us would get to know each other pretty well on this trip, I guessed. And for my part, it might not all be pretty.

After my performance, the town officials relaxed a bit. They were actually nice guys and seemed to buy our story about being from out of town. They shook their heads in amazement at my track pants and Riley's gleaming collar. They were fascinated by Riley's hair, our pale skin and blue eyes. Some kept their distance, but the head guy shook our hands and wished us a good stay in their village.

What a relief!

When the crowd dispersed, only one girl remained. She was about our age, with dark crinkly hair and super-smiley eyes.

"My name is Amunet," she said. "Welcome to our town." She bowed slightly.

"I'm Madison. This is Riley."

"Madison, Riley. These are names I've never heard before," she said, then grinned. "I like them. Where are you from?"

"Nubia," Riley replied so fast that I suspected it must be part of a cover story he'd worked on before we left.

"Nubia?" said Amunet. "I have seen many people from Nubia. None of them looked like you two."

Riley's cheeks flushed and he fell silent. He had a story but not much of one, it seemed. Time to do what I did best.

"We are from southern Nubia," I said. "Way down south."

She seemed to accept that.

"What are you doing so far from home?" she asked.

Riley cleared his throat, back in the game. "We are musicians, hoping to find work in the service of the wealthy."

"Musicians?" said Amunet. "Do you sing like Madison?"

"No-one sings quite like her," he said.

Amunet covered her mouth and giggled. "That's true. I have never heard anything like it before." I tried not to be offended. "And are you brother and sister?"

"Yes, we are," I said. Riley nodded eagerly. While I was no expert on Ancient Egyptian customs, I could guess a single girl and boy hanging out together wouldn't be the norm here. Saying we were related would cut down on awkward questions.

"Until you become established," said Amunet, "I would be honoured if you would stay in my home with my family and I."

"In your home? That's very kind of you," I said.

"We accept your invitation," said Riley. "And we'll contribute to your household in any way we can."

Amunet smiled and nodded. "That girl you spoke to before?"

"You mean the one I was sharp with?" I said. "I'm sorry about that."

"Her name is Sacmis," said Amunet. "She often makes people laugh—at others' expense. Today the laugh was on her."

Amunet's brown eyes creased with real delight. It seemed my poisonous outburst had made her day. And earned us a friend.

As we threaded our way through the narrow streets of the town, all heads turned to stare. I caught many shy smiles and it all seemed pretty friendly. I was just beginning to relax and think that all might actually be okay, when I looked up and saw Sacmis watching me from a first-floor window. Her lips were button-tight, her gaze colder than Mama Croc's.

I had made an enemy there. I hoped it wouldn't come back to bite me.

CHAPTER 9

Amunet's home was a single-storey mud house on the edge of town with a view of the Nile. A dark woman in a white dress with a striking silver necklace sat outside the house, kneading dough, as we approached. When she saw Riley and me, she reared back in fear.

"Mama, you do not need to be afraid." Amunet hurried over to her. "These are my new friends. Their names are..." She faltered.

"Madison and Riley," I offered.

It was a full minute before the woman recovered her voice. "I am honoured to meet you," she said. "My name is Sahara."

Riley and I smiled and nodded. Sahara ventured a small smile in return.

"This is my sister, Layla," Amunet said, pointing to a ceramic oven outside the house. We waited and, a moment later, a girl of around ten with one of those funky single-plait hairstyles peeked out from behind the structure.

"Hello, Layla," I said.

With eyes of terror, she ducked back out of sight.

"How are the dung bricks going, Layla?" Sahara called. "It will be time to prepare dinner soon."

"They're almost dry, Mama," a squeaky voice came from her hiding place.

"Dung bricks?" I said, unable to hide my distaste.

"They are a source of cooking fuel," said Amunet. "But what do you use in Nubia to create heat, if not dung?"

Oops. "Oh, we use dung too," I said. "Of course."

"Madison and Riley are a brother and sister from south Nubia," Amunet explained. "They have come to Egypt seeking work as musicians. I invited them to stay with us until they find their way in our country."

"You did right, my daughter," said Sahara. "We are happy to extend a warm welcome to our friends from the south. Please stay as long as you wish."

I wondered how Mum would react if I came home one night with a couple of weirdly dressed musicians who wanted to stay for a while. Then again, she was so busy with work these days, she might not even notice they were there.

Amunet showed us around the house. It was modest, to say the least. Dark inside, with a dirt floor, a single window high up, with no glass in it. The only furniture was a low table, a few stools and some rolled-up mats in the corner. There was a statue of a funny little man, recessed into one of the walls, with a couple of steps leading to it and bowls of food on the top step.

"That's our shrine to the god Bes," said Amunet.

"Bes?" I said.

"Yes, he's the protector of homes. He scares away evil spirits as well as scorpions and snakes." Evil spirits, I could handle. But scorpions and snakes? "You don't worship Bes in Nubia?"

"Oh, yes. I thought you said Tess."

There was another box-like room off this one, separated by a papyrus blind. "That is where my brother Razi sleeps," said Amunet. "Riley will share the room with him during your stay. You, Madison, will sleep in the main room with us."

"Great!" I said. *Oh, no!* I had to sleep on this hard floor, cheek by jowl with women I barely knew! Not good.

By the time we went back outside, Layla had found the courage to come out of hiding. She was too shy to make direct eye contact, but her gaze kept returning to us. We all watched Sahara knead dough on a ceramic tile, then shape it into balls and pound it flat. I noticed a lot of brown specks in the mix. At first, I thought they were some kind of seed. Then I realised they were grains of sand.

"Can I help you make the bread?" Riley asked.

"This is a woman's job," said Sahara.

"In our family, this is a job males and females share," Riley said, grinning at me, pleased to be able to sell a lie too.

It took a bit more coaxing before Sahara let him try. She showed him how to squeeze the mixture through his fingertips, then flatten and mould into rounds. I wondered what my friend was thinking—was it somehow connected with his plan in coming here?

As Amunet watched Riley work, it was easier to tell what was in her head. Riley's curls were tipped gold in the afternoon sun, his smile warm enough to turn the cool Nile waters to steam. There might have been thousands of years and a world of cultural differences between us, but one thing was clear to me—Amunet fancied Riley.

While the two of them finished making the bread, I went with Amunet and Layla to collect vegetables for dinner in the family's veggie patch. Making our way through the fields, Layla danced about, chattering happily. "What is your village like in Nubia? Bigger or smaller than ours? What family do you have? Is your father a farmer or a skilled tradesman?"

"You ask too many questions, Layla," Amunet scolded.

"I don't mind," I said. "Our village is smaller. Riley is my only sibling and my father is a ship-builder." (The last part was sort of true.)

A short, muscular boy, around ten, raced across my path as a tall, reedy boy chased him. The pair zoomed across two fields before the second guy crash-tackled his friend in an irrigation ditch. All around the fields, kids darted about in similar tip-chase games. They had the same hairstyle as Layla, heads completely shaven except for a thick plait at the side.

"That's an interesting hairstyle," I said.

"That is the sidelock of youth. All young boys and girls have it," said Amunet. "Do they not have this in Nubia?"

"It's not exactly the same," I said. "Not in my...village."

"I'm almost old enough to wear my hair long, like an adult," said Layla proudly.

"Really?"

When a sheep wandered onto our path, Layla shooed it away with big arm movements. It ran off, bleating a protest.

"What do children do for fun in your village?" she asked.

"Pretty much the same as you do here," I said. (She'd never believe me if I told her.)

"And do many boys in your village wish to make you their wife?"

"Layla! Do not ask such questions," said Amunet.

"None, as yet!" I said.

"Do not worry, Madison," said Amunet. "You are healthy and must surely be admired by all who have eyes. Someone will ask for your hand soon."

I seriously hoped she was wrong.

Approaching the river, we came upon a group of girls sitting around watching their friend do a strange performance. Her voice squeaked off-key, her arms flailed about, the other girls fell about laughing. I presumed it was some kind of Ancient Egyptian comedy till I caught the words she sang. They were from *Lean On Me*—the song I'd sung in the village. She was imitating me.

Layla slapped her hand to her mouth to stop a giggle escaping. But Amunet's expression was dark.

She stormed up to the group. "This woman is a guest in our town. Is this any way to treat her?"

"Sorry, forgive, forgive," said the lead girl.

"It's okay." I waved it away.

The girls bowed and murmured apologies, backing away, then scarpering.

"Many in my village do not like new or strange things," said Amunet. "But I do. Perhaps you will teach me your song sometime?"

"Sure," I said.

Layla spotted a friend of hers across the field and took off to greet her, leaving Amunet and me alone. Somehow, I got the sense Amunet had been waiting for this opportunity.

"Is Riley betrothed to anyone in your village?" she asked.

"No," I fired back by reflex. When her smile broadened, I realised that was the wrong answer. "He does like someone back at home. Although, they're not betrothed, as such."

Amunet pouted. "But does this woman want to make a home with him, have children, a family?"

"I'm not sure she's thought about it yet."

"Is this girl younger or older than me?"

"About the same age," I said.

"She should turn her thoughts to marriage before the gods stop granting her the gift of children."

What the—?

I was speechless for the second time today. For the second time in my life, actually.

"Riley should not give his heart to someone who will waste his time in indecision," said Amunet.

Reaching the veggie patch, we knelt down and began pulling out leeks and lettuces and some green vegetables I'd never seen before as Amunet explained that most Egyptian girls married at around fifteen and had children soon after.

"At sixteen, I am considered quite old to be unmarried," Amunet said. "Though I was almost married once—to Seth, the brother of Sacmis."

"Sacmis? The mean girl from the village?" I asked, yanking out a leek and shaking dirt off its fine roots. "Really? What happened?"

"I thought Seth would make a good husband," she said. "He was strong and healthy. I felt fortunate to have his attention. Then one day, at the market, I witnessed him being cruel to a slave girl."

She explained that the girl had stumbled and caused him to drop a goblet he'd just bought. In a rage, Seth told the girl he would make sure her master beat her for her clumsiness.

"That night, I told my parents I could not be happy with such a man," Amunet said. "They supported my decision and our betrothal was broken."

That was interesting and more enlightened than I would have expected from such an ancient culture.

"Well, good," I said with feeling. "Imagine being married to someone like that. And having Sacmis as your sister-in-law."

"His family was not happy about it," said Amunet, frowning. "They spread rumours around our village that I was fussy so other young men would stay away from me and I would be left without a husband to protect me. Sacmis said some things about me and my family that were not true."

"Poor Amunet!" I said.

"But I am hopeful I will soon find a more suitable man," she said. "My parents plan to visit a matchmaker in a nearby village soon if no suitor makes himself known."

"Well, that's good news!" I said. Though it sounded anything but.

"And my family would not mind at all if I were to marry someone from another country, like Nubia," she added excitedly.

Does she mean Riley? That she wants him as her husband? Seriously? I would have to get him to be mean to a slave girl and fast. I was trying to figure out just how to reply when I saw Amunet stiffen and frown at something behind me.

I turned to see Sacmis walking past our patch. She was with a young girl, presumably her sister. Like us, they had a basket and were collecting veggies for dinner. The look Sacmis gave Amunet was far from friendly. But she saved the best for me. Her almond eyes narrowed to slits, her lips pouted in an almost comical expression of hate.

"Hi there, Sacmis. Lovely evening, isn't it?" I said with a big smile.

Sacmis raised her chin and huffed off.

"You are being friendly to a woman who is my enemy." Amunet was hurt.

"No, I'm stickin' it to her," I said. "Don't you see? By being honey sweet to her, she can't say a word, though she knows I don't mean a word of it."

"Stickin' it to her!" Amunet tried the phrase on her lips. "I like this expression."

"Hello, Sacmis!" she shouted. "It's so good to see you, my very good friend."

Sacmis might not know what sarcasm was, but she could tell we were mocking her. As we giggled uncontrollably, she picked up a stone and hurled it at a crow and—*bang*—it fell to its death. That froze the laughter in my throat.

Though it seemed to delight Amunet, who chuckled all the way home.

CHAPTER 10

As Sahara and the girls got dinner ready—vegetable stew—I chopped a few things to help but generally felt pretty useless and wished there was more I could do to repay their kindness.

Just on dark, Amunet's brother, Razi, arrived home with three fish dangling from a stick. He was seventeen, with wavy hair and eyes like dark chocolate balls.

"This is Riley and Madison," said Amunet proudly. "They are from southern Nubia and will be staying with us for a while."

Razi gave a single nod. After that, he watched us wherever we went, his eyebrows tight. He seemed a serious guy who didn't smile easily.

Sahara slipped the fish into the oven for about ten minutes, and then dinner was served. We all knelt around a low table as she placed the pot of stew in the centre. When she removed the lid, a beautiful aroma, which was sort of sweet and spicy at once, filled the room. She gave each of us a piece of the flat bread that she and Riley had made, but no spoons, knives or forks. I watched to see what the others did. When the stew had cooled, they used a ladle to scoop it into a pocket in the bread, making a kind of stew sandwich, which was really tasty.

There was also a tray of cooked fish, served on something like couscous, which we ate with our hands, and plump, juicy figs to finish. We washed it down with a mug of very weak beer, which was apparently healthier to drink than the water and not really alcoholic.

I loved this communal way of eating, but it wasn't half messy. My hands were sticky and some of the stew dripped down my chin.

During dinner, Razi asked where we came from and why we were here. Riley and I answered as vaguely as we could, then batted the questions back to him.

"Amunet tells me you're a jeweller?" I said.

"Yes. My skills are not yet that of a craftsman," said Razi, "though my father is one of the finest in the area."

"You must be very proud," I said. "Where is your father?"

"He has been called to help on an important project for the Pharaoh," he said. "He is building a tomb like no other before."

"A pyramid?" Riley asked.

"Yes, with steps rising to the top, like a stairway to the gods. The Pharaoh honours our family by choosing my father in this noble work."

The words were effusive, but as he spoke his hands formed loose fists. Was it because of us or was something else bothering him?

"It must be hard on the family," I said, "trying to manage with him gone. Does the Pharaoh compensate well in his absence?"

"Compensate?" asked Razi.

"Yes, since your father's not here making jewellery, does the Pharaoh give you the money the family needs to survive?"

"She means surplus to barter," Riley leapt in. (He explained later that money in the form of a standardised currency hadn't yet been invented. The whole economy was based on trading goods.)

The family stared grimly ahead. "No surplus is provided in my father's absence," said Razi. "But we can take care of ourselves."

That night, as I lay next to Amunet on the hard floor, she told me the family was in trouble. A tax man was coming soon to collect surplus he said they owed and, with their jewellery business stalled while the dad was away, they wouldn't be able to pay.

"Can't you just tell this man your dad is doing the Pharaoh's business and you'll pay when he gets back?" I asked.

Amunet shook her head: "If we cannot pay, our case will go before some local officials. If we are found guilty, the punishment is a beating for the head of the family, which at present is my mother."

What? Sahara would be beaten because her hubby was off doing back-breaking public service for free? That wasn't fair. And Riley and I—two extra mouths to feed—were just what she didn't need.

In the middle of the night, I sat up, tense and tingly. From the corner of the room came a soft, scratchy sound. Someone was in here with us.

Slowly, I stood up, careful not to wake Amunet on one side of me or Layla on the other. There it was again—a scrape and a squeak. And then, in a shaft of moonlight slicing through the dark, I saw it—a giant rat. It was huge and ugly...and right there! I gasped, but no sound emerged. A hand clamped over my mouth so I could barely breathe. As I twisted around, I caught a swish of blond curls. It was Riley. With his free hand, he signalled me to *Shhh* and pointed to the front door.

We tiptoed out.

I wasn't sure what time it was, but it felt late. There were so many stars in the sky, I had to squint as I looked up. Around us, the village was still and dark with just enough starlight to make out the square shapes of houses nearby. The Nile River was a stripe of silver on the edge of the horizon.

"Rats!" I hissed. "Seriously? I'll never be able to sleep while we're here. How much longer are you planning to stay in Egypt, Riley?"

"I'm not sure," he said. "You see, I didn't just come here for a holiday. I wanted to help the Egyptians with a problem they have."

"A dental problem?"

"How do you know?"

"There was a toothpaste box in your lab. So what's the plan?"

"A lot of people in Ancient Egypt suffer from tooth decay," he said, "which could be avoided by regular brushing with toothpaste."

"So you're going to give them some toothpaste? Great! You brought those cartons with you? We can hand them over first thing in the morning and be out of here before lunchtime."

"It's not that simple," said Riley, pacing. "If I give them a manufactured toothpaste, they'll use it up and that will be that. I've studied the components, now I need to find local ingredients to produce the same effect. So they can make it for themselves. That might take a while."

"How long?"

"I'm not sure."

For a genius, the guy was maddeningly vague at times. And vague did NOT work for me at the moment. Not if it meant staying in this ancient culture with no flush toilets, running water or computers, and rats queuing up at night to nibble my toes. I needed an end date. And a better reason to stay.

"Why go to all this trouble?" I said. "Is it just to win another prize at the Science Fair?"

"No," he said. A tad too quickly.

"Aren't you bored with winning? Maybe you could try something new—like losing, for once. Just to see how it feels."

Riley folded his arms. "I have...*not* won things before, you know."

"Really? Like what?"

"Some sports things. A few science things, too. I know what losing feels like. I prefer winning."

That was interesting. And disturbing. It didn't fit at all with the clueless, puppyish image I had of Riley.

"What made you decide to come here for your first journey in the time machine rather than, say, going back a day in our own time? Or jumping into the future?"

"I never thought about going back a day in time," he said, scratching his head as though maybe he should have done that instead. "And I'm not sure I'd want to go to the future. I wouldn't want to know too much about what's ahead. Would you?"

"Well, of course I would!" I said. "If there's stuff to know, why wouldn't you want to know it, to change the bad things if you could."

Riley raked his fringe off his face. It stayed up for a few seconds, then flopped back down over his right eye.

"And you chose Ancient Egypt because...?" I said.

"Well, it's an interesting period in history," he said. "I had been considering it, along with Ancient Rome, medieval England and the Wild West. But then we went on that excursion and saw those mummies and you made that comment—"

"What comment?"

"Remember, we were looking at that mummy, the girl who died of dental abscess, and you said, 'If only they had toothpaste in Ancient Egypt, this would never have happened'. And I thought, well, that's smart. If I'm going to travel through time, why not do something to help while I'm there and fix a simple problem?"

For the second time today, I had a feeling of dropping from a great height. It had been *my* comment that had brought him here? Brought *us* here? A comment which, BTW, was not the least bit smart, especially when I made it to exactly the wrong person at the wrong time. Mega-mouth Maddy had done it again.

We stood silently in the dark. That was not so strange for Riley, who was used to being quiet. But it was weird for me. I was thinking about how much trouble my mouth had got me into during my life (though, to be fair, it had got me out of quite a bit too), when the rat shot out of the house and right past us. I literally jumped, then clamped my own hand over my mouth to stop myself screaming and waking the whole village.

"Just don't take too long figuring out the local toothpaste recipe, will you?" I said.

"If you want to, Maddy," said Riley, "we can walk down to the river, get into the time machine and leave right now. Just say the word and we'll go. Is that what you want?"

Yes, that is what I want! I could see my friends and family, go back to choir practice, my comfy bed. Back to where things were normal and safe.

"What do you suppose is happening back home?" I asked.

Riley frowned. "I guess our families will be worried."

Worried? That was the understatement of the millennium. Or two.

"But when we go back," he continued, "we could program the machine to land at exactly the same time we departed. And it will be as if we never left at all."

"So you could erase all their worry when we got home?"

He nodded.

That was something, at least. And in truth, I wasn't as desperate to leave anymore. Now that I'd got to know some Egyptian people, the whole experience seemed less daunting than at first. And maybe even the teeniest bit exciting?

Besides, I really did want to help the family with their tax problem. The thought of Sahara being beaten because they couldn't pay seemed so wrong to me.

"Why don't we stay for a couple more days?" I said. "You do your toothpaste thing, see what you come up with. I'll help the family with their tax payment."

"Are you sure?"

No. "Yeah. As long as we don't stay too long. Deal?"

"Deal."

Riley smiled. But it was weird. Clueless as he was about human emotions, I had the feeling he knew what my answer was going to be.

Of course, if we had left then, we would have avoided a donkey load of trouble that was *tramp, tramp, tramp*ing in our direction.

CHAPTER 11

I didn't think I'd sleep much the rest of the night. Not just because my rock pillow sucked, or because I expected to feel sharp teeth nibbling on my toes at any moment, but because my mind raced with schemes for helping the family to raise the tax payment.

Perhaps I could busk for some surplus? The Egyptians, if not exactly fans of my performance, had at least seemed riveted by it (much like you can't look away from someone vomiting). Then again, were they likely to throw wheat, or whatever it was they traded instead of money, into a hat after a performance? Probably not.

Perhaps Sahara could teach me to bake bread for the markets? Fresh loaves went down a treat at Crows Nest market. Then again, not everyone in Crows Nest was already an expert bread-maker themselves.

No, if I was serious about raising wealth, I would have to find something I could do that the Ancient Egyptians could not. How hard could it be? I had thousands of years of history to draw on. There had to be something. Anything. Anything at all.

A picture flashed to mind of the boys killing the crows around the crops with sling shots. And I had it! I would make scarecrows. I would introduce this revolutionary concept in avian control to Ancient Egypt and the family would clean up. All I needed was some sticks or reeds and a few old clothes. How could it lose?

Happy I'd be able help the family in the morning, I slipped off to sleep for a few hours. But I hadn't been up long when I realised my simple plan was not simple at all.

After eating a breakfast of honey and dates with some bread (alone, as Riley was nowhere to be seen), I turned my attention to Sahara. She was busy making clothes for me. And I mean busy.

Not for her a sewing machine, a bolt of cloth and a bit of know-how. No, to make clothes in Egypt, you had to start from scratch—literally. Scratching in the dirt.

The process began with the back-breaking work of hauling the flax plant out of the ground. Then you had to strip it, soak it, beat it and comb it till it was soft. If you had any strength left in your arms after that, you tied the ends of each strip together and then spun it around a wooden stick with a flat circular weight at the bottom until you had something resembling thread. Next, you pegged a couple of wooden sticks into the ground and wove the thread criss-cross, criss-cross until—*ta-dah!*—you had fabric. Then, and only then, did you start sewing—with a needle made of animal bone! And what a ghastly list of jobs had to be done to make those!

Getting clothes for the scarecrow would not be easy. There were few short cuts in Ancient Egypt. It was obviously going to be a day or three before Sahara finished making my Egyptian outfit. In the meantime, she lent me one of her dresses. It was a simple design: scoop-necked, long-sleeved, trailing to the ground with a rope belt at the waist.

"You cannot continue to wear only these *trackie-daks* and *T-shirt*," Sahara said with motherly concern. (Catching a whiff of myself, I had to agree.) "I am surprised you did not bring a change of clothes from Nubia with you."

"Well, it was kind of a spur-of-the-moment trip."

Her eyebrows climbed halfway up her forehead, wondering how a trip from southern Nubia all the way to Egypt could take anyone by surprise. What would she think, I wondered, if she knew how far we'd really come?

"Is there anything I can do to help today?" I asked.

Slowly, she smiled. In the Ancient Egyptian household, there were always chores to be done.

Soon after, Amunet and I made our way through the fields, clutching bundles of white linen clothing from the family which we were to wash by hand in the Nile River. Although, I didn't usually do laundry at home, I was keen to find an excuse to go back to the river so I could check the time machine was still where we'd left it.

We passed fields where bare-chested men worked the crops. Their copper-coloured skin was shiny with sweat—it was already searingly hot. Spotted cattle swished their tails constantly to shoo away persistent flies.

I noticed one older woman we passed waving a rope with a tassel on the end about her face and neck.

"I wish we had one of those fly swat things," I said, blowing two flies off my lips.

"They are the latest fashion," Amunet said. "Giraffe-tail swats. I'm afraid we do not have enough surplus at present to buy one."

Giraffe tail? Seriously?

A sharp earthy scent wafted over us, making my nose crinkle. What was it? Ahh...dung. Freshly laid.

"Do you know where Riley and Razi went this morning?" I asked Amunet.

"They have gone hunting," she replied.

"Hunting? Hunting what?"

"Some of the farmers have a problem with animals eating their crops. This must be taken care of."

"What kind of animals?"

"Hippopotamuses!" she said.

"Hippos! But...but they're dangerous, aren't they?"

Hadn't I heard that hippos, though vegetarians, were fiercely territorial with jaws that could snap you in half?

"Yes, many are killed performing this task," Amunet reported calmly. "Only the best and bravest hunters survive."

I stopped breathing as my eyes refocused on the horizon ahead. Several rickety papyrus boats rocked wildly on the water. The boats were overloaded with over-excited boys with spears all keen to show off their bravery and hunting prowess. Somewhere amongst that mad melee, I knew, Riley must be trying to keep his footing.

I knelt at the edge of the river and plopped the mass of white linen into it as my eyes searched the unsteady crafts for my friend. There were six boats in a semi-circle around a couple of hippos. Of course, there might have been more of the creatures, but you'd never know, as they could submerge themselves completely any time they wished. The only bit you saw was the pinkish-brown crown of their head and their beady eyes.

I had just spotted Riley on one of the boats in the centre when Amunet squatted down in front of me, frowning. "I don't know how you get your clothes clean in Nubia with that method," she said as mud and sand swirled over the material. "And look, you've got yourself all dirty." She wiped mud splatters off my face. "You'll have to do better than that if you wish to get a husband."

Amunet extracted a piece of clothing from the soggy pile, jiggled it about in the water for a while, then pounded it over and over on a nearby rock. I followed her lead. The material was heavy when saturated with water and after bashing it for a while, my muscles began to protest.

While I worked, I watched the hippo hunt. It was a mad affair. The men of each boat gabbled and shouted and poked spears at the hippos bobbing around them. There were eight guys on Riley's boat when two or three would have been plenty. The way the vessels swayed back and forth, it was only a matter of time before someone took a tumble. I was afraid Riley or one of the others might fall in and be killed. But I didn't want the hippos hurt either.

And then it happened. One boat rocked a bit too hard, throwing its occupants into the water. I jumped up as the air rang with shouts from the guys on the other boats urging their friends back on board.

After a tense few minutes, five managed to clamber to safety. But one did not. He was swept along by the current.

As he floated past, he looked right at me and shouted: "Please, I implore—". A mouthful of water drowned out the rest of the sentence.

"Oh mighty Osiris!" whispered Amunet.

"Doesn't he know how to swim?"

"To...what?"

Even swimming wouldn't save him if those hippos got to him first. I counted four pinky-brown heads moving his way. The hunters on the other boats weren't much use either. In their panic, the oarsmen were at odds. They were going nowhere fast.

"Is no one going to save him?" I asked.

"It's in the hands of the gods now," said Amunet.

Without pausing to think, I dived into the river. A brief shock of cold, then I swam as fast as I could out to where I'd last seen him. All that remained was a swirl and a few bubbles.

Treading water, I looked up at Riley, who pointed straight down. The guy must be beneath me. So I took a deep breath and duck-dived.

The water was murky but after a few seconds I saw him struggling not far away. His eyes were wide with terror and bubbles escaped his mouth in bursts. I swam over, grabbed his arm and kicked wildly for the surface. On my way up, I scanned the opaque water and saw a hippo sink to the river bottom and propel itself back up again.

We broke the surface and gulped down the air gratefully. The guy wrapped his arms around my neck.

"Can't breathe!" I croaked.

He loosened his grip a tad, but I had to kick doubly hard to keep us afloat. When a hippo head popped up not far away and he tried to climb onto my shoulders, I couldn't keep us up. So we sank like a stone.

I tried to fight the downward momentum, but I was rapidly tiring and the blue sky, which looked wobbly through the water, was getting further away. Down, down. My arms and legs felt like jelly, my chest was tight. We weren't going to make it.

But then we hit the sandy bottom and, following the hippo's lead, I pushed off as hard as I could. Bit by bit we rose skywards and, when my lungs felt as if they were about to explode, we broke the surface.

"Calm down and stay still," I said sharply.

"As you say," the guy said. "What must I do?"

"Can you float on your back?"

"I think so," he said.

"Then do it," I ordered. "I will guide us out."

I trawled my brain for the life-saving techniques I had learned in Little Nippers training at Bondi beach. Holding him by the chin, I kicked towards the river bank, though my progress was slow.

I glanced back and saw two—no, three—hippos after us. One opened its jaw, displaying huge brown canines that could crush us like toothpicks.

"Keep your eyes closed," I ordered.

So naturally the guy opened them and let out a scream that could have reached the 21st century.

Behind me, there was this strange kind of whooping noise, which I wouldn't have expected from a hippo, followed by rapid splashing. I wondered what it meant but dared not look back.

I expected to feel jaws scissoring through my flesh any moment. Would I even feel the bite? Maybe I wouldn't even notice my leg was gone till I tried to stand on the bloody stump. I pushed back these gruesome thoughts and focused on stroke, stroke, stroking towards the bank.

Then came the whoop again, louder and closer, followed by more frenzied splashing. I just had to look.

What did I find? That the hippos weren't the ones making the noise. It was Riley! He was on a boat, with just one other guy, yelping in that strange way as he churned the water with his pole and prodded the animals to divert their attention from us. But even this would not save us. The lead hippo was close enough for us to see our stricken faces reflected in its eyes. Slowly, it opened its massive jaw ready to bite.

"Oh, mighty Ra!" the boy gasped.

What came next was a blur, it happened so fast. Riley leapt out of the boat onto the barely visible back of the nearest hippo. He continued leaping from hippo to hippo as if they were stepping stones in a pond. I don't know who was more surprised—them or me.

Several snorted, one snapped—but missed. Unfortunately, the hippo closest to us paid no attention. I squeezed my eyes shut, expecting the worst. There was a splash and a grunt. When I looked back, Riley was in the water. He'd snapped his spear in half and rammed one of the broken bits vertically into the animal's mouth to stop it closing.

The Egyptian guy and I hit the river bank and surged out as we heard the wood crunch in the hippo's jaw. Looking back, I saw Riley was still in the water, trapped behind two hippos. He'd need to go around the animals to get to shore, which was dodgy enough, but then another hippo popped up right next to him.

"No!" I screamed, rushing back into the water as I shrieked and splashed wildly. The animals couldn't resist a peek to see what the commotion was about. While they did, Riley squeezed between them, headed for safety.

One hippo snapped its jaws as he went past. Too late. But the sound of that snap! I'd never forget it.

I thought the creature might follow us onto the river bank. The three of us—Riley, me and the guy I'd rescued—tensed, ready to run. Instead, the hippo gave us a beady-eyed scowl before slowly sinking beneath the surface.

From the other boats came a cheer. Some of the hunters jumped up and down in excitement, upending two more of the boats. *Idiots!* Thankfully, they all made it back on board, for in my weakened state I couldn't have helped.

Riley sank down onto the ground and closed his eyes.

"That was close," he said.

"You took a stupid risk back there," I said. "Thrusting your arm right into the hippo's mouth! What would I have done if you'd been hurt? How would I get back home?"

"Sorry," he said.

"So you should be," I said. "And by the way, thanks for saving us."

"Thanks yourself," he murmured.

I flopped on the bank beside him and closed my eyes. It took a few minutes for my heartbeat to feel anything like normal. When I opened my eyes again, Amunet was staring down at me, her dark hair dangling towards my face.

"Where did you learn to do that?" she said.

"Do what?"

"Move through the water like a fish."

"At school."

"Girls go to school in Nubia?"

I sat up and swept my wet hair out of my face. *Get your lies straight, Maddy.* "Sorry, not school. The pool. That's what we call the river near us. That's where I learned to move like a fish."

Behind her, I saw the guy I'd saved watching me and frowning. His sleeveless white tunic was soaked, his dark hair wet-pasted to his head. Even so, there was something about him—the well-defined jaw, thick lashes framing eyes like caramel swirls—that made it hard to look away.

"I am not accustomed to taking orders from a woman." His voice was deep and resonant.

"Well, I'm not accustomed to having to risk my life for clumsy people who fall into rivers full of hippos! So I guess it's a first for both of us."

I stood up to wipe the wet mud off my dress. It was a hopeless task, the grains were wedged into the weave. *Another heavy piece of cloth to add to the washing pile!*

When I looked back, the Egyptian guy had a *Terminator* eye lock on me. "Normally, you would pay heavily for such insolence," he said, "but today I will spare your punishment in gratitude for the service you have done me."

"Well, you're welcome," I said. "But before you go for a paddle again, can you do us all a favour? Learn to swim. So someone doesn't have to take a bath in their clothes to fish you out."

Amunet shook her head rapidly in warning. I sensed Riley standing up slowly next to me, ready to step in if he needed to.

But I had this. I'd dealt with bullies before and arrogant guys who thought they could order me around. The best way to handle them was to stand up to them. So I held the guy's gaze, folded my arms and gave him a "Not cool dude!" headshake, daring him to say more.

He turned away for maybe a minute. I saw his chest expand and a muscle on his jawline clench. I was a little worried that maybe I'd gone too far. But when he turned back, he laughed as if it was all a big joke.

"But where are my manners?" he said, all charm. "Before I say another word, I should thank you. For saving my life. You were very brave."

"It's okay," I said, waving it away. *No biggie.* No need to fuss.

The other boats had reached the shore by now. The boys rushed over to check on the guy, all talking at once. I thought I saw a couple bowing.

"Is he someone special?" I asked Amunet.

"He is the son of the great vizier."

"What's a vizier?"

"He advises our Pharaoh on matters of business. His family has a beautiful home and many servants."

So, he was a rich accountant's son? So what?

"His family has been searching for a suitable wife for him for some time," said Amunet. "He has travelled all over the land and met many beautiful girls. But none has captured his heart."

I looked around and saw that the guys from the boats had formed two lines, like a guard of honour, with an open path

between them. At one end was the rescued guy, at the other end—
me. He looked straight down the line at me, smiling broadly.

"Until now," I heard Amunet say behind me.

Slowly, he stalked forwards, like a cat approaching a
fishbowl—with me the fish, trapped inside.

Uh-oh.

He stopped in front of me. "My name is Phoenix. I give
thanks to the gods for sending you here today." He held out
his hand, inviting me to take it. "And you are...?"

All heads turned my way, stupid half grins on their faces.
Amunet's was the silliest of all. Riley was the only one not
smiling. Because he knew, as I did, that *that* look, on *this* guy,
at *this* point in history, could mean only one thing. Trouble.

But what could I do? The guy wanted a name. It would
be rude and possibly even fatal not to give him one. So I took
his hand and shook it firmly.

"My name is Sacmis. Pleased to meet you."

CHAPTER 12

"Was that a good idea? Giving your name as Sacmis," Riley asked as we walked back through the fields, clutching armloads of clean white clothes.

"You think I should have given my own name?"

"No," he said. Though it sounded more like a yes.

"Trust me, we do not need that kind of complication," I said. "Sacmis is welcome to...what was his name again?"

"Phoenix."

"She can have Phoenix and his massive ego. And all the problems he'll bring her way. You and I should just do our job here, get the toothpaste happening, help Amunet's family with the tax and leave. Clean and simple."

It was late afternoon by the time Amunet and I finished the laundry. I couldn't remember ever being so tired. The sky was a pale blue, the heat had eased a smidge. But the smell of dung was sharp, catching in the back of my throat.

All the farmers were gone from the fields, replaced by dark-haired young women collecting veggies for their families' dinner. Kids with thick plaits like ship's ropes ran through the fields, sunlight glancing off their shiny scalps, shouting and laughing with their friends. And everywhere I looked, people pointed to me and whispered behind their hands.

"I wonder what would have happened to Phoenix if you hadn't been there," Riley asked.

"He would have drowned, no question."

"Are you sure? Was it possible someone else might have saved him, or he might have saved himself?"

"No way. He was going down in that river and almost out of air when I yanked him up again."

Riley nodded slowly. "You know he's the grand vizier's son?"

"Amunet said that was some kind of business manager for the Pharaoh? Is that like an accountant or something?"

"I think it's a bit more than that. From what I've read, the vizier is very close to the Pharaoh. And the Pharaoh is like a king, here. Like a god, actually. He's really powerful."

"Oh."

Then maybe I shouldn't have brushed him off so quickly. Perhaps he could have used his influence to fix Amunet's family's tax problems. Still, a guy like that would probably create more problems than he solved. Overall, I reckoned we were well rid of him.

"Did you get a chance to check on the time machine while we were there?" I asked.

In all the excitement, I'd forgotten to look. *Du-uh!*

"It's safe," Riley said. "All systems functioning."

"That's a relief."

Riley and I walked along in silence. Which was okay, for a while. But when it went on for too long, I looked over and saw my friend's lips twisted to one side and his forehead buckled.

"Spit it out!" I said. "What's on your mind?"

"Nothing. It's just, well, Phoenix was lucky you were there today."

"Yes, and...?"

"And if you hadn't been there, then..."

"Then what?"

He chewed his lip, then looked over at me. "You've read books on time travel?"

"Yeah, of course." Or, at least, I'd seen a couple of films.

"Those stories always stress that you shouldn't change the past in case it affects the future significantly."

"Significantly?"

"You know: if you change one thing, it changes something else, and so on and so on. Like a ripple effect."

"Yeah?"

"It's just that you saving Phoenix today could be quite a change to history."

"Well, what was I supposed to do? Let him drown?"

"No, I guess not." Sounded like a yes to me.

"Well, maybe you're the sort who can stand by and watch someone drown for the sake of science," I said, "but I'm not."

We carried on walking, dry earth crunching loudly beneath our feet. It was ridiculous to think anything *I* did could have much impact on history. I was just an ordinary high school girl, not some heroic figure from history.

"What about the toothpaste thing you're trying to do?" I said. "Won't that affect a lot of lives, too?"

"I suppose. But not as significantly."

"But that girl mummy in the museum died of tooth abscess, didn't she? If she had toothpaste, that would have changed her life quite a bit."

"Mostly it's just hygiene," he said. "A way to stop people having so much toothache in their lives."

At that point, Amunet and Layla raced over to greet us. "Did you see the hippo's teeth?" said Layla.

"Yes, unfortunately!" I said.

"How much do you think it would have hurt if it bit you?"

"Layla! Please!" Amunet scolded. "What a question!"

The little girl blushed, but couldn't stop. "Were you really, really scared?" she asked.

"Yes, I was," I said.

"Do not bother Madison. She has had a tiring day," said Amunet.

"Sorry." Layla bowed her head in apology. "May I help carry the clean clothes?"

Layla grabbed half my load, then raced up ahead (dragging the white linen through the dirt) to report back to her friend, who kept turning back to look at me with big eyes of awe.

"Layla! The clothes!" Amunet shouted, shaking her head in frustration. Riley raced ahead to take some of the load off the girl.

"I am sorry my sister has plagued your ears with her childish questions," Amunet said.

"It's okay, I don't mind."

But then Amunet had a few of her own. "What did you think of Phoenix? Weren't his eyes beautiful? What about his muscular arms, his commanding voice?"

"He was okay, I guess."

For some reason, I thought of Jamie Fletcher then and wondered what he was up to. Would he even notice I was missing? Probably not. Phoenix reminded me of him in some way. They both had too much confidence in their own power to impress.

Amunet ran ahead, and I caught up with Riley, who was stroking a non-existent beard. Something was bothering him. As it bothered me too. But like the words to a song you can't quite make out, I couldn't say exactly what it was. It was just a feeling that we'd missed something. Something big.

"The vizier should make a generous offering to the gods for bringing you to the river today," Amunet called back. "For if you had not come with me to help clean the linen on this day, his only son would now be at the bottom of the river. And his line of succession would be at an end."

CHAPTER 13

"Our village has never seen a more heroic act than yours," said Sahara as we ate dinner with the family that night. "Imagine, a girl rescuing a man in mortal danger! But how is it that you are so strong in the water?"

I tried to fob her off with luck of the moment, lots of water play as a kid, but she wouldn't let it go.

I turned to Riley. "It looks like we'll have to tell the truth," I said. He almost choked on his mouthful as I began my tale of how the Nubian god of water called Aqua-marinus (the best I could do at short notice) had visited our family one evening in dreams and instructed Riley and I on how to stay afloat in the river and in water rescue techniques. "She told me this was in preparation for an important future event."

"That event," said Razi excitedly, "was undoubtedly the rescue of Phoenix, son of the vizier!"

"And you should have heard the way Madison spoke to Phoenix," said Amunet. "The goddess Tawaret has never heard a woman speak to a man this way before, much less a person from a village speak to one so high born. At first, I thought he would have you whipped. Or worse. But he seemed to like it. In fact, he seemed to like you very much indeed."

Everyone stopped mid-chew to stare at me.

"So why did you tell him your name was Sacmis?" she asked.

"Well, I...umm..." I dug deep within the lie bank but came up empty. Just as the silence was getting embarrassing, rescue came from an unexpected source.

"My sister is almost betrothed to someone in Nubia," Riley said. "Nothing is formal yet, but my parents are negotiating the terms of the union in our absence."

I nodded vigorously to confirm this. *Good one, Riley.*

"You did not mention this before?" said Amunet.

"Well, as nothing's happened officially," I said, "I didn't want to count my chickens, you know?" Blank looks all around. *Oops. Counting your chickens before they hatched* was an old expression, but not that old it seemed.

"That is," I continued, "I thought it would be bad luck to say anything to you about my betrothal until it has been sealed." They nodded in unison. Bad luck, they understood.

"But why did you choose Sacmis, of all names?" asked Razi.

"Well," I said, taking a long swig of my drink to buy some thinking time, "I knew Sacmis was not Amunet's friend. So I thought a union with Phoenix might mean she and her family would have to move far away from here, somewhere you may not encounter them so frequently."

In truth, it was the first Egyptian girl name that popped into my head at the time.

"But are you sure, Madison, you don't want Phoenix for yourself?" said Amunet. "He's rich and important and very handsome. He may prove to be a better match than the boy from your village."

"And high-born men like him rarely choose those from humble backgrounds," Sahara added. "This would be a great honour for you."

"No, my heart belongs to another," I said.

"I understand," said Amunet quickly. "Where the heart goes, you cannot but follow." Her gaze drifted to Riley, who was ladling stew onto his bread and didn't notice.

As we finished eating, some men from the village arrived with gifts for the family—a stack of fresh flat bread and a generous basket of vegetables.

"This is to thank your guest for her brave deed, which brings honour to our village," said a super-short man with gappy teeth. "We believe you were sent from the sky by the god Ptah himself to bring glory upon us all."

He was right—I did come from the sky. But my god of travel was Riley Sinclair.

CHAPTER 14

For the next few mornings I was awoken before dawn. I staggered out of bed—well, got up off the floor anyway—nibbled some fruit and bread for breakfast, then joined the rest of the family already hard at work making goods to trade at the next market in the main square.

My family back home would have been amused to see me smiling and saying a polite "Good morning" when I usually grunted and threw things at anyone who woke me too early.

My family. Just the thought of them made my stomach tighten and twist like the linen we'd washed by the Nile. Homesickness. I'd never experienced anything like it. I mean, I was a bit yearny for home during school camp but, in truth, it was my bath I missed most. I longed for some warm perfumed bubbles to wash off the week of camp grime. Now, as I notched up almost as long in Ancient Egypt, I would have traded any number of scented soaks for an evening laughing with Mum, Dad and Gran. I could hardly bear to think of what they'd be going through back home with us missing. It was only because Riley had promised to reverse time and erase their pain that I was able to carry on.

Between us, we'd agreed to stay a few more days to help boost the family's market earnings. But as soon as they had cleared their tax debt, we'd be off—him to fame and glory with his time machine, me to my pyjamas, my family and friends and a huge bar of chocolate. I could hardly wait.

Thankfully, making goods for the market did take a lot of time and focus, so there wasn't too much chance to mope. We each had our own projects. Once Sahara had finished the two dresses for me—one plain like hers, the other pleated, with colourful stones around the collar—she began making more to sell at our stall.

Riley helped Sahara bake bread every afternoon. And on market day morning, they planned to get up extra early to make some for the stall. I noticed he'd fashioned a kind of linen hood over the stone slab where he worked the dough.

"Let me guess," I said. "That stops sand getting into the bread and ruining people's teeth?"

Riley grinned and nodded. *Clever.* And when he finally came up with the local recipe for toothpaste, it would be even more amazing. But though he searched every spare moment, a few key ingredients were still proving elusive.

Layla was hard at work, too, making dung bricks to trade. When I heard this, I gritted my teeth and offered to help. The feel of it squishing through my fingers was beyond revolting. And the smell? It was pretty gross at first, but after a while I barely noticed it, which was perhaps more disturbing. We made lots of bricks and the process got really repetitive. So I suggested we try different shapes: circles, squares and pyramids of dung. Then we moved onto animals: crocodiles, dogs and hippos. Eventually we got really ambitious, and sculpted shapes of gods: Horus the falcon, Anubis the jackal, and Sobek the crocodile. I thought it was pretty artistic and

Layla was really excited...until we showed Sahara. She didn't say anything, but the withering look she gave ensured all the rest of our bricks were the standard rectangular variety.

Razi worked all the daylight hours making jewellery to trade. He said the pieces weren't up to his father's standard, but I thought they were pretty and wouldn't look out of place on a modern market stall. He made single- and multi-strands of beads, as well as several brooches in the shape of beetles.

"They're cute," I said. "Are they ladybirds?"

"That is the scarab, or dung beetle," he explained. "It is a symbol of fertility or new life." Dung was a symbol of new life? *Seriously!*

My favourite piece was a pendant shaped like an eye and inlaid with a blue stone. "This is the eye of Horus," said Razi. "He protects against evil."

I had my own personal project too. I had made, with Amunet and Layla's giggling assistance, a prototype of a scarecrow. We found some old broken spears to use as the frame. We made a head from reeds, with black river stones for eyes, and dressed the scarecrow up in my track pants and T-shirt. It was sure to cause a stir.

But would it bring in any surplus to help pay the family's tax bill?

On market day, we got up while it was still dark, loaded our wares into wicker baskets, with rolled-up mats to display them on, and hurried into the village. The dung bricks went ahead on a donkey borrowed from a neighbour.

Lots of others villagers had the same idea. The streets were thick with people pushing past each other to get to the best spot for their stall.

"Hey, you know who'd really like to be here now?" I said to Riley. "Lauren. She loves markets."

"Lauren who?" he said. I looked over to see if he was joking, but there was the usual clueless look.

"Honestly, Riley!"

By the time the sun rose, the streets were heaving with people haggling over prices or spruiking their wares. Not surprisingly, fresh fruit and vegetables were big sellers. A few stalls offered cooked food—mostly stew in pocket bread. Some ready-made clothes were on sale, though nothing like the volume in modern markets. And some sold cloth, including one man who went about draped in shiny silver material. One of my favourite stalls sold papyrus, though as most people couldn't read or write, the product wasn't exactly walking out the door—unlike Sahara and Riley's bread, which was gone in under an hour.

There was some really wild stuff too. Leopard skins with the head still attached, elephant tusks and a platter made out of a crocodile's bottom jaw. *Gross!*

In the main square, people crowded round to watch some sort of show. Riley and I pushed through the spectators, expecting to see some local musicians or dancers. But that's not what it was.

Three men, with ebony skin and bulging muscles, stood in a line, hands and feet bound, as an older man with a sleazy smile addressed the crowd.

"Gather round," he said. "Come, view this week's prime human merchandise. Fine specimens for you to procure today."

"Procure?" I said. "Wait, they're not...?"

Riley nodded grimly. "Slaves."

"So this is a slave auction?"

"Look at the arms on that middle one," a man in front of us whispered to his friend. "He'd be useful at harvest time. He could do the work of many beasts."

"But the man on the right looks more youthful," said his friend. "He may not be as strong, but he would give his master many more summers of labour."

The auctioneer dragged the first offering forward by his rope handcuffs, prodding him with a stick to get him to turn slowly for the crowd's inspection. "This man is a prisoner of war who fought bravely for his leader," said the seller. "For the right price, he could be yours to take home today."

The prisoner looked up just then, straight at me. His eyes were so dark they were almost black, and dull—all spark of hope extinguished.

"This is terrible," I said, not that softly. A few people looked around at me.

"It's not just Egypt who has slaves," Riley whispered. "A lot of other places do too."

"Well, it sucks."

One by one, the men were sold off. Each winning bid was greeted by polite applause from the crowd.

"But don't go yet, people," said the auctioneer. "For we have saved the best till last."

The best? No, the worst. An Egyptian girl, no older than fourteen, was led into the arena. Head hung low, she stood trembling before us. "This girl offers herself today to the highest bidder," said the seller.

I searched the faces of the men and women around us, expecting shock or outrage. But there was none. Selling a fourteen-year-old girl was not that unusual, so it seemed. The auctioneer pinched her chin between his fingers, forcing her head right to left for inspection. She squeezed her eyes shut, but the tears snuck out, streaking her cheeks.

"She volunteered herself for sale today to help her family," said the auctioneer, "which shows she has a dutiful nature. One day, she may make a good wife for one of your sons and produce many fine children. Or, she may simply be used as a servant for many years to come."

"Used?" I said. "I can't watch this. We have to do something."

"No." Riley gripped my arm and whispered: "Nothing you say or do will change the way these people think. All that will happen is we'll get into trouble. And then..."

He licked his lips, but he didn't need to say it. If we were in strife, we might not be able to help Amunet's family with their tax. Or worse, we might never get back home. I couldn't risk either of those outcomes. There was nothing I could do. Except give the man a really dirty look.

The bidding was fierce with at least six bidders. The woman who won had filmy eyes and a turned-down mouth.

"That girl is from the next village," Amunet said. "She offered herself as a slave to raise money for her family's unpaid tax."

PAULENE TURNER

"She was traded for a tax bill?"

I watched the new owner leading the girl down the road. The slave girl's shoulders shook with sobs and, when she was too slow, her new mistress shoved her in the back, making her stumble.

"Poor girl," I said.

"Do not worry," said Amunet. "I know in other lands slaves are treated cruelly, but here they have many rights. They often become part of the family or marry into it. And, one day, their owners may grant their freedom or they may buy it back for themselves."

I hoped Amunet was right, that the girl's new masters would be kind and her family would soon find the wealth to buy back her freedom. But most of all I hoped that, come next market day, it would not be Amunet or Layla in the arena being sold off to clear their tax debt.

It was crucial that we did well here today.

CHAPTER 15

By mid-morning, though, things were looking pretty good. Layla's dung bricks had sold out, as had the extra clothes Sahara made. And Razi had a slow but steady stream of customers for his jewellery. In payment, we got a couple of geese for dinner (we'd have to kill them ourselves), some silver, a bolt of golden fabric, some oil and grain.

I'm sorry to say, by late morning my scarecrow was still up for sale. Though it did draw lots of curious people to the stall. And while they were there, they sometimes found other things to buy instead.

Around noon, Amunet and I met up with some girls from her local dance troupe to start warming up for a show. They had practised all week for their performance here. It wasn't because they were expecting people to throw coins or goods to them, as with buskers from our time. They wanted to catch the eye of a rich person looking to hire a group of entertainers for a party or private dinner. Recorded music had not yet been invented so live performers were in demand for dinners and parties for the wealthy.

In between my dung brick and scarecrow projects, I had practised with Amunet's troupe and had given them all a good laugh too. They couldn't believe a girl, even one from southern Nubia, could be so hopeless at their style of dancing. After a while, though, I caught on to the rhythms of the swirling, seductive steps and the howling songs.

"Now that I have learnt your music and dance," I said during one rehearsal, "it's time for you to try one of my Nubian songs."

So, I taught them *Lean On Me* and a few more modern moves. They caught on pretty fast too, once they stopped giggling long enough to listen.

Today, our group of six dancers would try our luck in the market square and see how many offers we received.

"Over there looks like a good spot for our show," I said, pointing to a clear, flat space just beyond the stalls.

Amunet looked over and licked her lips. "Maybe we should delay the performance, practise some more and return next month."

A few of the girls nodded eagerly.

"No, we're here now," I said. "We're doing this. You're just nervous."

We cleared sticks and stones from the ground, then got into our start positions. One girl had a harp, another some wooden pan-pipes. The rest of us had tiny metal clickers between our fingers.

When people saw us preparing, they drifted over to watch, causing a wave of panic to run through the group again. Once more, Amunet suggested waiting till next month "when we are truly ready".

"No." I shook my head firmly. "We're ready now."

"What if people laugh at us?" said Amunet.

"They won't."

"What if we make a mistake?" said another girl.

"We know the dance routine well," I said. "We'll be okay."

They took their start positions and I counted us in: "One, two, three…" No one moved. "Come on girls. We'll lose the audience!"

Before us was a sea of dark and bald heads, with one wavy, blond head bobbing forward. Riley burst through the crowd, carrying an empty grain vat.

"I thought I might keep the beat with you on this? Is that okay?" he said.

"I'm not sure," I said. "The girls are pretty nervous."

"We would be delighted for you to join us, Riley," said Amunet. "Get ready, girls!"

The routine kicked off weakly. A couple of the dancers banged into each other and stopped, but I kept the others going and, by the end of the first song, we got our act together. Another dozen or more people came over to watch for the second dance. That went well too, with the audience clapping enthusiastically. The girls began to relax and enjoy themselves. Amunet was the happiest of the lot—especially with Riley, whose drumming did give our routine a boost.

Halfway through the third dance, I spotted Sacmis in the middle of the second row. She wasn't smiling. It wasn't just spite, I knew, but professional jealousy too. Sacmis had a dance troupe of her own in another part of the market. We were competing for the same rich clients.

When her eyes met mine, she gave me the full-witch treatment—slitted eyes, lips comically taut. I nodded and beamed at her as if I was her best friend—stickin' it to her again. Her response was incendiary.

I saw her hand jerk over her head and a shower of stones bounced around our feet. One by one, the girls cried out and began hopping about in pain. The music stopped.

"I'm bleeding," said one.

"Ahhh!"

"What was that?" said Amunet.

I trod on something small and sharp. *Ow!* Crouching down, I saw it was a stone—razor sharp—specially selected to put us off our steps. As all the girls hopped about in pain or sat on the ground to dig out sharp stones embedded in the soles of their feet, the audience wandered away. Furious, I looked around for Sacmis. But she had vanished.

"What a...girl dog!" I said to Riley.

"You should probably take it as a compliment," said Riley, "that she sees you and the troupe as a real threat."

"She's right," I said. "I am a real threat."

We checked everyone's feet. There were no serious injuries—just minor cuts and major embarrassment. "Better clear all the stones away before we start again," I said.

"Again?" said Amunet, and all the girls look surprised. "But we cannot dance again this day. We have been shamed."

"It is not us shamed by this. It's her—Sacmis. And we're not going to let her ruin our show," I said. "Get up, get ready. We'll start again in five minutes."

I steered Riley through the market crowd. "We need to find Sacmis. And make sure she doesn't do this again."

"Are you thinking of getting some kind of revenge?" Riley asked. "They say the best revenge is living well. In this case, it would be to dance well—better than Sacmis's troupe."

"Yeah," I said, "we'll do that, but we need something more to remind her not to mess with us!"

I thought Riley might say we should move on, not look back, *blah blah blah*. Instead, he went quiet and still, his forehead wrinkling just a tad, like the hallway rug at the end of the day. This was the look he got whenever his science brain fired up.

"Wait here," he said, and rushed off.

It was kind of thrilling imagining what my genius friend might come up with. Would it be a powder to make her break out in an itchy rash that spelled *KICK ME QUICK?* A pill to whip up a wind storm—from her rear end? Or a drink containing truth serum so the whole world would see the poison in her mind? Whatever it was, I knew it would be awesome.

In a relatively short time he was back with something gathered in the folds of his shirt.

"What is it?" I asked.

"You'll see!" He grinned. "Come on."

I followed him to the far end of the market where Sacmis's troupe was performing to a large crowd. Sacmis was centre-stage making snake eyes at all the guys. When she saw us, the smile froze on her face. She watched Riley crouch down and line up on the ground six brown balls, about the size of large marbles, almost perfectly spherical.

I squatted next to him. "What are they?"

"Mud balls. I'm going to flick them at her feet."

"Mud balls?" I was unimpressed. "You're going to make her feet dirty? *That* is the plan of the greatest scientific mind of our time?"

He closed one eye and flicked the first ball. It rolled straight and sure towards Sacmis, stopping just short of her feet. Then he did the same with the other five. They all got close to her, but none touched her.

"Oh no, you missed!" I said.

Sacmis looked down at the balls, then smiled back at us, savouring a moment of triumph before stomping on all six balls, *in...time...with the...song.* Her pretty smile grew wider with each stamp. I was starting to get really annoyed when I saw her face change. A crinkle, then a deep trench formed on her forehead, and she began hopping about in pain.

"Mud balls with mashed chilli centres," said Riley. "Oh and I put some of the stones she threw at us inside them. They would have cut the skin providing multiple points of access for the chilli juice."

The chilli would burn the skin like the fires of Hell without doing permanent damage—except to her image.

Sacmis's face twisted in pain. Spotting a man in the audience with a drink, she snatched it off him and poured it over her foot. It cooled for a few seconds (unlike him—he was furious), then the heat must have flared again as she raced through the crowd in search of further relief.

By now, everyone was laughing.

"Nice move, Sacmis! Was that part of the routine?" called one joker.

"That was a hot dance!" said another—me, actually.

Riley and I grinned at each other. Those blond curls might make him look like an angel, but there was at least a bit of wicked in him. I liked it.

We raced back to our own crew and started the show again. After a couple of songs, we were back into the rhythm and had quite a big audience.

"Let's do *Lean On Me* girls!" I said. "One...two...three!"

A man at the front with ears like jug handles thrust his bottom lip out in horror and confusion. The whole crowd appeared to be bewildered. It was a style of music they had never heard before. Gradually, though, they warmed up. Some began trying to clap the rhythm with me, which drew others over to watch.

We did our best performance ever.

As we danced, I caught the eye of a guy in the second row. In his thirties, maybe, with a trimmed beard and a twinkly smile, he nodded a greeting to me and whispered something to the woman next to him. She looked over and smiled.

Our last song got heaps of applause and even a few cheers. Amunet and her friends were beyond thrilled—squealing, jumping about and hugging each other. Caught up in the moment, Riley and I went to hug each other too, but pulled back at the last moment.

"Good job," I said, punching him lightly on the shoulder.

"You, too."

We kept smiling at each other in this goofy way. It was the buzz of the moment, I suppose.

"Maddy," he said, "there's something I've been meaning to say to you."

"Yes, Riley?"

He looked down at the ground and took a slow breath, then cleared his throat and looked up at me. "I want to tell you...that is, I've wanted to tell you for quite a while...that I—" he cleared his throat "—I really like—"

"That was admirable!" The twinkly man from the audience appeared at our side. "A feast for the eyes and ears! You are all to be commended for your formidable talents."

"Well, thank you," I said.

"My name is Azizi."

"And I am Dalali," said the woman with him.

"We are servants of the grand vizier. And we come to you with an invitation."

As Amunet and the girls rushed over to listen, the man told us the chief vizier was having a large birthday banquet at his home the following week. "We would be honoured if your troupe would perform for the vizier on his special day," he said. "If you are not previously engaged?"

"Amunet is our leader," I said. "You'll have to ask her."

Azizi turned to her, bowing and grinning. "What say you, Amunet? Will you grace the vizier's home with your presence and that of your lovely dancers?"

Amunet pulled herself up to her full height and appeared to consider it coolly. "Tell the vizier it would be our great pleasure to perform at his party."

So an agreement was reached. And Amunet seemed like a cool-headed, professional negotiator. But the guy had only moved a few steps away before she began bouncing about again, wild with excitement.

Back at the stall, the scarecrow was still up for sale, which was disappointing. Sahara said a lot of people had been curious about it. But so far, no-one had made an offer. I thought I'd give it one last try.

"Roll up, roll up!" I shouted. "Who would like this lovely scarecrow? He'll keep the birds off your crops so you can keep the kids working on the dung bricks!"

Parents passing chuckled at this. Kids didn't find it that funny.

"Why waste time and energy throwing rocks at birds," I called, "when a look from this scary guy will send the crows flapping in fear!"

A dozen people slowed down to listen now, a mix of men and women with half-grins on their faces. Riley came over to watch, too, Amunet trailing him like a lovesick puppy.

"I call this model Uncle Joe," I said. "Because it looks a lot like my uncle—but much more handsome!"

Laughter burst from the crowd! They were easy to please. But what would make them go a step further and buy the thing? I had it!

"This design will not only scare the crows, it will bring good luck to the owner." Egyptians were superstitious. I'd play to that. "Just as the spirits of our ancestors rise up from their graves, so these scarecrows are a symbol of rising from death...for all eternity."

People glanced sideways at each other. A woman, small and bony like a bird, spoke first. "I will give two pieces of gold for this scarecrow," she said. "That is more than it is worth. You are robbing me."

Sahara smiled and nodded to me. I was tempted to take the gold, but there was something in the woman's eye—a glint of greed. I had watched Gran playing poker often enough to know a bluff when I saw it. The woman wanted the scarecrow and was prepared to pay more than her first offer. I just needed to figure out how much more.

"Two pieces of gold?" I said, as if surprised. "But think of how many days of labour it will save and how much more time you and your husband will have to spend with the children."

"There's one reason NOT to buy it!" a man called out to general cackles.

"Then think of all the crops that will be saved," I said, "of the surplus vegetables you will be able to trade at the next market if the crows fly past your patch and onto someone else's."

"All right," said the woman. "I will give you three pieces of gold and some grain to make bread. That is my final offer."

Sahara beamed now—this was good. I didn't want to blow it by pushing too hard. But there was more to be had here. I could feel it.

"And look at the exotic clothes on the creature," I said. "Whoever buys this, ladies and gentlemen, will have the only one of its kind in the village. No, the only one in the country. Wait, no! The only one in the world. How many times can any of us truly say, we were the first?"

People went quiet.

"I will give you five gold pieces and some oil," said a man with only one good eye and a sunken socket.

"Seven gold pieces and four fish for tonight's dinner," said another, displaying a mouthful of grey teeth.

"Ten gold pieces and this," said a man with a head like a bowling ball. The "this" made me forget to breathe.

"What is it?" said Sahara. "It is gold, but with such a strange pattern. Is it Nubian?"

In his hand was an Australian two-dollar coin.

"Where did you get that?" Riley asked the man.

"From that man over there!" He pointed to a tall blond man in a striking outfit of gold cloth. When he saw us looking, the man took off into the crowd.

"You have a deal, sir," I said to my buyer. "Sahara will sort you out. Will you excuse me for a moment?"

I jerked my head at Riley and the pair of us charged after the man. His pale hair was easy to follow in this dark-haired crowd.

"Wait!" I shouted after him.

He didn't look back but kept moving, suspiciously fast, like he was running away. We got to the main square, which was thick with traders packing up or negotiating last-minute deals. I scanned each person in the square. Once. Twice.

"Do you see him?" I asked Riley.

He shook his head. "He's gone."

"But how did he get away so fast?"

We hurried back to catch the buyer, who had roped in two men to help him carry the scarecrow.

"Who was that man with the gold coin?" I asked. "Did you know him?"

"No."

"Did he give you his name?" Riley asked.

The man frowned. "He said he was the son of Peter."

The son of Peter? *Hmmm*. That rang a distant bell.

As the three of them proceeded along the street, a crowd of curious people followed them.

"What is this circle?" Razi asked, inspecting the Australian coin. "It's beautiful. Is it Nubian?"

"Yes," I said. "It's not worth much in itself, but perhaps the taxman might find it interesting."

"You got a good price for your scarecrow," said Sahara. "You must use it to trade for something you want."

"No, no," I said. "This payment is for you. For your family's kind hospitality."

Sahara tried to argue, but I insisted. Finally, she hugged me tightly. "Thank you, Madison and Riley. We have all done well today. Perhaps tonight, I will not have to see the taxman in my dreams."

"Thank the gods for that, for it is not a pretty sight," said Razi, making a face and a rare joke.

"Do you think one of us might have dropped that coin," I asked Riley as we walked home, a little way behind the others. "Could this 'son of Peter' have found it on the ground somewhere?"

"Not much chance I dropped it," said Riley. "I checked and double-checked my supplies before we left Sydney. What about you?"

Could the coin have been in my back pocket when I jogged over to Riley's that night? "It's possible, I suppose."

"If not, that would be...interesting," said Riley.

"Interesting, how?"

"It would mean that someone else besides us is time travelling."

"Interesting" was one word for it. "Alarming" would be another. A "mind-blowing earth-shattering disaster" was closer to the truth.

"But you probably just dropped it," said Riley.

CHAPTER 16

We slept in the next morning. It was almost light when we got up. *Luxury!* We were slower than usual to get going, just kicking back with a drink and some fruit as we talked over our success at the market the previous day.

Razi was in the best mood I'd seen him in. He smiled a lot and chatted about our dance performance. He even did his own imitation of the steps which had us all laughing. "It was a day of good fortune when my sister Amunet met our friends Riley and Madison in the village," he said.

"And for us," I added quickly. "Do you think we got enough surplus yesterday to cover the tax bill?"

All eyes turned to Sahara. "We will know soon," she said. "However, I am hopeful we will have sufficient to pay our tax. With many thanks to the generous contribution from our friends." She gave us a motherly smile.

It was hard to believe only a week ago, I'd been rushing to choir practice in Crows Nest. Now here I was, living with an Ancient Egyptian family who I'd grown quite close to in a very short time. I'd be sad when I had to say goodbye. Which could be soon after the family settled their tax bill.

When Riley said he was going for a walk, I jumped up and went with him. We passed the family's veggie patch and continued on to a tangle of wild-looking weeds he wanted to investigate.

"How is the toothpaste coming along?" I asked.

"I'm almost there," he said, squinting at the plants. "Just a couple more ingredients and it'll be done."

"And the tax payment is sorted, so I guess we'll be off home soon?"

Riley nodded as he reached for a dark red leaf in the middle of the patch, ripped it, sniffed it, studied the membranes, then discarded it.

"Riley, do you get, you know, homesick?" I asked.

He turned to me, eyes super-pale today—a reflection of the morning sky. "No, I know this won't be forever. Why? Do you?"

"Me? No, of course not," I said. "I mean, it would be nice to have a glass of water from a tap. And see my friends. And family."

"Well, I see only one parent at a time these days, anyway," he said.

His parents had separated about nine months before. And not in a good way.

"That must be...weird."

"I'm getting used to it," he said.

He leaned over and pulled a twig off a brownish plant. It had half a dozen rounded leaves with tiny prickles on the underside. "My sister, Tanya, says I shouldn't stay at Dad's because he's the one in the wrong."

I didn't know the details but I'd heard things had got kind of nasty between his mum and dad in the courts.

Riley tore the prickly leaf and milky liquid trickled out. He sniffed it, then threw that away too and stared out at the blue-grey waters of the Nile. "But all I know is that Mum and Dad both love us. And they're both hurting."

What could I say to that? I was just glad my parents weren't breaking up and tearing me in two along the way. Although to make that sort of decision, they'd have to be in the same room long enough first. Since I turned fifteen, they'd each taken a bigger role at work and we never seemed to be together that much anymore.

A flare of sunlight to my left dazzled me. I put a hand up to block the glare and squinted through my fingers to see where it was coming from. In the middle of the fields was a human sacrifice on a cross. At least that's what it looked like from here. Moving closer, we saw it was the scarecrow, wearing my Sydney clothes, its reed head lolling to one side. A crowd of men and children stood around watching solemnly, like they were waiting for the scarecrow to "do" something. As Riley and I went by, their unsmiling faces followed our progress.

"What's the name of the Egyptian god with the falcon head again?" I asked.

"Horus," said Riley.

"We'd better pray to Horus to keep the birds away from their crops. And those farmers away from us."

By the time we got home, Sahara had laid out all the goods we'd acquired from our day's trading. We had silver, oil in ceramic vats, sacks of grain, gold and silver cloth and a couple of vases.

"I believe that should cover what we owe," said Sahara, smiling. "Babu should be satisfied."

"Babu?" I asked.

"That is the name of our tax collector," she said. His name had sucked the good mood out of the room.

"Did you find those blue stones you were looking for yesterday?" I asked Razi.

"The lapis lazuli?" He nodded. "I was fortunate to get them from a market trader named Karim, who came from a land far away."

"So now you can finish off the piece for your buyer?"

"No, not I. For it is a special piece, commissioned by a wealthy man to present to the chief vizier at his birthday celebration. Only my father can do this just right. Though he will have to act quickly, as the vizier's party is just two days after he is due home."

"That's the party where we'll be dancing," said Amunet, treating us to a twirl. Layla tried to copy her sister but lost her balance and toppled over, giggling.

"I can hardly wait," said Amunet. "Are you excited, Madison?"

"Yes, I'm looking forward to it."

That was a lie. Riley and I should be a long way from here—in time and space—by the time the party came around. Not that it wouldn't have been fun to do the show with her.

"I must make you girls some beautiful costumes to dance in." Sahara stroked Amunet's hair. "Something which will draw all eyes to your performance."

"I certainly hope to catch the right person's eye," Amunet said, looking at Riley. Unfortunately for her, he was focused on some soil he was rubbing between his fingers. *Sorry Amunet, in a contest between soil and a pretty girl, the dirt wins every time with Riley.*

"What is the piece of jewellery your father is making, Razi?" I asked.

"It is an ankh," he said. "Let me show you."

He unwrapped some white cloth to reveal a silver necklace with a symbol like a Christian cross, except that there was a loop on the top part of the stalk.

"The loop represents the sun," said Razi. "The line through the middle represents the watery line at the edge of the horizon. It is where the blue lapis lazuli will be set by my father." He pointed to some recessed spaces on the crossbar.

"It's very beautiful," I said.

"It is indeed," came a gravelly voice from behind.

And that was when I got my first look at Babu, the taxman. He was muscular, with a smooth-shaven head and eyes like possum poo—brown and lightless. Bare-chested, with not a single hair visible, in a crisp white sarong, he might have been handsome if not for the sneer that had set on his face from overuse.

"Let me see the necklace," he said. He held out his hand. It wasn't a request.

"It is not for you," Razi replied. "It is a gift for the vizier."

"Fear not. I will not harm it," Babu said, smiling. "For where would be the profit in that?"

Razi held the piece on the cloth for Babu to see. The taxman's face drifted forward, his tongue flicking out excitedly before he snatched.

"What are you asking for it?"

"That is a matter between my father and the purchaser," Razi said. "And before you ask me who that is, I would not tell you even if I knew."

Oh no! I might not have been super-clued in to the social rules of the time, but even I knew this was the wrong tone to strike with the tax monster!

"It is a beautiful necklace," Babu agreed. "You will get a good price. And I will take my fair share of what you receive." He thrust it back at Razi, all interest gone.

"Your work takes you far from home, Babu," said Sahara. "You must be hungry and thirsty. May we offer you some refreshment?"

Babu gave a single nod and Sahara jerked her head at Layla and Amunet, who rushed off to fill his order.

"And do you have the tax you owe, madam?" he said. "For it falls due today."

"I am pleased to say we can pay you in full." Sahara brought out a stool for him to sit on and she and Razi carried out the goods for his inspection. Amunet gave him a cup of the watered-down beer as Layla offered bread and dates. Babu slurped his beer and tore at his bread. He chewed the dates open-mouthed—totally gross—then sucked his teeth noisily as he turned to Riley and me.

"And you are?" He looked me up and down.

"My name is Riley," Riley said, jumping in. "This is my sister, Madison."

"The pair from southern Nubia! I have heard much of you. I believe you were with Amunet yesterday when her dance troupe had the honour of being engaged for the vizier's party."

The guy was well-informed. Which was disturbing. If we had been in my time, I might have replied: "What's it to you, Bat Poo!" But, call me a social genius, I guessed that might not be in the family's best interests today.

"We were honoured to perform for the people of the town," I said, "and doubly honoured to receive an invitation to dance for the vizier. I pray we will bring him pleasure on his special day."

Babu smiled slightly and licked his lips. He liked that answer. It was nice and subservient. However, he did not like the glares Razi gave him or the way he dropped the final bag of grain onto his lap, just that bit too hard, making him grunt.

"By anyone's calculations, that is more than enough to pay our bill," said Razi.

Babu's eyes lazily perused the pile. "That is adequate for what you owe, this month. However, it does not cover next month's bill."

"Next month?" Razi scowled. "What has that to do with anything?"

"You were late with this month's payment," said Babu. "I need to teach your family to meet your future tax obligations punctually." With his little finger he picked a chunk of date out of his front teeth and sucked it down. "So here's what is going to happen. I will make an estimate now of what you owe for next month. I will base it on the payment this month, plus extra to allow for the sale of this exquisite necklace and the rewards Amunet might anticipate as a member of her most admired dance troupe. And I will need the payment early."

"How early?" asked Razi.

Babu carved numbers into the dirt floor with a stick as he calculated, muttering to himself the whole time. He was like something gross on the internet you really didn't want to see but couldn't look away from.

"Hmmm. Double this month's payment should cover it," said Babu. "And I will take that payment now."

"Now? But we do not have it," Sahara stammered.

"That is a most unreasonable request!" Razi said. "How do you expect us to comply when you have taken all we have?"

Sahara dropped to the ground, clasping her hands towards Babu. "Please, I beg you, we will pay our share. But we need more time."

"I could take that lovely necklace you were boasting about just now," he said, "and call it settled."

"No," said Razi. "It would dishonour my father if he failed to deliver the jewellery to his customer, as promised."

"Very well, then," said Babu, running a hand over his scalp, "I have a suggestion. Because I have grown fond of your family and would hate to see this lovely woman suffer—" he made fake eyes of sympathy at Sahara "—I could overlook next month's tax burden."

"Would you do that, Babu?" Sahara's bottom lip quivered.

"If your daughter Layla were to come to work as my personal servant," he said.

What the—? I'd heard Mum and Dad talk about tax audits with dread but this was beyond awful. Sahara gasped. Layla began to cry, and Amunet pushed her sister protectively behind her.

Razi roared in frustration and launched himself at Babu. But he didn't lay a finger on him because Riley crash-tackled him to the floor, then sat on him, pinning him down.

"Get off me!" Razi shouted.

"Their father will return within a week," I said over Razi's protests. "May we beg an extension until that time?"

"Ahhhh," said Babu, a smile breaking over his face like a plague. "I knew there was something I'd forgotten. I have to inform you that your father's return has been delayed. The Pharaoh was so impressed by his hard work, he invited him to continue at the tomb for a further month. This is a great honour for your father and your family."

Uh-oh. Now they were in real trouble.

Razi roared again and redoubled his efforts to shift Riley and get at Babu, but Riley could not be moved. The rest of the family stood by, stunned.

Which just left me to do the talking.

"Hey, Babu," I said, like he was my best friend, "want to see something special?" I held my hand out, fist clenched, palm up. Slowly, I uncurled my fingers to reveal the Australian coin. Babu stroked his neck as he checked it out, then gingerly reached over for it. I pulled my hand back at first, then held still and allowed him to take it. He rubbed the ridges on the engraving, studied the picture on the coin with something close to awe.

"What are these strange creatures on this circle of gold?"

"In southern Nubia, where I come from—" I began, with no clue how this sentence would end "—there is a legend of two mythical gods. The first is a creature that bounces called a kangaroo. The second is a flightless bird—an emu. Between them, they carry a magical shield that bestows good luck on whoever possesses the coin."

Babu was entranced. So was everyone else—especially Riley—wondering where this was headed. The tip of Babu's tongue flicked out. I'd hooked his interest. Now I just needed to reel him in. What would someone like him want? He was greedy, unlikeable. Ah, I had it.

I took the coin back, holding it between my thumb and index finger, within his reach.

"Only a few of these golden circles exist. They have the power to bestow good fortune and desirability upon their owners. That is why they have come to be known as—*love coins*."

Babu's eyes grew to twice their size. Brown Smarties on white dinner plates.

"All this can be yours," I said, "if you give the family another month to settle next month's tax."

He reached out to take the coin. I whipped my arm back. "Do we have an agreement?"

"I'll give you two weeks," he said.

And grabbed.

CHAPTER 17

"New plan," I said. "We stay a week or two longer, just until we help the family get the payment they need."

"Are you sure you want to do that?" said Riley.

No. "Yes, of course." I couldn't leave them like this. With the prospect of Sahara being beaten or Layla forced to become Babu's servant. "But as soon as we have enough surplus to put them in the clear, we go. Whether you've finished the toothpaste or not."

A pause, then Riley nodded. "Whenever you want to leave, Maddy, just say so."

That was reassuring.

"So, any ideas on how to get the payment together?" I said.

Riley twisted his lips to the side. "I'll think on it while I work."

Clutching a ceramic bowl, he headed off into the fields to continue his search for toothpaste ingredients. As he walked down the dry hill, dust ghosts swirled at his feet. I had to fight the urge to call him back and tell him I'd changed my mind, that I wanted to go home right now.

I'd sounded brave enough talking to him about staying longer, though I felt anything but brave. I thought I'd be safely home by now. With my family and friends. In my comfy room, trading stupid jokes with Lauren. Hockey practice, homework, my playlist. It had all seemed so ordinary and uninspiring when I lived it every day. I'd been busting to break out, have some kind of adventure, a change from the relentless routine of school life. But from where I stood now—on top of a hill, overlooking the Nile River, in Ancient Egypt—my old life didn't seem nearly so boring.

"At least we will still get the payment for our engagement at the vizier's party," said Amunet.

I nodded and forced a smile. I thought they'd be doing that show without me but now I would be part of the troupe.

"And we still have the necklace for the vizier," Sahara said. "Razi must finish it in my husband's absence."

"Will the buyer be okay with that?" I asked.

"I will pray to the gods to guide Razi's hands so the buyer will not notice the difference."

"Do you think that will be enough for Babu?" I asked.

Sahara smiled. "Perhaps."

But the way she said it sounded more like, *Perhaps not.*

Amunet and I were due across town for a rehearsal. On the way there, we came upon a large crowd in the main square gathered for a *kenbet*, or local court. A woman around Sahara's age stood quivering before three old men.

"The woman has done something wrong," said Amunet, "and the village elders are deciding how to punish her according to the Pharaoh's rules."

A few whispered words to the girl next to her and Amunet had the whole story. This was a tax case, like ours. The woman's husband had been away serving the Pharaoh at the pyramids when a tax bill fell due. She paid with sacks of grain, but some of the sacks were later found to have been bulked up with sand.

I looked around at the crowd. Most were quiet and still, their faces full of pity. With one exception—a muscular man in the front row clutching a gold coin. *Babu.* The woman was one of his clients. And from the look on his face, this was a part of the job he really enjoyed. Not only that, but he seemed to think it was a good place to make new female friends. He wore a twisted *how-cool-am-I* grin as he talked to the women around him, rubbing the *love coin* between his fingers. For luck.

I slipped behind a tall man so Babu couldn't see me. Once he realised the coin wasn't working, that no magic on earth was powerful enough to make him attractive, I did not want to be the first person in his sights.

The oldest of the official men stepped forward. He was tall and super-thin, like aged parchment stretched over old bones. "We find the defendant guilty." His voice was shaky. "For her crimes, we sentence her to thirty strokes of the cane."

A great wailing erupted from some adults and children in the front row—the defendant's family, I guessed.

"Nooo! Please don't!" A little girl's high-pitched voice cut through the wall of sound, breaking everyone's heart.

The official enforcer arrived—a young man with muscles on his muscles and a long, thin stick. He forced the woman to her knees. "Prepare to accept the Pharaoh's punishment," he bellowed.

The woman trembled as he ripped the back of her dress open, exposing her bare flesh. She lowered her head and squeezed her eyes shut.

And it began.

There was a loud *whoosh* as the stick cut through the air, then a *thwap* as it struck her back. The woman howled like a wounded animal. And so did her family. The first blow made a long deep cut, and bright red blood flowed like water from it.

One of the older girls in the family began to gag and pushed through to the back of the crowd to vomit.

"This is horrible," I said.

Amunet squeezed my arm for comfort and pressed her lips together.

The woman cried out at each of the first dozen lashes and sank a little lower each time, until she was flat on the ground, face in the dirt. After that, the screaming stopped. Somehow, the silence was more chilling. Her family's crying had faded to sniffles and hyperventilating gasps. The man continued to lash the woman even after her eyes closed in unconsciousness—or worse.

The crowd was silent, though many wiped away tears. The woman in front of me held her friend's arm so hard, her nails dug into the flesh, drawing blood.

By the time the man finally threw the stick down and rolled his shoulder, which must have been sore from all the thrashing, the woman's back was a mess of torn flesh. Blood freckled her face and clumped in her hair, though her lips were pale pink, verging on white.

I felt strangely cold and more than a little nauseated myself. Especially as I considered that, in two weeks, if we didn't manage to raise the extra tax payment, it would be Sahara in the circle of punishment, beaten half to death.

But surely not? Babu wouldn't do that to such a lovely, hard-working woman, would he?

I glanced over at the tax inspector. There was no pity in his looks. He whispered to the young woman beside him and his lips curled into a flirtatious grin. As I watched, she slapped him sharply across his face and stormed off. He touched his cheek, then looked with confusion at the coin.

Someone in front of me laughed and his eyes snapped our way, fixing on me.

"Time to go, Amunet," I hissed.

We raced through the streets, haring round corners, leaping over donkey poo. I wanted to put as much distance as possible between myself and that gross spectacle of "justice". When there was no sign of Babu in pursuit, we slowed to a normal pace.

"What can I do to help raise money for the tax payment?" I asked Amunet. "Can I make something for the market stall?"

"There are no markets before the payment falls due."

"What else? Could I do cleaning, perhaps?"

"People do their own cleaning," said Amunet.

"Cooking?"

"Cooking? You?" She raised an eyebrow.

I groaned. "There must be something a girl can do to earn surplus in this town."

Amunet thought about it, then smiled. "There is one thing."

CHAPTER 18

And that was how, the next day, we found ourselves among a throng of women outside the sprawling home of a rich government official on the outskirts of the town, waiting to audition for a job as "mourner" at his funeral.

The sun had just risen. The heavenly scent of baking bread wafted over to us, almost—but not quite—covering the smell of mud and dung. Palm trees lining the wall around the house cast long shadows, providing much-needed shade for the two dozen or so women chatting about the prospect of a morning of mourning.

Being paid to pretend to grieve over someone you didn't know seemed weird to me, though Amunet said it was normal in Egypt. The greater the wailing at a person's funeral, the more prestige went to the dead person, she said. What a dead person would want with prestige, I couldn't imagine. But this strange custom gave us a chance to add to our surplus and help Sahara pay the tax bill. So I was happy.

The heat was building, but the women stayed cool as they waited. Many of them had worked together before. And they all deferred to a woman named Jamila, in her twenties, who was *numero uno* in the mourning business, it seemed.

I watched Jamila for a while, with her big smile and theatrical arm gestures. There was a take-no-prisoners air about her and an animal alertness in her heavily made-up eyes.

"Is this your first time, girls?" she asked Amunet and me.

"Yes," I said. "We're a bit nervous."

"I remember my first time," she said. "I was so nervous. I never expected to get the job. But when I saw the family's grief, I was so moved. I think they responded to that genuine emotion in me."

"So who is the...err...?" said Amunet.

"The stiff?" said a woman named Kanika with a long thin face. "A rich man who looked after the Pharaoh's wealth. Lived forty-five years."

"A ripe age," said Jamila. "One which a humble villager will rarely attain."

Kanika agreed.

"So what goes on at the funeral?" I asked. "I'm not from around here."

Jamila explained that the man who had died was an advisor to the Pharaoh, a man called Nuru, and he had already been dead for seventy days.

When he first passed out of this world, his servants took him to the House of Beauty, which I guessed was like a funeral home, where they washed him, pulled his brain out with a hook (tick to Jamie Fletcher) and discarded it, then placed his liver, lungs, stomach and intestines into separate jars. What was left of the body, they stuffed with a chemical similar to salt to dry it out, then rubbed his skin with ointment and coated it with a sticky resin like glue or wax. Finally, they wrapped

Nuru in linen bandages and placed him in a painted coffin with a mask on his head.

It was only by preserving the physical body through mummification, the spirit—or *ka*—would be able to live again in the afterlife, Jamila explained.

"The man was swimming in surplus," she said. "He spent the past ten years building a tomb and filling it full of jewels and riches that he might want to spend on the other side. If we're chosen to be official mourners, we will join Nuru's family and friends as part of the procession to the tomb."

"How many of us will they employ?" Amunet asked.

"Sometimes they take ten or even more," said Kanika. "Sometimes just a few. Depends on the budget."

"And what do we have to do to get the job?" I asked.

Jamila and Kanika exchanged a look for just for a second. It was too quick for me to read.

"Just between us," said Jamila, leaning in, "what they look for is soft, genuine emotion. Dignified sniffling is in, wailing and breast-beating is out. But keep that to yourself."

She winked and Amunet and I smiled, feeling fortunate to have been let in on the secret.

Not long afterwards, an official emerged from the house and a terrifying cacophony began. Women, who had been calm and cheerful only moments before, raised their heads skywards and wailed. Tears flooded their faces, eye makeup streaking down their cheeks, their noses frothing and bubbling with emotion. The noise they made sounded barely human. And the volume? *So much for sniffling. Thanks for nothing, Jamila!*

Some of the women worked in pairs, I noticed, taking it in turns to kick each other in the shins to inspire yowls of genuine ear-splitting pain.

Jamila was the worst. As I watched her, I remembered a nature documentary I'd seen in which a snake had devoured a mouse. It didn't chew, just took the creature down in one go, dislocating its jaw to fit it in. Her mouth was just like that, so wide I reckon she could have swallowed poor Nuru and his coffin whole, no problems.

And while she screeched, decibels above the rest, she couldn't resist a little sideways smirk at me that said, "Sucked in, Sniffles!"

But she didn't know what she was up against. I'd been on Movie World's biggest roller coaster—the Terminator—three times. I'd been on more scary water slides than she'd had hot stews. When I opened my mouth and performed, she knew she was dealing with a pro. Once I had the official's attention, I toned things down to the sniffle she'd suggested and summoned up genuine tears. It wasn't hard. I just had to think of my friends and family back home and water flowed freely from my eyes.

A man tapped me on the shoulder—I was "in". Jamila made it too, and Kanika and two others who gave Oscar-worthy performances.

But Amunet was not chosen. Smiling bravely, she said she would spend the day rehearsing with the troupe and see me back at the house later.

What a wild day it was. First, they dressed us. I still wore white but my garment had a thick collar of red, blue and brown stones. They made me wear a wig of dead-straight black hair cropped to the shoulders, just like Cleopatra, then put really thick kohl on me—an eyeliner made from something like soot mixed with oil— and gave me a cool gold snake bangle for my arm.

There were about twenty family members in the funeral party and at least twice as many servants, carrying things to place in the tomb. We took our position at the back of the procession, where we wailed and tore our hair out as if it was our best friend in that coffin. Interestingly, we were the only ones expressing any emotion. After seventy days of embalming processes, I guess Nuru's family and friends had come to terms with his passing.

At various spots along the way, a man I presumed was a priest, with a very tall hat, muttered strange incantations, which Jamila said were magic spells to help Nuru pass into the afterlife. The tomb was a big stone building that looked more like a museum than a grave, on the edge of the river. Two men did a ceremonial dance at the door. Then they performed the opening of the mouth ceremony, touching the mummy's mask with a crooked stick which was supposed to be a magical instrument allowing Nuru to breathe in the next life.

We weren't allowed inside the tomb. I wouldn't have wanted to go in anyway—it all looked pretty dark and dingy in there. But from what the girls told me, Nuru had been one of the richest men in Egypt and, for the past ten years, had filled his grave with things he wanted to take with him. I guess they didn't have that expression: *You can't take it with you*. I saw servants going inside with platters and vases, the man's favourite chair, plates of his favourite food and a mug of beer.

I imagined Nuru coming back to life, pausing to sit on his chair and have a nibble and some beer before going on to take the gruelling test to pass into the afterlife.

First, Jamila explained, he would have to face the Goddess of Truth, called Maat, and make a negative confession of all the bad deeds he had NOT done in his lifetime (I did NOT copy Lauren's science homework, and did NOT pretend to be sick from school just so I could line up for some concert tickets, that kind of thing). Then his heart would be weighed on scales held by Anubis, the jackal god. If he passed the test, he would enter the Field of Reeds, a kind of paradise. If not, his heart would be devoured by a beast called Ammut, which was part crocodile, part lion, part hippo. Poor old Nuru. I truly hoped he'd been a good boy in his lifetime.

The last part of the ceremony involved sealing up the tomb with rocks and incantations.

"Like that's ever going to work!" Jamila said. She explained that tomb robbery was common in Ancient Egypt. "It is not a question of *whether* this tomb will be robbed, but *when*."

"I don't know about that," Kanika said. "These days there are methods to deter robbers. Only the other day I heard of a group of thieves who were rained upon by hundreds of poison darts. They died in excruciating pain."

"That's right," Jamila said. "And there was also that group that took the wrong turn inside the chamber and tumbled into a pit of snakes."

"But if they died inside the tomb, how did you ever find out about it?" I asked.

"Some of them made it out alive," said Kanika. "But not for long." She drew a line across her throat with her index finger and made a hacking sound.

"You mean they were...?"

"Let me put it this way," Jamila began. "By the time the officials had done with them, they were a whole head shorter."

The two women cracked up at this, but I didn't find it the least bit funny. In a world where a lot was riding on making it through the afterlife, tomb robbery was a huge crime, it seemed. In fact, the women told me, officials took a dimmer view of it than they did of murder.

After sealing the tomb, all the funeral guests adjourned to a big tent by the river for food and drink. By then I really needed it. I was super-hungry and almost hoarse with wailing.

"So will we be seeing you at all the big funerals from now on?" Jamila asked as she ate a brown dip, something like hummus, with bread.

"If there are any in the next couple of weeks, I might be there," I replied. "Probably not after that."

"Why only for two weeks?" Kanika asked. "You have the makings of a magnificent mourner. You could rival the great Jamila herself."

"After two weeks, it will be too late," I said. "The damage will be done."

I explained that the family I was staying with had been hit by an unreasonable tax bill while their father was away. That was why I was here—to help them pay their bill.

"Perhaps the tax officer will wait for his money if you explain the circumstances," Jamila said.

"Not this tax inspector," I replied, frowning.

"What did you say the officer's name was?" Kanika asked.

"Babu," I said, in unison with the women.

"He is a very bad man," Kanika added. "He always targets the families of those men away from home doing the Pharaoh's work. His favourite pastime is watching helpless women being beaten for unreasonable tax demands."

"Would you excuse us for a moment, Madison?" asked Jamila.

She and Kanika gathered the other mourners and moved away to whisper together. Their eyes flickered my way from time to time, so I knew they were talking about me. At the end, they came over together. "We are in agreement," said Jamila. "We will give you half of the payment each of us receives here today to help the mother of your friends stay out of trouble."

"What? But don't you need the payment for yourselves? For your own families?"

"Her need is greater at present," said Kanika. "None of our husbands are away right now. We women have to stick together against greedy officials."

And that was what happened. When they paid us our gold and silver at the end of the day, all the mourners gave me half of their earnings, which I thought was pretty cool.

Jamila gave me all of hers. "On one condition," she whispered. "That you promise not to make a career out of mourning. I like being the most sought-after mourner on the circuit."

CHAPTER 19

As I made my way back home, I saw a familiar blond head at the river's edge. Riley was squatting down, staring at the mud as if it held the answer to all of life's biggest questions—which it probably did.

He looked up just then, spotted me and smiled. "Hey, how was the funeral?"

"It was the most fun funeral I've ever been to," I said. Thankfully, it was the only one, so far. "And look what I got for it!" I jangled a heavy purse with my payment.

"Well done," he said.

"What are you doing?" I asked. "Making mud pies from the looks of things." In front of him were rows of mud-balls the size of a fist.

"Just an experiment. I'll show you." He picked one up and threw it down hard on the ground. It splodged and sort of broke apart, and that was it.

"What's it supposed to do?"

"Just wait," said Riley.

A wisp of smoke snaked upwards, then another and a couple more until a localised mist had formed around us.

"Interesting. What's it for?"

"It was just an experiment with soil stability and—" Riley froze mid-sentence, mouth open. He did this a lot as he got distracted by his scientific thoughts. It was really annoying.

"And?" I prompted.

As the mist broke up, I saw he was staring at the fields.

"Oh," I said.

The lone scarecrow in the fields was lone no more. Three others had sprung up during the day. This new idea had caught on, much to the annoyance of a dozen boys standing around, arms crossed, bottom lips thrust forward in a sulk. They were the crow killers but now they were out of a job and not happy about it.

When they saw me, one of them pointed. "There is the maker of crow-scarers!" he shouted. They started towards me, shoulders squared, hands forming loose fists.

"You'd better take off, Maddy," Riley said, stepping in front of me.

"What do you think they'll do?"

"I don't know. Just go! I'll talk to them."

I took off the other way. As I looked back, I saw Riley flinging mud balls onto the ground. The strands of smoke rose up to create a thin wall of fog between me and them, giving me cover to escape. Riley was freaky-good with soil.

Splodging through the wet mud along the river's edge, I ducked behind trees and crops where I could to stay out of sight. But surely the boys weren't that angry? A scarecrow was a good thing—it would help their families. They'd realise that eventually. Though "eventually" might not be soon enough to save me now.

On my right was a hill. Perhaps if I ran up to the top, I could lay low, literally, and get a head start if I saw anyone coming after me. I glanced up to see how high I'd have to climb and was shocked to see a familiar face peeking over the edge, smiling at me. It was a tall man with a blond beard in a billowing gold coat. This was the mysterious son of Peter from the markets and the source of the Australian two-dollar coin.

"Hey! You!" I called out. "Wait! Can we talk?"

He ducked back out of sight. So I started up the hill. Grabbing tufts of dried grass, scrabbling at the rocks and clay, I managed to haul myself up the side of the hill and over the top. Before me was a wide, open space, backed by rows of bushes, but no sign of the man anywhere. He must have rushed off. Why would he run from me?

In the gravel near my feet, the sun caught the tip of something shiny buried in the dirt. Squatting down, I grabbed the hard end and pulled it up to find it was a metal spoon, slightly bent, with two stars engraved on the handle. I'd seen spoons like this before. I'd used them myself—at the Crows Nest soup kitchen.

And then I knew. The guy on the hill was the same "homeless" man I had met on my way to choir practice, who I'd taken to the soup kitchen. Not the son of Peter, as our buyer at the markets had called him, but Peterson. He'd smiled at me the same way then, as if amused by something only he found funny.

Was he here today by accident? Or design? Did he drop the spoon on purpose, as a clue?

I couldn't be sure. But one thing I was certain about.

Like us, Peterson was a time traveller.

CHAPTER 20

I was still standing there, staring at the spoon, when I got that prickly feeling, like I wasn't alone.

Turning, I saw five beefed-up Egyptian men swaggering my way. They wore grubby white sarongs and silver bands on their muscular upper arms. Their heads were shaven. And they had matching sneers.

A couple of them hurried forward and grabbed my arms.

"Let me go," I said, struggling hard. Their grip tightened. "Ow, that's hurting. What do you want?"

From behind the group came a man in a creepy golden mask painted with a falcon head—the god Horus. It couldn't have been Peterson. This man was shorter. His tunic was crisp white. His arms and legs were thinner and paler than the others. They were the brawn of the outfit, he was the brains.

"Where is it?" he whispered in my ear.

"Where is what?" I asked, trying to sound braver than I felt.

"You know what," said the man.

He must have been talking about the purse of gold and silver I'd earned today. It was tied to my linen belt, concealed in the folds of my dress. Was he going to rob me? That sucked! Sahara really needed this money.

"I don't know what you mean," I said, hoping to stall as long as I could.

"I don't think you want to play that game with me, girl," said the man. "You won't win. And you might get hurt."

Mum's voice popped into my head, telling me money was not as important as a life. If a burglar struck, I should give them what they wanted and walk away. I sighed inwardly as I realised she was right. And anyway, I really had no choice here.

"The pouch is on my belt," I said, expecting to feel him fumbling for it and tearing it off. But he made no move to take it.

"I'm not interested in gold and silver," he whispered. "I want...the other thing."

What *other thing* could he be talking about? Except...? *No, it can't be.*

"Riley's time machine," he whispered.

How could he know about that? Who was he? I tried to peer through the mask's eyeholes to see who was inside. It was too dark to tell.

"I don't know what you mean?" I said.

"Tell me where it is and I won't have to hurt you."

I really didn't want to get hurt, though I couldn't tell him where the time machine was. If he took it, we'd never get back home, never see our friends or family again. No way could I do that.

But I could hardly tell him to shove his stupid mask where the sun didn't shine. These guys did not look like the sort to take bad news well. My only option was to lie.

"We hid it in the village," I said. "I'll take you there."

The man stared at me for a while, his dark eyes blinking through the holes, assessing me.

"Very well," he said. "But if you're lying, you will regret it."

I tried to look strong, though everything inside me felt like it was melting. My heart, my lungs, my ribs were turning to soup, sliding down to somewhere around my knees. What would he do when we arrived in the village and there was no time machine? I just had to hope that between here and there, I'd get an opportunity to cry for help or run away.

The guys frogmarched me down the hill and along the river bank, the man in the mask staying so close he kicked my heels whenever I slowed down. About halfway to the village, the guys fanned out around me—two in front, two to the side, one in the rear, blocking all escape. The masked man gripped my elbow. "Don't try anything stupid."

"Who are you? How do you know about the time machine?" I got no answer. But I caught a scent of something sour. Not dung, but something else unpleasant and, weirdly, familiar. I sank into silence as I looked for opportunities to escape.

"There she is—the crow-scarer," someone shouted. I couldn't see the speaker, but it was a boy's voice.

Next thing, stones flew at us, pinging off the skulls of my captors, banging on their arms and backs until they were forced to crouch down and shield their heads with their hands. The angry boys from the fields were throwing rocks at us, I guessed. Or perhaps just at me. I spotted Riley among them, briefly, before—wham—I got hit in the cheek. *Man, that hurt!*

"Keep moving," the masked man said, squeezing my arm hard.

Mist seeped from some of the rocks they'd thrown until a thin fog formed around us.

"What is this, the work of demons?" one of the men up front called.

"Yes, it is a demon! And it's coming for us!" I replied. "You'd better run!"

The masked guy slapped me on the side of the face so hard I saw stars for a few seconds.

"She's lying," he shouted. "Stay calm. This is nothing but a trick."

But he was too late. I'd spooked the guys. Three of them ran off.

"Oh great!" the masked man muttered.

Up ahead we heard thudding and a growl, followed by hysterical screams. As the mist broke up briefly, I glimpsed hippos charging past, less than a foot away. The three guards who'd run off now lay on the ground, their limbs at odd angles. We must have stumbled onto a hippo run—the path between the river where the hippos swam and the land where they grazed. I'd heard about these in biology class. It was not a good place to be.

The masked man hauled me back, gripping me tighter as a couple more of the creatures thundered past.

"Stay where you are," he shouted at the remaining two guards. But they were babbling in terror and couldn't wait. They made a dash for safety. There was a *thwap* and a *thump* and more cries for help, followed by several loud *thuds*. Then silence.

I turned away, feeling sick. I couldn't look. Even the masked guy groaned, though whether in sympathy at their suffering or frustration at their stupidity, I couldn't tell. Throughout it all, he never once relaxed his grip on me. We waited a few minutes in case any more animals appeared, then he shoved me forward.

"Quickly," he said.

Skirting the unconscious—or dead—guards, we got off the hippo path as fast as we could.

On the other side, more rocks flew our way, each one trailing a plume of smoke that combined to form a thick fog around us. Inside the veil, it was moist, like fine rain, and smelt of damp earth.

"Where is the machine?" the man whispered, his lips tickling my ear. "Relax your mind and make a picture in your head of its hiding place."

Although I didn't want to, I found myself thinking of the reeds by the river where we'd hidden the machine. And the cloak, covering it, which made it seem invisible.

"Yes, yes," he said. "It is a clever place to hide it. But where exactly? Show me."

What was this? Telepathy? Because I didn't believe anyone could read minds. Even so, I tried not to visualise the spot where the time machine should be. But the more I tried not to think of it, the clearer the picture formed in my head.

"Maddy, where are you?" It was Riley's voice. I was so happy to hear it, though I couldn't tell where exactly it was coming from. The masked guy clamped his hand over my mouth.

"Thank you, my dear," he whispered, then shoved me forward and vanished into the mist.

I staggered about, stumbling in splodgy mud, splashing in puddles, until someone grabbed my wrist.

"Let go!" I tried to yank my arm back.

"Maddy, it's me."

Riley's hair was damp, his face and clothes speckled with mud. But I was so happy to see him! I launched myself into his arms. He tensed, then began to relax.

"I was so scared," I said.

"You're okay now," he said, hugging me a little tighter.

"Riley, the man wanted the time machine."

Riley frowned. "How did he know about that?"

My friend was quiet as we walked alongside the river, and I told him how the man had pretended to read my mind and then thanked me before he left, like I'd revealed something to him.

"Is there any chance he did read my mind?" I asked.

"None at all," said Riley.

"That's a relief," I said. I'd thought the guy was bluffing. "But how did you find me?"

"When you left, I tried to talk to the scarecrow boys and calm them down. They were angry because they'd lost a good job—keeping the birds off the crops—and gained a bad one."

"Dung bricks?" I said.

Riley nodded. "I tried to tell them that with the surplus from the extra dung bricks they sold, their families could have more things they liked. But by then, they were interested in my mud balls."

"Distracted, you mean?"

Riley showed the boys how to make them. While they were up to their elbows in mud, one of them had seen me walking by the water with a group of local men known to be bad news.

"I asked if they would help me save you," said Riley. "They're really strong and accurate throwers, which was useful. And with the extra mud balls they made, we had plenty of ammunition."

We were almost back to the village now, but as we started up the dusty hill, I pulled him back. "And you're absolutely positive he couldn't read my mind?"

"Yes," said Riley. "Still," he turned back to look at the river, "no harm in making sure."

And we were off. Jogging back past the crops and along the river again. Despite how tired I was, I kept up with my friend. For the last hundred feet, I went flat out like I was in a race. Soggy mud squished between my toes and splashed up my legs, but I didn't care. My neck, my chest, were so tight with terror, I could barely breathe. And Riley was right beside me. For all his scientific cool, he was just as keen as me to make sure the time machine was safe.

A quick glance around to check no-one was watching and he slipped into the forest of reeds. I saw him moving around, his forehead puckered with worry as he swept the stalks aside, searching for the invisible time machine.

"Got it," he said, a smile breaking over his face. "It's safe."

I sank down in the mud and closed my eyes. I couldn't move. Or speak. For at least half a minute.

"Admit it, you were scared, weren't you?" I said on the way back. "A small part of you was worried mind-reading was actually possible."

"No, not really," he said.

"Well, if that's true, why the Olympic sprint at the end?"

His lips stretched into a grin. "I still believe it's impossible to read minds," he said. "But, as a scientist, if I find evidence that contradicts that belief, I'd have to reconsider."

"I have evidence," I said. "My gran reads my mind all the time. Which is not ideal."

He chuckled. "You're talking about facial tics and tells. Body language? Yeah, that is a kind of mind reading. Which I'm not good at."

"It's not that hard," I said. "You just have to pay attention to the signals people send, weigh them up against the situation you're in, taking into account the sender's possible motivations and what you know of their past behaviour."

"I always think people mean what they say," said Riley.

"Big mistake," I said. "That'll get you into trouble one day."

As we walked back to the house, I told Riley how I'd spotted Peterson on the hill before the guys attacked. And how I'd met him once before in Crows Nest.

"He's a time traveller, like us," I said.

A storm of emotions swept across Riley's face—the smooth look of shock, the rumpled forehead of worry and a divot like a cut between his eyebrows as his scientific brain tried to figure out how it might be possible.

"Does that mean your time machine isn't the first one in the world?" I asked. "Did this Peterson invent it before you?"

"Not necessarily," he said.

I wouldn't normally let him get away with such a vague and baffling comment. But, after the day I'd had, I couldn't face one of those twisted time discussions. And besides, we were approaching the village and scents of spicy stew and baking bread were wafting out, demanding priority over all else. I was starving.

I was just about to speed up the hill when Riley held my arm. I looked over to find him doing lip yoga again—mouth twisting left, right.

"What is it?" I said. I was tired and hungry. Whatever he had to say, he'd better say it quickly.

"Before we go in, I need to tell you, Amunet said something today. Something that made me think she might like me."

Of course she liked him. She liked him plenty. I'd hoped he wouldn't notice. *Deny, deny, deny.*

"Are you sure you weren't imagining it?" I said. "I mean, we don't really know their customs here, the signals they send if they like someone. Could you be reading too much into it?"

He pressed his lips together and couldn't meet my eye. "She said she loved me with her whole heart and that if I asked her to marry me, she would say yes a thousand times."

Hard to read too much into that.

"And what did you say? I hope you told her you were betrothed to someone in our village?"

"No," he said. "I didn't think of that. I said I was in love with someone else."

"Well, that's not bad," I said. "But it won't put her off. Because if there's no formal commitment, she'll think she still has a chance."

"I said I'd been in love with this girl since I was small, that my heart belonged to her alone. That there was no one in the world like her and though I knew I was not worthy of her right now, one day, I hoped I would be."

Whoaah!

"Pretty good," I said. "How did you come up with that? Did you get it from a film or fairytale? Or what?"

He shrugged.

"You did well," I said. "But, generally, when constructing your lie, you should remember K.I.S.S. *Keep it Simple, Stupid.* The less complicated you make it, the easier it is to sell. In this case, being betrothed would have been simpler and more effective."

I thought it was good advice. But Riley's jaw locked tighter than an ancient tomb. He was upset—that much was clear. But I had no idea why. Was it because I'd insulted his lying skills?

And then I realised, this must be how Riley felt most of the time. Clueless. It was a new experience for me, one I didn't care for much at all.

CHAPTER 21

Sahara threw her arms around me, tears in her eyes, as I presented the purse I'd earned from the mourning job.

"I thank you for all the family, Madison," she said. "May you live long and have many sons." (She meant well.)

"So, Mama, do we have sufficient surplus now to pay Babu?" asked Amunet.

"If we are able to sell the necklace Razi is working on for the vizier," said Sahara, "then, yes, I believe it should be enough."

Amunet sank back with relief while Layla jumped up and down, pumping her arms heavenwards with joy.

"You are very kind, Maddy," said Amunet later. "I had hoped to call you sister one day, but I fear it is not to be."

She glanced Riley's way and looked so downcast, I felt truly sorry for her. Hopefully, she'd get over him quickly when we left.

As we ate dinner, everyone wanted details of the funeral—what I wore, how many mourners there were.

"How dark was it in the tomb?" asked Layla. "Was it scary?"

"I didn't go in," I said. "But, yes, it looked scary."

Razi was interested in what riches the servants had carried inside and the security in place around the tomb.

"Did you hear of any traps that might be set to catch tomb robbers?" he asked.

"No, but from what the other mourners said, lots of tombs have them," I said.

"What kind did you learn about?"

"Why are you asking, Razi? You're not thinking of breaking in, are you?" Sahara said.

"No," he said. "Though it would solve a few tax problems in the future."

"My brother, do not even say such a thing!" Amunet was angry. "What if someone hears and reports you to the authorities?"

"You know what the punishment is if you get caught for tomb robbery, right?" I said.

"Everyone knows that," Razi replied. "But we have our tax payment now. There is no need for me to take such a risk."

"I hope you would not consider such a thing, even if we had no payment." Sahara frowned. "Think of us. How would we bear your loss?"

"Don't worry, Mother." Razi kissed her cheek.

Mid-way through the meal, some farmers came to visit us. They brought vegetables, grain and beer as gifts to the family, to thank Riley—who, it turned out, had spent part of his day building a hippo fence to keep the animals off their crops. My friend explained later that he'd smeared a rope with chilli seeds and juice, effectively moving the creatures further downriver away from the farmers' fields. It was good for the hippos, as it meant there was no more need to hunt them down. And for the farmers too.

One of the men in the group was Sacmis's father, who told us with great pride (and a good deal of boasting) about a deputation from the vizier that had come to his home to request Sacmis's attendance at the vizier's birthday party.

"They even brought her fine clothes and impressive jewels to wear to the occasion," he said.

"That is a great honour for your family," Sahara said. "Are you acquainted with the vizier?"

"No," said the man. "That's the strangest part. All we were told is that the vizier's son was most admiring of my daughter and anxious to ensure her attendance at the event. She swears she has never met him before. All we can think is that he must have seen her from afar and fallen in love."

As he spoke, I felt eyes turning my way. Layla stopped mid-chew, mouth open, to gape at me.

"That should have been you," said Amunet when the men had gone. "Phoenix, the vizier's son, thinks he has invited you to the party, because you gave the name of Sacmis when you saved his life."

"What will he do," said Razi, "when the wrong girl arrives to accompany him?"

It was a good question. I didn't like Sacmis much, but I didn't want anything seriously bad to happen to her on my account.

"And Madison will be at the party, too, don't forget," said Sahara. "As part of the dance troupe."

"Do you think he'll recognise you?" asked Layla.

"No, he shouldn't."

I mean, I would just be a member of a dance group employed to entertain them. How closely would someone as important as Phoenix look at any of us, mere servants? Not that closely, surely? And anyway, Phoenix had met me for only a short time, when I was dripping wet. I'd look quite different at the party.

I was pretty confident I'd be safe.

I looked at the dress I'd worn during the day and shook my head. It was so dirty. It would take a lot of pounding to get that clean. And there was a bug on it—a weird-looking fly which seemed to have died and stiffened into the material.

I showed it to Riley thinking he might find it interesting as a scientist. He scratched at it and tapped it. And froze.

"Oh no!" he said. "This is a tracking bug. I've seen some of the prototypes for these at the science lab where I work. But this one seems more advanced than any I've seen before."

"What? That can't be right!"

I grabbed the dress off him and clawed at the insect. It made a slight *ting* sound like it was metal.

"How did it get there?"

"Someone must have put it on you," said Riley.

"Well, who would have—?" I began. And then I knew. "The guy in the mask! It had to be him!"

"Oh no." Riley's words were soft but the big-eyed open-mouthed look that went with it screamed trouble. "Remember how he was talking about telepathy and reading your mind?"

"Yeah?"

"And then we went back to the reeds to check on the time machine." Riley swallowed with difficulty.

I gasped. "We've led him straight to it. We have to go back and move it. Right now."

"We can't do anything until morning," said Riley. "It'll be too dark."

"What about a burning stick?" I said. "Couldn't we use that?"

"It's windy tonight. The fire will blow out before we get down the hill."

"Well, come on," I said, "a scientist like you must be able to make a bit of light when we need it?"

Riley bit his thumbnail, his eyes losing focus as his mind turned inward for ways to create light. Once he got that look, I knew it wouldn't be too long before he'd find an answer.

By bedtime, though, he still hadn't come up with anything. *Of all the times to be out of ideas!*

I felt so helpless, lying there on the ground, listening to rats shuffling about in the dark when our time machine had already been stolen or soon would be. I'd been lying there forever—well, for almost half an hour—when Riley tapped my arm and gestured for me to come outside.

He held a ball of light the size of a soccer ball. The outer covering was white linen with reeds like small struts to hold the shape. Inside, it glowed.

"What have you got in there? A candle?" I asked.

"Glow-worms; a dozen of them. It was the best I could do."

"Okay. Let's go."

Creeping out of the house, we began making our way through the fields. Riley's light ball gave off a quivery golden glow that was pretty but not that effective. Luckily, though, it was a full moon that night, so we could kind of see where we were going.

I had to fight the urge to run all the way back to the river. But in such dim light, I'd only have ended up in a ditch. So I stuck to fast walking.

Riley led the way to the reed patch, then headed in. *Crunch, crunch, splodge, crunch.* I waited for the sound effects to stop and his head to bob up with a report that he'd found the machine. But minutes later, he was still thrashing about.

"Are we sure this is the right spot?" I asked.

"It's hard to be too sure in the dark," he replied. "But I think so."

I stomped into the reeds to join the search, slopping through the mud, slapping the plants aside. A few snapped back and scratched me.

"Ow!"

"Stop, stop!" said Riley.

"You found it?" I was excited.

His face was pale and serious in the moonlight. He shook his head. "It's not here."

He paused to catch his breath. "The time machine's gone."

CHAPTER 22

It took every bit of my strength not to lose it at this point—not to dissolve into a heap right there, helpless and wailing, on the dark river bank. I bit the inside of my cheek and dug a nail into my thigh to create the kind of pain that would stop me thinking about the things I'd lost with the machine—like my ability to go home and see the people I loved. Would I truly never sit on the sofa in our living room and watch Mum laughing, machine-gun style, at some joke on *The Truth About Dating*? Or see Dad barbecuing in that silly apron with the pug face I gave him when I was ten?

A tear rolled down my cheek and I wiped it away before Riley could see. Poor guy had lost as much as me but must also be feeling the guilt of dragging me into this mess with him. Whatever happened, I wouldn't say anything mean or blame him for this outcome. Because how would it help to add to his mountain of misery?

I snuck a peek to see how he was coping. And could not believe it. He was grinning and shaking his head.

"Clever! Didn't see that coming," he murmured.

"Clever?" I repeated. "What do you mean?" My flinty tone should have warned him. Or the death stare I sent his way. As usual, he didn't read the signs.

"Planting the bug and coming out with all that telepathy

stuff so we'd go and check on it—and lead him right to it," he said. "That was smart."

"Yes, it was," I said. "Especially as we had a scientific genius on our team, and we still fell for it."

That wiped the smile off his face. He was starting to catch my dark mood now.

"This is all your fault, Riley!" I said. "You've ruined my life. I won't ever see Mum and Dad, or Gran, or my friends ever again. Because of you. Why did you have to invent a stupid time machine anyway? Wasn't that a bit of overkill for a school science fair?"

"I don't know. I just—"

"Well, you should know. Anyone who invents something that epic should know a whole heap more than you seem to. And why did you have to bring me on this stupid trip with you anyway?"

"Bring you?" He opened his mouth, then closed it again, but made no reply. If I was him, I'd have slammed back, "I didn't invite you. You jumped into the machine without asking for my consent!" But that wasn't Riley's style.

"I'm really sorry, Maddy," he said. "But this is not the end. You will see your family again."

"How?"

"The machine is password protected," he said. "He won't be able to get it off the ground. That will give us time to find it and take it back."

That was something. But was it enough?

"What if he cracks the password? Or if he doesn't, but we still can't find him or it ever again?"

"Well, if that happens...I'll build another one," said Riley.

Sure you will, I almost said. Although you might have to wait a few thousand years for the parts to be invented.

"He won't have long to work it out either," said Riley, smiling as if this was good news. "If he hasn't cracked the password in five days, the machine will be useless to him."

"Why?"

"Because the time gateway will close."

"Time gateway?"

Riley explained that he'd opened a gateway from Sydney to Ancient Egypt for one month from the date of our departure. After that time, the gate would close and the guy wouldn't be able to get back through.

"He won't get through? But we still can, right?"

"Err," he said. "Well, no, actually."

"What? How come you never mentioned this before? That we had a deadline?" The word *deadline* danced around in my head, taking on a whole new, literal meaning.

"I thought we'd stay for only a week or two, so the gateway didn't seem to be an issue."

Not an issue! That we could be locked out of our own time zone! Seriously!

"Maybe a gateway isn't even necessary," Riley said, making a mental note for future variations. But if we didn't find the machine soon, as far as I could tell, we wouldn't have much of a future!

"Riley," I began, my jaw so tight I could barely get the words out, "is there anything else you haven't mentioned that is crucial to *our survival?*"

I didn't breathe as I watched him bite his bottom lip and mull this over. After way too long, he shook his head. "Don't think so."

"So, basically, we have four or five days to find the machine and return to Sydney in it, or the time gateway will shut and we'll be stuck here...forever? Is that about right?"

Riley scratched his chin. "Well, yes, in theory."

I wanted to kill him then. The only thing that stopped me was the knowledge that, if we did find the machine, I'd need him to operate it to get me home. But if our deadline passed and this time gateway, which he'd never mentioned before, closed with us on the wrong side of it, he was a dead man. He'd be keeping company with Nuru and the other mummies buried beneath the ancient sands for thousands of years. And I would personally perform the brain extraction in the time-honoured Egyptian way!

"Don't worry, Maddy," said Riley. "We'll find the machine. And if we don't? Well, I'll figure something out."

Chapter 23

I couldn't sleep when we got back. I tossed and turned on the floor till my shoulders and hips felt bruised, then gave up and went back outside for some air. I was still pacing as the sun rose, its golden rays gobbling up the darkness.

I can do this. I could hold my nerve and stay cool until the time machine situation was resolved, one way or another. The idea of the "another" way made my stomach twist and writhe like a pit of Egyptian vipers.

Razi got up with the sun to work on the necklace for the vizier's party. It looked good so far. The stones were vibrant blue, polished smooth and set just right. Even so, he batted away all my compliments. "I will never be as good as my father. I am only fit to sew the soles of a donkey's shoes."

I understood his tension. A lot depended on him finishing the job and landing the sale. If he succeeded, his family would be free and clear in terms of tax. If not? None of us wanted to think about that.

Sahara was busy sewing something. She wouldn't let us see what.

"It's a surprise," she said with a twinkle.

Surprises drive me insane so, although I knew I shouldn't, I kept contriving ways to take a peek.

"Here's a refreshing beverage for you while you work," I

said, moving her way with a cup. Amunet took the drink and blocked my path and my view of Sahara's work.

After breakfast I tried again.

"I can't eat all my dates," I said. "Here, Sahara, have the last one." As I tried to pass it over, Amunet snatched it off me with an *I-so-know-what-you're-up-to* look.

I even tried the "Look, someone's waving behind you!", but Amunet blocked me again.

"Please, Madison!" she said. "Exercise patience. Or you'll spoil the surprise!"

Patience. There was that word again. On my list of least favourites, along with "eventually", "in good time", "time will tell", "time gateway". And so on.

At least I'd made Amunet smile, if briefly. Today, she was unusually flat. Every time she looked at Riley, her spark of joy dimmed a little more. Though I doubt Riley noticed. He was locked into his own thoughts as he assembled his mini-laboratory for testing toothpaste ingredients. When he went to leave, I followed.

"I'll come with you."

"No, please, Madison," said Amunet. "I beg you, stay. For we must rehearse our dance with the others."

"I think Riley needs my help, don't you?" I said.

He licked his lips and nodded. Not that convincingly.

Amunet grabbed my arm and, with a quick look back at Sahara, hustled me outside. "Please! I am sick with worry about my mother and what Babu may do if we fall short of our tax payment. We must get this dance right so we will be paid handsomely and my mother will be beyond his reach."

I was torn. I wanted to head out and search for the missing time machine with Riley, but Amunet was desperate.

"It's okay, Maddy," said Riley. "I've got this."

"Okay, then. See you later."

"Hopefully, when I get back, I'll have good news," he whispered.

I watched him stride through the fields, blond hair flaring in the morning sun. Somehow sensing my gaze, he turned and raised his arm in farewell.

Did I think he'd get the time machine back? He was smart, really smart—but not in that devious sort of way he might need to steal it back from a thief. That was more my thing. I should have gone with him. But for now, I'd have to trust Riley to search on his own.

Around mid-morning, Amunet and I met up with the other four girls in the troupe, who were jittery with excitement and nerves. They really wanted this to go well, as did I. If I was stuck in this period for the rest of my life, I'd need some way to make a living. Performing was one option. Others included bread-making, sewing, dung sculpting or finding myself a husband before I got too old.

The rehearsal went well. The group was tighter and more in sync.

During our first break, Amunet sat next to me on a low stone wall as we shared a drink from a leather pouch. She was distracted and on edge and I got the feeling she had something she wanted to say.

"Good rehearsal," I said to warm up the chat. "We are

going to rock the vizier's world tomorrow night."

"My aunt has found a possible husband for me," she said.

"Really? Who?"

"A man of seventeen years, a farm worker, good and strong and a loyal son. He lives in a village half a day's sail from here."

"Good news!" I said in a *that-is-so-not-good-news* sort of way. I knew I should be happy for her. She could fulfil her dreams of being a wife and mother. But it was hard to get excited when, if she lived in my time, we'd be hanging out, talking about music and guys, catching films, doing stupid, fun stuff for years before anything got too serious.

"What's he like? Is he handsome? Funny?"

"I don't know," said Amunet. "I have not met him."

Imagine marrying someone you'd never met! What if you didn't like them? If they were cruel? Or stupid? And you were trapped with them for the rest of your life?

Somehow, though, I didn't think that was Amunet's main worry. She'd grown up accepting marriage to a stranger as a normal thing. No, her problem was that she had fallen for Riley, big time. But he hadn't fallen back. Which had to suck.

"Do you think there is any chance that, with more time, Riley will forget this other girl and find space in his heart for me?" Her toffee eyes pleaded for an encouraging answer. I didn't want to hurt her, but she needed to hear the truth.

"There's no chance at all," I said. "I'm sorry, Amunet."

"Who is this girl?" she said. "He seems devoted to her."

"Yeah," I said, still weirded out by how Riley—awkward, cold scientist with little on display in the way of emotions— had described this grand love for a non-existent girl in such romantic terms. *What was it he said, again?* That he'd been in love with her since he was small. That his heart belonged to her alone and, one day, he hoped to be worthy of her. *Wow!* Where had that come from? Was it possible he was describing real feelings he had for someone? But who? Lauren? He could barely remember her name. And I hadn't noticed him checking anyone else out round school, though I guess he might have hidden it from me. It was more likely to have been something he saw on TV or in a film. Which was weird enough. I thought he only watched science programmes.

"Does this girl he spoke of feel the same way about him?" asked Amunet.

"Well, I'm not sure."

Amunet shook her head in disgust. "If she is not careful, she will lose him. Someone else will realise his worth and steal him from her."

Her voice cracked at the end. She didn't cry, but I could feel the effort it took to hold back the tears. It was a relief when dance practice resumed and we could just focus on the moves again.

CHAPTER 24

The day seemed especially long as I waited for Riley's return. As the sun began to set, I scanned the horizon but could see no sign of him.

He finally appeared in the doorway as we sat down to dinner, mud clumped in his hair and smeared over his white tunic. The instant his eyes met mine, I knew—he hadn't found the time machine. The tiniest of head shakes confirmed it. I tried to take the news well, but I felt like I was falling off a cliff.

As the family talked around me, their voices seemed distant and hollow. I took a slow breath, which sounded unnaturally loud in my ears. Then another. I told myself to stop fretting. We would get the time machine back or Riley would build another one. This was only a setback. We'd have another chance to look for it, perhaps even as early as tomorrow. The gateway wasn't closed...yet. Next time, I would go with him. And we would find it.

I pushed the food into my mouth, forced myself to chew and swallow, chew and swallow. But I barely tasted it. I tried to laugh and nod and make appropriate responses to the conversation, though it was hard to focus on their words. My mind kept drifting back to home and how much I missed it. And how stupid I was to have jumped into the time machine the way I had without even asking what it was first. I just couldn't believe that I might never see the people I loved again. I wouldn't believe it. Somehow, no matter what we had to do to get there, Riley and I would find our way back home. This, I promised myself.

By the time we'd finished eating, I was calmer.

Then Riley plonked a bowl with a yellowish paste in the centre of the table.

"What's that?" asked Sahara.

"It is called toothpaste," he said. "It will remove grains of sand from your teeth and preserve your teeth for years to come."

I smiled and nodded. *Good job.* I knew he could do it. Ironically, now that both the toothpaste and tax problems were solved, we would have been free to leave right away—if we'd still had the time machine. When we did find it (note—I said *when* not *if*), we would be free to blast off immediately.

"Try the toothpaste," Riley invited the family, gesturing towards the bowl.

Razi frowned. "Do we eat it?"

"No," said Riley. "You put it on a brush or your finger." He scooped a blob of the yellowy gunge onto his index finger. "Then you rub your teeth front and back like so."

Riley demonstrated, then rinsed his mouth with the beer and spat it into an empty bowl. As one, the family winced.

"Would you like to try?" he said.

At this point, I think even Riley, clueless as he was, could see they would rather have had their brains hooked out through their nose. It was only their respect for him that prevented them saying so.

"Err, I will try," said Razi bravely. He imitated everything Riley had done: scooped up the paste, rubbed it around his mouth, struggling to hide a look of revulsion, then took a mouthful of liquid and swallowed the lot—toothpaste and all.

"You're supposed to spit it out," I said.

"But, if you'll excuse me saying so, Riley, that is impolite in our country," said Razi. Then he clamped a hand over his mouth to stop the whole lot coming out again in one big heave.

"Would you like to try?" Riley asked Amunet and Sahara. Layla shook her head and covered her mouth.

"No, thank you, I'm quite full at the moment," Sahara said.

"Me too," said Amunet.

Riley and I exchanged worried looks. This was the whole point of coming to Ancient Egypt, to help people with their teeth. Now it seemed they didn't want to be helped. They probably didn't even know they had a problem. It was only with the distance of thousands of years that we could draw conclusions about their society's dental health.

"I'll have a go," I said.

So I rubbed the paste back and forth over my teeth, resisting the urge to screw up my face in displeasure. It tasted revolting. Of course, at home, the toothpaste-makers put in things like mint to improve the flavour.

I held the paste in my mouth for as long as I could then grabbed my cup, swilled some of my drink around in my mouth and—*whoosh*—spat the lot into a bowl. The family looked grossed out. But I had to admit, after weeks of no brushing, it did feel good.

"How do your teeth feel?" I asked Razi.

"Mmmm. They feel smooth and fresh," he said.

"You should do that every morning after breakfast and every evening before you go to bed," said Riley. "And then you will have less teeth trouble."

He sounded like one of the dentists visiting our school to talk about "Protecting Your Smile". And his lecture had about as much effect. The family looked at him blankly, but none of the girls made a move to try it. Not even love-struck Amunet.

After dinner, I made an excuse to go outside and jerked my head at Riley, signalling that he should follow.

"So, what happened with the time machine?" I asked.

"I followed the bike tracks until the sand covered them completely, then I fanned out in all directions and asked people if they'd seen anyone wheeling a strange machine around."

"And?"

"And nothing. I did find this though," he said, and he raised his arm.

"You found your arm?" I was perplexed.

He moved it round a bit more and I caught a flash of shimmering material.

"The invisibility cloth that was over the bike!" I said.

"It must have slipped off the bike and the thief didn't notice," he said. "At least it means he won't be able to hide it easily."

"How do you know he didn't just blast off out of the time period? Maybe the tracks disappeared because the machine went straight up into the air."

"He'd have to crack the password to do that."

I folded my arms, tipped my head and studied my friend. "Tell me the password isn't Riley Sinclair. RSinclair, RileyS or anything like that."

"No-oh," he said.

"Riley1, Science Fair Project. Einstein rocks?"

"No."

"What then?"

"It's Madison16," he mumbled into his chest.

Oh. That was weird. "Sixteen because...?"

"That's your age."

I nodded slowly. "Well, that should be safe-ish." As long as whoever took it didn't know our names or how old we were. Although, I had a feeling they might.

Well, this was...awkward. Riley used my name as his password?

"I'll come and help you look tomorrow," I said. Riley nodded sombrely. "Congrats on the toothpaste, by the way, though I have to say, it tasted disgusting."

"I can add some elements of flavour, if that's the problem."

But it wasn't. It was the whole vibe of the thing. The Ancient Egyptians had never brushed their teeth and could see no reason to start, especially when it involved putting tasteless paste in their mouth and spitting it out so impolitely. If this were to work, we had to give toothpaste a good image and promote it at a society level. How in the name of Isis, Osiris and all things Egyptian could the two of us do that?

"We are going to a big event tomorrow night—the vizier's party," said Riley. "I imagine some important people will be present. Maybe if we get them interested, others will follow?"

"Seems a long shot," I said. "But it's the only plan we've got. So it's worth a try."

CHAPTER 25

We headed off early the next morning to continue searching for the time machine. We spoke to dozens of people within a wide radius of the place where we'd hidden it, but no one had seen a thing. I just didn't see how that was possible.

"What next?" I said.

"Not sure," said Riley. "Let me think on it."

Major heart sink. Riley had run out of ideas. I think he was as crushed as I was, but I couldn't talk about it right now. To put it into words would somehow make it more real.

"I have to get ready for the show tonight," I said. "Are you coming?"

"I need to sort out a few things with the toothpaste first," he said.

At least the pressure was off regarding the tax payment. While Riley and I were out looking for the machine, it seemed Razi had a surprise visit from the prospective buyer of the necklace. The man had studied it carefully and pronounced it more than acceptable, promising to pay the agreed price at the party tonight after he presented it to the vizier. Which meant the family's tax problems were almost over.

"I told you he'd like it," I said.

"The buyer must have faulty eyes to view my work as acceptable," said Razi, smiling. "Thank the gods for his poor sight."

Now, Sahara revealed her "surprise". She had made dresses for all the girls in the troupe from the gold cloth she'd got at the markets. They were sleeveless, with long skirts split at the sides to allow movement. Colourful stones, donated by Razi, decorated the collars.

"Oh, mother," said Amunet. "They are more beautiful than the stars in the sky."

"I feel in my heart the vizier's party will be very special," said Sahara. "A night to remember."

Amunet wanted to rehearse again. I told her we shouldn't, as yesterday's run had gone so well, but she insisted. In my experience, last-minute rehearsals were usually disastrous. And this one was no exception. We were off-key, banged into each other and tripped over our own feet. It was just pre-show jitters, I knew. But Amunet freaked big time.

"I cannot remember a single step," she said. "I fear that last night, as I slept, a snake slithered into my brain. Now I am as graceless as a camel with boots of dried dung. We must send a messenger to the vizier, explaining we are ill and cannot attend the party."

"No, we're going," I said firmly.

"But if we make a mistake? The vizier might punish us. Severely."

"You think he'll chop our heads off if we miss a step? Will you listen to yourself!"

"I cannot do this," said Amunet.

"Yes, you can."

"Stop this, Amunet," said Sahara. "You look beautiful, you dance well. The vizier will be very happy on his birthday night. But only if you keep your promise to go to his home and entertain him. No more talk of snakes or sickness."

We got into our gold costumes. One of the girl's mums had brought black, shoulder-length wigs for us and helped us tie dozens of tiny plaits into them, weighted at the bottom with small stones "to make your hair swing more attractively". Sahara did our makeup, in that Egyptian style, with the black kohl eye-liner creating a shape like cat's eyes.

When we'd finished, I felt so Cleopatra. (Didn't I wish I had my phone now? This would so be my new profile pic.) Now we just had to put on a good show.

With that thought, my stomach did some dance practice of its own.

CHAPTER 26

Late in the afternoon, we began the trek along the river to the vizier's home. It was still sweaty warm and everything at the edge of our vision trembled in a heat haze. The perfumed oil Sahara had sprinkled on us just about covered the ever-present stench of baked clay and dung, though the oil's scent was sickly sweet.

The six of us from the troupe walked loosely in a group with Sahara and Layla up ahead. They were coming to the party too. They'd been hired to help with the food, as had many women and girls from the village. It was great news, as not only would they get to see us perform, but they'd earn more surplus for the taxman. Every bit helped.

As we trekked along the river, I spotted someone waving and jogging towards us. It was Riley, almost caked in mud. His blue eyes looked like chunks of lapis lazuli through the brown mud mask.

"You look...nice," he said.

"I wish I could say the same about you," I said.

"You look like a mud monster." Layla began to giggle.

"Arrrrgh!" Riley surged at the girl, who shrieked and reared back, helpless with laughter. "I'm almost done here," he said. "I'll clean up and catch you up later."

And he took off.

A bit further along we came upon an impressive sailboat. It was painted black with gold trim on the railings and deep-red sails. Its all-male crew was immaculate in crisp white sarongs, with bob-cut wigs, their muscular forms gleaming with oil or sweat—or both.

As we watched, two of the crew members helped a woman aboard and onto one of two elaborate chairs, like thrones, on a raised platform in the centre of the deck.

"Is that Sacmis?" Amunet squinted towards the river.

"Yeah, I think it is."

In a white dress with shimmering gold thread, her hair plaited and decorated with shiny beads that caught the light, Sacmis looked good—and she knew it. As she turned to look at us—or rather to watch us looking at her—she smiled.

"Look at her!" Amunet scowled and shook her head. "She looks like a snake who just swallowed a fat rat." I couldn't have said it better myself.

Presumably she was on her way to the party as Phoenix's guest, though I couldn't see him aboard.

"Though when the vizier's son finds it is not you on the boat, Maddy, but an impostor who has taken your place, then Sacmis may feel more like the rat sliding down the snake's throat."

Amunet cackled, but I didn't feel great about it.

We had another hour of trudging along the hard, dry ground before we first glimpsed the vizier's home. As big as our whole village, with a wall all around it, lined with palm trees and lush vegetation, it truly looked like an oasis in the desert.

Merchants led donkeys loaded with goods—presents for the vizier, or kitchen supplies—round the back to the servants' entrance. So we followed.

"Welcome!" Azizi and Dalali, the pair who had picked our dancing troupe in the marketplace, waited by the entry for us. They smiled and bowed.

"Each and every one of you looks very beautiful." Azizi beamed. "We are excited about your performance tonight."

"Let us show you around," said Dalali.

They led us through the house, pointing out features as we went. A large family shrine dominated one room; a drinking well featured in another. We passed a wine-making area and some horse stables. It all seemed strange at first, but when I thought about it, the shrine was like the family photos on the wall, the well was like our sink, the wine-making room was the ancient version of the wine rack. And the horses were the cars in the garage.

In the centre of the house was a large courtyard garden with exotic plants, sculptures and water features. As we inhaled sweet scents of flowers and listened to the rush of water in a fountain, the girls were big-eyed with awe.

"Are we still in Egypt?" said Amunet. "Or have we all passed through the underworld to a paradise beyond?"

"Pretty sure it's still Egypt," I said.

"I am happy the vizier's home pleases you." Azizi glowed on his master's behalf.

We passed the kitchen, which looked insanely busy with red-faced men and women, frazzled boys and girls, rushing about to shouted commands.

"There's Layla!" said Amunet.

We waved and Layla jumped up and down with excitement until a stern woman grabbed her by the plait and dragged her back to work.

The last stop on the tour was the Grand Hall, an impressive room with high ceilings and walls painted in shiny blues, greens and golds—and enough tables and bench seats to accommodate more than a hundred people, which was slightly unnerving.

"Here is where you will perform." Azizi gestured to a wide space in the centre of the hall. "Will it be adequate for your needs?"

"Oh yes, that will do nicely," I said.

"We hope to bring joy to the vizier with our performance," Amunet added.

An impressive wooden table, painted black with matching chairs, sat directly in front of the dance floor. The seat in central position was impressively carved and painted gold.

"Let me take a wild guess," I said. "That's the vizier's seat?"

"Correct," said Azizi, like a game-show host. "As you see, you must dance well because he will be close enough to notice your mistakes."

At the sight of our stricken faces, Dalali tutted. "Do not listen to his teasing. The vizier knows nothing about dance. Just smile at him and he'll be happy."

"May the gods give you wings on your feet." Azizi bowed and left.

We spent a few minutes working out how we'd enter for our dance and move about on the floor. It was a pretty good space, despite two large, round pillars in the centre. Just as we finished, we saw Sacmis being seated at the special table—three seats along from the golden chair. Her earlier confidence had vanished. She sat with her hands tightly clasped in her lap, her gaze fixed in terror upon the ground. I liked her much better this way.

"You really should have given Phoenix your true name, Madison," whispered Amunet. "For it would be an honour to be seated at the head table with all the important people."

"No," I said. "I'd rather hang out with you."

Though it was flattering to think it could have been me and that Phoenix might have wanted me beside him at such a big event. Presumably, he would take the seat next to Sacmis? *Hmmm.* That would put him only a few feet from the dance floor—close enough to recognise me if he looked hard enough. I'd have to keep my head down.

"Have you ever thought, Maddy, that the gods have a plan here?" Amunet whispered. "You gave Phoenix a false name to keep him away. And yet, as you dance, you will be close enough to hear him tear the meat from the bones of the animals he eats."

CHAPTER 27

As the guests arrived, Dalali got us to help out with the drinks. I carried a tray of goblets and Amunet had two jugs—one of wine, one of beer—to fill them.

"This is so exciting," said Amunet.

Most guests, male and female, wore white outfits with elaborate jewelled collars and black wigs. Quite a few had gold head-pieces or headbands with snakes or colourful stones moulded into the centre.

A tall woman with cheekbones like quotation marks took a goblet from me and smiled. And *Eeoo*! Her teeth! They were a mix of brown and yellow, like an old piano keyboard. She was in her twenties, but from the looks of it, she'd be toothless by the time she turned thirty. At least that was something Riley could fix if he got word of his toothpaste out tonight. A big *if*.

And speaking of Riley, he wasn't here yet. I really hoped he hadn't got so carried away with the mysteries of mud that he missed the party altogether. We needed him on drums. I needed him to get me through this.

"What are they serving over there?" I asked Amunet, pointing across the room.

A couple of servers held trays of wobbly brownish blobs, which they offered to all the female guests. I thought it was jelly or some strange Egyptian delicacy until I saw one woman put it on her head and leave it there as she went about socialising. Other women did the same.

"They must be scent cones," said Amunet. "I have heard of them, but I've never seen them before."

"Scent cones?"

"They're made of animal fat mixed with fragrant spices and herbs. As they melt, their glorious aroma is released into the hair. Aren't they elegant?"

Ancient Egyptian women liked fat dripping through their hair?

Well, stick me in a painted box and call me Tutankhamun! This was one wacky place.

"Riley, where are you?" I muttered.

"Your brother will be here," said Amunet. "He will not let you down."

I wasn't so sure about that. The room was full now and still no sign of him. I was imagining what I'd do to him if he didn't get here on time—it involved mud, lots of it, being shoved down his throat—when I heard a deep voice behind me.

"How do I look?"

"You look wonderful, master," said a second male voice. "If I was that girl, I would fall in love with you instantly."

Through the strands of my wig, I saw Phoenix, the vizier's son. He was peering across the room towards the table where Sacmis sat, waiting. A man I presumed was his servant walked beside him.

"Look!" said Amunet. "There's Phoenix. Isn't he handsome?"

And he was, in a brutal kind of way. Unlike most others in the room, he wasn't wearing a wig and his dark hair was thick and shiny. He wore a sarong of gold cloth and a matching short cape clipped at the neck with a scarab clasp. But the most striking part of his outfit was the leopard skin draped diagonally across his back, its head resting on his right shoulder.

"I tried to dress more simply than usual," Phoenix told the servant. "For Sacmis may be overwhelmed by too much splendour."

"She is lucky to have the chance to command your attention," said the servant, "if only for an evening."

"As I recall my last meeting with her, I believe it is I who am lucky to have her attention for the evening," said Phoenix, "for she is a most unusual woman."

Amunet covered her mouth to stop giggles bubbling out. "Did you hear what he said? About *you*. For you are the Sacmis he is talking about, the one he expects to have by his side this night. Oh, Madison, I believe the vizier's son truly admires you."

"Shhh. He doesn't even know me."

Though I had to admit, I did kind of like it and wanted to hear more.

"I hope she has more control over her tongue tonight," said the servant, "so I do not have to cut it out for you, master."

Amunet gripped my arm.

"I have never needed a weapon to tame a woman's tongue before," said Phoenix. "But keep your knife sharpened just in case."

Between the bobbing heads, I saw a glint of white teeth. I think they were joking. But if so, it was some kind of Ancient Egyptian humour I didn't get at all.

Amunet and I stayed close, but not too close, to Phoenix as he made his way to the table. His progress was painfully slow. Everyone passing stopped him to give their birthday wishes for his father.

"Look at this goblet!" A jowly man in a gold skull-cap demanded my attention. "Gods! It's filthy! Get me a clean one immediately."

I hurried to the kitchen for a fresh tray of goblets and made my way back through the crowd just in time to catch Phoenix's first look at Sacmis.

One minute he had this big-eyed expectant look, the next it froze and kind of melted into disappointment. His brow crinkled slightly, his mouth drooped. Though it was just for a few seconds. Then his cheeks expanded into a broad smile again as he bowed to her.

"Did you see his face?" said Amunet. "He was not happy. Do you think he'll have her beaten?"

"He wouldn't, would he?"

"He is the vizier's son. He can do whatever he wants."

After watching them together for a few minutes, though, a beating seemed unlikely. Phoenix was all charm, she was all modesty. She hadn't met his eye once, as far as I could tell.

Whatever. They were no longer my problem. And they were welcome to each other.

After the guests had been through the buffet—like a plague of locusts—they sat back, ready for some entertainment.

"It is time to perform, ladies," said Azizi.

"What is my first step?" Amunet's voice trembled. "I can't remember a thing."

"It'll come to you," I said. "Just stay calm."

Most of the girls were sheet white—quite a feat when your usual colour is caramel. They prayed to all kinds of Egyptian gods to guide their feet. Lining up at the entrance, I was worried a couple might actually break down in tears.

"Take a deep breath, everyone," I said. "We'll be fine. It'll be fun." I sounded more confident than I felt.

A quick look round the corner and I saw all the tables were full. Lots of jet-black heads and white-white outfits. And, in the second row, was someone I hadn't expected to see—Peterson, our fellow time traveller. As his eyes met mine, he nodded and gave me that smile like he had some private joke going on. *Just my luck.* He was right there, but, as I was about to go on stage, I couldn't do a thing about it.

"The drummer? Is he not coming tonight?" Azizi asked.

I was about to say no, I didn't think so, when the room went quiet. Everyone looked around to see why, their heads swivelling towards the entrance as they watched someone make their way into the hall. It was Riley, clutching his vat drum. His blond hair was now, thankfully, clean, and looked almost white in dramatic contrast to the dark heads around the room.

He wore the tunic Sahara had made for him, of silver cloth, tied at the left shoulder. It showed off his blue eyes and paler colouring. I noticed several women watching him with curled lips and predator's eyes. As he set his drum down on our stage and took his place behind it, Phoenix watched him too, jaw clenched, as if sensing a rival.

But Riley didn't notice a thing. He turned to me with a big puppy smile, ready to play. Despite how annoyed I was with him for being late, my cheeks stretched into a grin.

"The drummer's here now," I said. "Okay, ladies, time for the show."

But now it was I who seized up. I couldn't move, couldn't remember my first step. I tried to slow my breathing to steady my nerves, but somehow I wasn't getting enough air and had to gulp down lots of panicked breaths. I was hyperventilating.

"Calm yourself, Madison." Azizi placed a reassuring hand on my shoulder. "Relax your mind and picture the dance in your head. You will be fine."

I did as he said. Closed my eyes. Made my mind a blank, a whiteboard. Took one deep breath. Released it slowly. Then another. The girls began playing the dance music. *Okay, I have it!* I could see the steps in my head.

We hit the stage. Nerves sharpened our senses and made our timing and movements more crisp and accurate. After a few minutes, I relaxed and began to enjoy myself. When we finished the first dance, the audience applauded warmly. Azizi, who was filling the guests' wine glasses at the top table, looked over and gave me an encouraging smile.

Our second dance was better. By the third, the guests shouted their enthusiasm. The vizier, a rotund man in his forties, with more makeup on than me, was having the best time of the lot, whooping and clapping.

Then came the final song, *Lean On Me.*

Riley began the beat on the drums. We started clapping. I gestured for the audience to join in, but they sat there, unsure what to do. The girls in the troupe looked over anxiously. This song always worked best with audience participation. So I appealed directly to the vizier on his golden throne. "Sir, would you join us?"

From the back of the room came a gasp, followed by a hiss of whispered mutterings. *Uh-oh.* Was it bad form to address the top man directly? The vizier frowned for a few seconds, then grinned and clapped. *Clap, clap.* He giggled, loving it, though his timing left a lot to be desired.

"And you, sir?" I implored Phoenix, on his left. As soon as his eyes met mine, he startled. And the corners of his mouth crept into a grin. Like a snake who had spotted a rat in the corner, one that now had no hope of escape. I should have known even in this wig and costume, my blue eyes would give me away.

Now, the whole room was clapping. For when the two top guys were doing it, no one dared remain still.

As we took our bows for the final song, people went wild. The troupe's position on the party circuit was secure.

In the back room, Amunet and the girls literally jumped with joy.

"That was so much fun," said Amunet. "I can't wait to do it again."

"You will not have to wait long," said Dalali. "For I have already had requests from guests to discuss new dates for your next performance."

Sahara, who'd been serving drinks, came by wearing a proud mother's smile. "Girls, that was wonderful." She hugged Amunet, then me. "I hope you can stay together as performers for a long time to come. Madison, how soon are you expected back in Nubia?"

"In Nubia?"

"How long can your family spare you?"

"I...err...don't know."

And, just like that, my good mood vanished. I looked over at Riley, who gave a tight smile. Even he seemed to feel the force of her question. Now that the time machine was gone, neither of us knew when we'd be going home. Or *if* we ever would.

I hurried out to the courtyard garden for a few moments alone. I needed to calm down, get a grip on myself, push those dark thoughts back. They wouldn't help me find the time machine or make a life here if that's what we had to do.

Before I even got to the garden, I felt tears streaming down my face. I kept picturing my family and friends at home, trying to come to terms with my disappearance. Trying to move on with their lives but not managing it because nothing made any sense.

"What is the matter, Sacmis?" a honeyed voice came from behind. "Or should I call you Madison?"

I wiped my cheeks and turned to find Phoenix, half in, half out of the moonlight. "Are you crying?" His voice was more tender than I would have expected.

"No. I think I'm getting a cold." I sniffed loudly to strengthen the lie.

He smiled wryly. "You know, in this land, it is not wise to lie to someone of high rank. You told me your name was Sacmis. Now I am sitting with one woman when I was hoping for another."

"I didn't lie," I said. "Sacmis...is my middle name."

Shadows slipped into a dimple on his chin I hadn't noticed before. "You are a woman of mystery, Madison Sacmis," he said. "Where are you from?"

"I'm from Nubia, south Nubia."

"I have known many women from southern Nubia. None were like you. Where are you really from?"

He was sharp, I'd give him that. Which in the circumstances was not good. I didn't know enough about the geography of this area or time to bluff it out. I had to stall. "As you say, a girl needs to have some mystery."

He prowled around me, the dead eyes of the leopard on his shoulder staring into mine, cold and unfeeling. By contrast, Phoenix's eyes were full of light.

I moved away, along a path between the garden beds. A sweet scent floated up from a flowering bush, then something damp and earthy. Phoenix took a path parallel to mine, slipping in and out of the shadows like a jungle cat.

"You are not afraid of me, are you?" he said.

"Should I be?"

At the end of the path, I turned a corner and passed a three-tiered fountain. I strained to see him through the foliage and listened for the crunch of his feet on the gravel path to tell me where he was.

"You have no need to fear me," he said, appearing right next to me. "So tell me. Where is your home?"

"You wouldn't believe me if I told you," I said.

"Try me," he said.

"I'm from a land down south, way down south. Weeks sailing away from Nubia. It's called Australia."

I wasn't sure why I said it. I guess I figured, what harm could it do? Sometimes it was easier to tell the truth than a lie.

"I have never heard of this land, Australia. Tell me about it." He sat on the edge of the fountain to listen.

So I told him about Australian animals—the koalas and the kangaroos and the emus—and the Opera House right on Sydney Harbour. How we liked to swim in the ocean, go for picnics in parks. How we were really into equality of race and gender. And everyone having free speech and a fair go. He listened intently, taking it all in.

When I finished, he smiled. "Are all the girls in Australia like you? So direct and unafraid? If so, I must pay a visit there very soon."

My cheeks burned. Thankfully, in the dark, the glow wouldn't be too obvious. I stole a glance at Phoenix. His smile was so warm and natural that at this moment it was hard to believe he was a high-born guy from an ancient era.

"Maddy?"

Riley was on the other side of the fountain, his hair ablaze in the moonlight. "Are you okay?"

"She is with me," Phoenix boomed. "Why wouldn't she be okay? I can look after her better than a servant with a drum."

This was weird and somewhere I did NOT want to go.

"If you don't mind, I'd like to hear from Madison herself," said Riley.

"I'm fine, Riley. I'm coming in now."

As I started to move away, Phoenix caught my arm and smiled. "It was very nice to talk to you, Madison. I hope we may speak again soon."

The way he looked at me made me feel *something*. When I wanted to feel nothing. The moonlight softened his features, making him look strong yet vulnerable. Even the leopard on his shoulder looked more kitty-cat than natural-born killer.

"I hope I didn't interrupt anything before," said Riley as he handed out fresh goblets to the guests. I followed along with jugs of drink, smiling and refilling them.

"Actually, you did," I said. "And thanks for that."

Riley grinned.

"How's the toothpaste plan going?" I asked.

"It's ready," he said. "I just need to have a word with the vizier."

"Oh, that's all?"

My sarcasm was wasted on him, but it was there. "Riley, I might not be an expert on Ancient Egyptian customs. But it seems to me there's no way a servant could just walk up to the vizier and start chatting about toothpaste. And even if you did approach him—and didn't get hauled off to be flogged, or worse, for being so bold—would he like the concept any more than Razi and our family did?"

"If he had a chance to try it with the taste modifications I've made," said Riley, "and with allowances for local manners, I think there would be a chance."

"What allowances for local manners?" I asked.

Before he could explain, though, Azizi was standing in the middle of the dance floor, calling for silence.

"Ladies and gentlemen," he said, "on behalf of the vizier, we wish to offer you something unique tonight. The vizier's son would like to demonstrate his superior hunting skills. To make it interesting, he would like one of you here tonight to challenge him to see who is the better hunter."

For no reason, I had a really bad feeling about this.

"Who among you considers himself worthy to challenge the mighty Phoenix?" Azizi shouted.

There was a long pause, then one young boy rose to his feet, propelled there by his father on his left and his brother on his right. He was about eighteen, thin but serious. As polite applause crackled around him, he said something to his father and tried to sit down, but his relations kept him up. He nodded solemnly to Azizi.

Three more contenders popped up, looking equally uncomfortable. And who could blame them? Even if they wanted to compete with Phoenix, it was awkward because (a) the guy was probably a good hunter and hard to beat, and (b) even if you could beat him, the birthday boy might not be happy about his son being shown up in front of his friends. All four of the contenders, it seemed to me, were balancing on a tightrope over a pit of danger.

Phoenix walked to the centre of the room and stood beside Azizi. "I see five men on their feet who think they can beat me," he said.

Five men? Everyone looked around, confused. *One, two, three, four.* Could Phoenix have miscounted? Now he glared at each contender in turn, a staring match he won every time. They stood straight, arms by their side, faces colouring as they waited to see who he chose.

"I choose you," he said coldly to the fifth contender. His head snapped right—a direction no one expected. People leaned forward in their seats, brows ridged with confusion, to glimpse the mysterious fifth contender. There was no one standing over that side of the hall.

Correction. There were no guests standing over there. But plenty of servants, handing out drink and fruit and nuts. His eyes lasered onto one carrying a tray of goblets. *Riley.*

CHAPTER 28

It took Riley a minute or so to realise Phoenix was looking at him, that he was the chosen contender. I would have freaked out at that point, but not Riley. He nodded calmly, put the tray down and moved to the centre of the stage to stand beside his opponent.

There was a hiss of whispers all around the room. From the looks on faces, I got the idea it was not usual for a high-born guy to challenge a lowly servant.

Azizi swallowed nervously and cleared his throat. "And what is your name, challenger?"

"I am Riley Sinclair." A collective intake of breath. *What a weird name*, everyone probably thought.

Phoenix clenched his fists, flexed his arm muscles and narrowed his eyes at Riley.

"Where are you from?" asked Azizi.

"I come from a land down under," Riley said.

Everyone with a voice in that hall began chanting: "Phoenix! Phoenix!" Including Amunet. I looked over at her with a *WTH* look. She shrugged. Okay, I got it. Anyone cheering for Riley would be in trouble.

"Phoe-nix, Phoe-nix!" I joined in. Riley did not look impressed.

Two servants carried out a rustic-looking wooden cage. Inside, a small furry animal, long-bodied, like a ferret, darted about in fear.

"In a moment, I will open the cage," said Azizi. "The first of the two contenders to fell the mongoose will be the winner."

They were going to kill that cute animal for sport? *Gross!* Phoenix couldn't help it, I suppose. Brutality was considered manly around here. But Riley had better not hurt the creature or I'd be really annoyed.

Riley's brow wrinkled just slightly. I got why. In order to win here, he would have to (a) kill an innocent creature and (b) show up the vizier's son at his dad's birthday party. The safest thing to do was let Phoenix win, but I remembered Riley saying how he preferred winning.

"Choose your weapons," said Azizi.

Phoenix whispered something to Azizi, who signalled to a servant. A few minutes later, the man appeared with a lethal-looking spear. This was the vizier's son's weapon of choice. Meanwhile, Riley ran out into the garden, returning with a large flat stone he'd found there. *Good idea, Riley! Choose a weapon not guaranteed to kill.* Still, it was a big stone. If it hit the animal with any force, he might just as well have speared it.

"If you win, Riley Sinclair," said Phoenix, "what would you like as your prize?"

"I...err..." Riley looked around the room. "I would like five minutes of discussion with the vizier."

"That is not possible," said Azizi. "You must choose another prize."

"I agree to your terms," said Phoenix, overruling him. "And if I win, I take your sister, Madison, as my personal servant."

What the—? I was not a prize to be won. Nor was I Riley's to give away. Riley looked over at me as he chewed on his bottom lip. *Oh nonono.* He wasn't going to…? He wouldn't, would he?

"Agreed," said Riley.

What the—?

Azizi opened the cage and the mongoose shot out super-fast, ducking under the guests' feet, weaving around chairs and beneath tables. People screamed and kicked up their legs as it approached. It wriggled into their sleeves and down their shirtfronts, and lifted one woman's wig off completely to reveal a bald, polished scalp—which might have been amusing, in that jeery *Funniest Home Videos* kind of way, if the poor creature hadn't been running for its life at the time.

Meanwhile, Phoenix watched intently, gripping his spear till his knuckles were white. Riley clutched his stone, arm across his body, like a Frisbee set to fly. Neither one blinked. When the animal came to a stop in a clear space between two tables—*whoosh*—they loosed their weapons.

I saw the whole thing as if it was in slow motion. Phoenix's spear travelled straight and sure for the mongoose's heart as Riley's rock glided in the same direction. The rock just clipped the spear, sending it fractionally off course, before knocking a wicker bread basket off the edge of the table. The basket fell, flipping on the way down and trapping the mongoose underneath. The spear landed on top of the basket, its weight making escape impossible for the animal.

A moment of silence, then the hall erupted into wild applause. The animal was alive but trapped by the basket. The vizier declared the contest a draw.

"Would you like the privilege of killing the creature, Riley

Sinclair?" said Phoenix, now magnanimous and cheerful.

Riley paused. "As the gods have sought to spare its life," he said, "should we not spare it too?" *Nice one, Riley!*

"Free the mongoose!" Phoenix commanded.

I cheered, though I was the only one who did. As the servant lifted the bread basket, the creature bolted away so fast it was a blur.

"My friend, you are the guest," said Phoenix, "so I will leave it to you to decide whether we both win and gain those prizes which we have worked for. Or we both lose and obtain nothing."

Riley turned and looked at me, eyes bulbous, biting his lip.

"We both win," he said, mouthing "Sorry" at me.

Well, he will be when I finish with him.

More applause and cheers followed. Everyone was happy with the result. Except me. Now Phoenix turned to look at me, the same way he'd looked at the mongoose a few minutes earlier. Only for me, there was no hope of escape.

CHAPTER 29

I only had time to see Riley, toothpaste kit in hand, sitting down next to the vizier before Phoenix grabbed my arm and took me into the garden.

"So, now you are mine," he said. "I won you fairly in a bet witnessed by everyone here tonight." His grin was as big as Christmas morning. Which made me even more cross.

"Only problem was you made that bet with Riley, not me," I said. "I am not his to gamble with, which means the whole thing is null and void."

"He is your brother, is he not?"

"Yes," I said. A fake brother. Soon to be a dead and dismembered fake brother. How could he do that to me? He must really want to succeed in this toothpaste mission. Note to self: never get between Riley and success.

"Brothers have authority over their sisters in this country," he said.

"Well, they don't where I come from."

"So you refuse to be my servant?"

"Yes, I refuse," I said, trying to appear confident, although I was a tad worried it might be a really dumb thing to say in this time and place.

"As my servant, you will live here in the house with us," he said stiffly. "If you wish, I can move some of the other girls around and ensure you have a room to yourself."

"Oh great!" I said. "I'll be a special servant—one that all the other servants hate. Fantastic!"

Phoenix tilted his head, brow furrowed. He might not be used to sarcasm, but he caught the chill in my tone. "You do not wish a room on your own? Would you prefer to share with some of the other girls?"

He just didn't get it. What could I say to make it clear to him?

"I don't mind whether I have a room to myself or share with other girls," I said, "just so long as I'm free to do as I please when I get up in the morning."

"I see," he said. "You wish to be *free*. But, as my personal servant, your duties would not be burdensome. You will accompany me on *picnics* and watch over me whenever I go near the water."

He raised his eyebrows, coy now, pleading just a little. At least he didn't expect me to sew or cook or make his dung bricks.

"Occasionally, I will permit you to wash my feet," he said, the dimple making a reappearance. "I am sure you will enjoy that."

He was grinning now. But how was that funny?

I tutted loudly and looked away, arms folded tightly.

"I am very fond of you, Madison," he said, stepping closer and stroking my hair. *Uh-oh.* I stepped back, afraid for different reasons now. The right side of my head felt tingly all along the path he'd traced.

"Yeah, well, forcing me to be a servant is a strange way to show it."

I shot off along the path away from him. He took a parallel one, but skirted around and headed me off at the end.

"How do people show each other their feelings where you come from?" he asked. "In this...*Australia*. Please, I wish to know more of your customs."

In the moonlight, his skin looked velvety, his eyes glossy, like microwaved chocolate. I cleared my throat and wished I could as easily clear my head.

"Well, in my country, we have a saying: when you like someone, set them free. If they come back, they're yours. If they don't, they never were." (It was something I'd read in a birthday card once—only it said "love", not "like".)

"Can you explain the meaning of this saying?" He looked genuinely confused.

"It means you can't force someone to like you. They have to give you that affection of their own free will."

Phoenix paced, shadows sinking into vertical creases on his brow. He turned to look at me several times, jaw clenched, eyes narrowed. *Uh-oh.* This wasn't looking good.

"Very well," he blurted out. "I release you, Madison, from your obligations as a servant. Perhaps some time you will return to me of your own free will. I pray to the gods for that day to arrive soon. For I do desire it most greatly."

His eyes locked on mine and I found I couldn't look away. "Until then, I bid you good-night." He bowed and left me.

That was...unexpected. And strange.

When I returned to the main hall, I saw him talking to the guests, Sacmis by his side. I was relieved but a little sad too. The truth was I didn't totally dislike the guy. If we'd been in Sydney and he'd asked me on a date, I might have said yes. *Might.*

Here, in Ancient Egypt though, there was no such thing

as a date. Women were wives or servants. And not much in between. So that was that.

I looked across the room and spotted Riley with the vizier and a few others at the table. The older man held something like a vase, with a narrow top and wide bottom, to his mouth and spat into it. That must have been what Riley came up with to remove the embarrassment of spitting out the toothpaste. Clever.

The vizier frowned, then smiled. He embraced Riley and patted him hard on the back. Then he gathered a few other older men to try the toothpaste, too. They all looked dubious at first, but after going through the process, they became joyous, grinning and laughing. And whenever Riley spoke, they leaned forward to listen.

Has he really done it? Launched toothpaste to the ancient world? Fantastic! Though he wouldn't get to enjoy his success for long, because as soon as he'd finished with the vizier, I was going to murder him for using my freedom as leverage for his win and almost turning me into a servant. *What a low act!*

Azizi carried a tray with just two drinks on it—one for the vizier and one for Riley—to the pair to celebrate. He was being invited to toast with the vizier like an equal, not a servant. But as the older man reached for his goblet, he accidentally knocked it over. It crashed to the ground, spilling the wine on the floor.

Everyone rushed forward to help. Azizi gabbled and bowed as Riley passed his goblet to the vizier.

It was then I remembered—Peterson the time traveller was here somewhere. I had to find him. I did a quick scan of the room but couldn't see him. I'd just started looking more carefully when Razi appeared beside me, bright-eyed and smiling.

"How is the evening progressing?" he said. "And congratulations on your performance."

"Thank you," I said. "It's all going well."

I glanced over and saw the vizier with his hand on Riley's shoulder, like a favoured son, drinking from his goblet. Near them Phoenix and Sacmis stood together talking and I felt something weirdly like jealousy ripple through me. *Get over yourself, Maddy.*

"It's all good," I said. "And with you? Is the sale of the necklace on track?"

Razi nodded. "My client will present it to the vizier shortly. We will receive payment tomorrow."

His gaze slid past me to a servant girl, around sixteen, who smiled coyly back at him. Romance was in the air.

All was well with the world.

Until it wasn't.

A ghoulish scream sliced through the laughter. Everyone froze.

"Oh, master! Please, somebody help!" Dalali called.

The vizier slid to the ground, his face turning blue, his eyes bulging and white froth oozing from his mouth. And he made this awful gagging sound as he choked. Two well-dressed men in gold wigs with heavy makeup pushed through the crowd and knelt beside him. But they were too late.

The vizier was dead.

The party was over. In more ways than one.

CHAPTER 30

Phoenix ordered all the guests out of the room as he ranted and raged about his father's death. Black tears from his eye kohl streaked his face like war paint as he called on the gods to tell him why his beloved father had been taken from him and begged them to send violent retribution down upon the murderer. His servants whimpered and cowered at the force of his rage. I was pretty scared too.

Ragged with emotion, he turned and extended his arm, his finger pointing at Riley.

"You!" he shrieked. Two strong guards flew at Riley, seizing an arm each. "You poisoned my father. And now you shall pay."

"I didn't kill him," said Riley.

"My father trusted you! He tried your paste for teeth and has now paid with his life. He departed this world in great suffering—we all saw it. But now, Evil One, Bringer of Death, you shall suffer too, and far more than my father. Bring me my hunting knife!"

The servants scattered in terror, like cockroaches on the kitchen bench at night, to search for the weapon.

"No!" I shouted. Everyone turned to look at me, shocked by a servant speaking out.

"Riley did not kill your father, Phoenix!" I said. "It couldn't have been the toothpaste. Or the other men who tried it would be dead too." I got the words out quickly in case anyone tried to silence me mid-sentence.

"That is the sister of the Evil One," said a guard. "She may have been in on his plan. Perhaps she should be punished too."

"Leave her out of this!" Riley shouted.

Phoenix came over to me now, his dark eyes locking onto mine. He stayed like that for a minute or so, his gaze shifting around my face examining each feature, as if committing the details to memory. There was arrogance in the casual tilt of his head, fury in his clenched jaw. But in his misty eyes, I saw only pain.

Without shifting his gaze from my face, he pointed to a man beside him.

"You tried the paste for teeth," he said. "How do you feel?"

"I feel fine," said the man. "And my breath has never been fresher."

Phoenix took a deep breath and let it out slowly. He seemed deflated afterwards, smaller somehow. No longer a tyrannical ruler, just a teenage boy who'd lost his dad.

"I'm so sorry about your father, Phoenix," I said.

He pressed his lips together, trying to hold the emotion back. "Release Madison and Riley," he said softly.

The guards looked about, confused, as if they'd misheard.

"Now!" he screamed.

He put his head in his hands, rubbing his eyes and sniffling. But when he looked up, there was a rock-hard resolve in him.

"Who was the servant who brought the wine to my father?"

A tense silence followed.

"Tell me!"

"It was Azizi," Dalali stammered. "He served the wine, master."

"Bring Azizi to me!"

But though the vizier's servants and friends searched all corners of the sprawling mansion, Azizi could not be found.

My guess? He'd run off into the desert to hide. And who could blame him? If he was caught, it was doubtful anyone would be interested in proving his guilt before Phoenix got busy with his hunting knife.

After that, we stumbled home in the dark. I felt hollowed out by all the day had brought—the loss of the time machine, the nerves of performing, the terror of retribution from Phoenix.

Riley and I lagged behind the others so we could have a private talk.

"I really didn't think we'd get out of that," I said.

"You saved my life tonight, Maddy," said Riley. "Thanks."

"It's okay. Even though you almost turned me into Phoenix's servant."

"Sorry about that. I thought you'd be able to talk your way out of it. He seemed to like you."

"That doesn't make it okay."

"I'm really sorry. But it was the only way I could think of to get to speak to the vizier."

And look how that had turned out.

"Poor vizier," said Riley. "He was a nice man."

"Poor Azizi, if they ever catch him," I said.

Poor Phoenix too. He'd lost his dad. There were no winners tonight.

"What happened exactly?" I asked.

"One minute, the vizier was well and in good spirits," said Riley. "Then he dropped his cup, and I gave him mine—"

"You gave him yours?"

"He drank the wine, and..." He shook his head, frowning.

"You know," I said, "what with everything going on, I forgot to tell you I saw that Peterson guy at the party."

"Peterson, the time traveller? Really?"

"Just before we were about to do our dance, I spotted him in the crowd. He smiled at me, like it was all a big joke. Do you think he had something to do with the poisoning?"

Riley frowned. "Maybe, but he would have had to sneak into the kitchen, find out which goblet was the vizier's and slip the poison in."

"And given he's so tall and fair, someone would surely have noticed," I muttered.

"But why would he even want to kill the vizier?"

I couldn't think of a reason, but what did I know? I knew nothing about the guy except that he was a time traveller with a twisted sense of humour.

"Any idea who else might have wanted the vizier dead?" I said.

"He's a powerful man," said Riley. "He probably has loads of enemies."

Well, yes. And...? An idea was buzzing around in my head like a fly you couldn't swat away but couldn't ignore either. "The thing is, Riley," I said, "the poison wasn't in the vizier's goblet. It was in yours."

Even in the dark, I saw the whites of Riley's eyes expanding as he turned to me. "That had to be a mistake," he said. "I mean, no one would want to kill me."

"Well, we don't know what Peterson wants. He might be after you. And the man in the mask who tried to kidnap me? He mentioned you by name. Maybe he wants to kill you."

"But it had to be someone with access to the kitchen," he said, thinking practically.

"True. But, I never saw that masked guy's face. For all I know, he could have been there, disguised as a servant."

"If he has our time machine, though," said Riley, "then, presumably, he got what he wanted. Why go to all the trouble of killing me?"

It was a good point. If he took off with our time machine and left us behind, Riley and I were as good as dead in our time anyway.

"Except he didn't have the password," I said. "So he couldn't get off the ground. Hey, you don't suppose he had some kind of antidote to the poison. And was planning to trade it for the time machine password?"

"Seems a bit complicated," said Riley.

"Did you see any strange servants hanging around when you got the drinks?" I was excited now, sure I was on to something. "If he did have an antidote, he would have to have been close by to administer it in time."

"I didn't notice anyone close by," he said. "Except Azizi."

"Well, it couldn't have been him. There must have been someone else. Think."

Riley looked over, his brow creased. "How are you so sure it wasn't Azizi?"

"Seems unlikely," I said. "He's such a nice guy. Do you know one of the other servants told me that on market day, Dalali wanted to book Sacmis's group to perform at the party. It was Azizi who persuaded her our group was the better choice."

I intended the words to come out in support of the guy, but somehow, they had the opposite effect.

"So, you're saying Azizi was instrumental in getting us to the vizier's party," Riley said. "And he was the one who brought the poisoned drink out."

And it hit me. Like a blind camel slamming into a pyramid.

"Before the girls and I started performing," I said, "I was freaking out a bit and Azizi gave me a pep talk. He said, 'Relax your mind and picture the dance'. They were the same words the masked man used when he kidnapped me. 'Relax your mind and picture the time machine'. Ohmygod, Riley! Azizi and the masked man are one and the same."

"So Azizi stole our time machine and tried to poison me?" said Riley. "Then he must be a time traveller too."

"What?" That felt like seriously bad news. "Azizi and Peterson are both time travellers? But how is that possible? Did someone invent a time machine before you?"

"Not necessarily. They could be from the future, in more advanced versions of my machine."

"From the future? Which *hasn't even happened yet*? But how is that possible?"

"Well, it depends whether time is linear or non-linear," he said.

"Huh?"

"Think of a journey from the past to the future," said Riley, "as being vertical rather than horizontal. Not so much a train travelling along a track, but something more like a building with different floors and the time machine is like a lift going up and down between them."

"Huh?" I looked up at the star-speckled sky stretching endlessly above me. I wasn't sure what I expected to see—the underside of a future time, maybe? "Are you saying that all the times—past, present and future—are going at the same time, rather than one after the other?"

"It's a theory."

A ridiculous one.

"And Azizi might have travelled down in the lift of time," I said, thinking aloud, "to try to kill you—in a machine that was more advanced than yours but based on the one you invented?"

"It's possible," he said.

It sounds totally impossible to me.

"Well, why would he even need your machine then?" I asked. "If he had his own improved version?"

Riley frowned. "I can only think he's trying to change something about the origin of the event—that he wants to alter something about how the time machine first came into being."

We were quiet the rest of the way home, listening to the rhythm of our footsteps—*crunch, crunch, crunch*—on the dry earth and the suck and slurp of water at the river's edge. The moon followed at our shoulder, like a spy eavesdropping on our conversation.

While I struggled to get my head around the whole time thing and the idea that some time-travelling assassin was here trying to alter the origin of a future event, one thing was clear to me. Time travel was dangerous. And if a lot of people did it, it could be catastrophic.

Because how could you be sure of anything ever again? You'd go to bed at night, not knowing whether the world would be the same when you woke up. Or whether someone might have gone back in time and changed something in your past, even something small, like whether your parents went to the party where they first met. Or your grandparents did? Or your great-grandparents. Those changes could ripple through the timeline, changing more and more things along the way, till everything was wildly different when it caught up with you the next morning.

If you even existed anymore.

It was terrifying when you thought about it. And Riley should have thought about it a lot harder before he started all this.

"Riley," I said, "are you sure you want to put this project into the Science Fair this year?"

"No," he said. "Though I don't have anything else to enter."

"How about a translation pill? Or a cloak of invisibility?"

"Well, the pill is top secret and the cloak...is nothing that new."

"So try losing this year. Like the rest of us." It wasn't a suggestion.

As we approached the village, I wrenched my mind back from these end-of-the-world problems to those here and now in Ancient Egypt, where all the good things Amunet's family had hoped for at the start of the evening had pretty much turned to dung.

"Do you think the vizier's death will mean Razi won't get paid for the necklace?" I said.

We had our answer as soon as we stepped through the mud-brick doorway. It was there in Sahara's tight smile,

Amunet's too-happy voice and Razi's posture, as stiff as a freshly wrapped mummy. Bad news. Possibly, the worst.

I took Razi outside and asked whether the buyer would still pay him. He shook his head grimly.

"Well, at least we can give the necklace to Babu as part of what we owe," I said. "That should be enough, don't you think?"

"Do you think a single necklace will be enough for someone as greedy as Babu?" he asked. "Especially when he knows we were unable to sell it."

"But we have our payment for the dancing tonight as well," I offered. "And Layla and Sahara's payments for their work, as well as the gold and silver from my day as a mourner. Won't that do?"

"I hope so," he said, staring across the fields towards the Nile, a slash of sliver against the charcoal sky.

I heard a sniffling coming from behind the beehive oven. Peering around, I found Amunet on her knees, crying. "I can't bear to think of anything happening to Mama," she said. "Or of Babu taking Layla as his servant."

Neither could I. But surely that wouldn't happen?

We wouldn't let it happen.

CHAPTER 31

The next morning, we went about our chores as usual. And though from time to time we discussed the vizier's party and his death, we avoided all mention of tax payments or Babu.

Amunet had that same brittle breeziness going on. Sahara was quiet but efficient. Razi was super-distracted. Every time someone asked him a question, they had to repeat it at least once.

"Do you want to go and look for the time machine?" Riley whispered. Of course I did, but something held me back. It was a feeling Razi was about to do something stupid.

Around mid-morning, he slipped out of the house. No-one else noticed, but I did. I followed him out and watched him take off across the fields.

"Riley, can I have a word?" I leaned back inside and gestured for him to come out.

As he did, I grabbed his arm and hurried him along with me. "Razi's up to something. We have to stop him in case he makes things worse."

We took off through the fields after him, alert and ready to duck behind crops or rocks for cover if we needed to. But Razi didn't look back once.

When he got to the water, he turned right and jogged along the river bank. We followed for about fifteen minutes under a scorching sun. Sweat zig-zagged down my back and plastered my hair to the back of my neck. Then he started uphill, through a rubbly grey landscape towards a derelict mud hut at the top.

Riley and I followed him part way up, keeping low to stay out of sight. As he approached the hut's entrance, someone emerged to greet him—a young guy, muscular, with shoulder-length wavy hair. It was Lisimba, one of Razi's close friends who we'd met on our first day here. The pair talked for a while, then another guy came out. He had a shaven head and was chunky too, though not as well toned.

"I think that's Seth, Sacmis's brother," said Riley. "He was on the boat with us the day you rescued Phoenix."

"Seth?" The same Seth, I presumed, who had been engaged to Amunet till she broke it off because of his cruelty to a slave girl at a market. "I thought the families were on bad terms. What's Razi doing with him, I wonder?"

When the three guys went inside the part-ruined building, Riley and I hared it up the hill. We crept as near to the front door as we dared. But, though we could hear voices inside, we couldn't make out the words. We needed to get closer.

Around the back of the house was a high window, which seemed our best chance. Though getting up there would not be easy—it was really high. First, I tried standing on Riley's interlaced hands, but when that didn't get me high enough, I had to cling to the window ledge and balance my feet on his shoulders.

"Don't make any sudden moves, will you?" I said.

"Can you hear them in there?" he whispered.

"Shhhh."

I listened. Hard. Murmurs gradually turned to words then sentences. Thankfully, I didn't need to listen for long to get the general idea. It was just as I feared.

"You can let me down now."

I began easing myself down, but stumbled midway, landing with a thump and a grunt. Inside the house, the voices stopped.

Minutes later, the guys emerged, fanning out around the building to check no-one was eavesdropping. They didn't see Riley or me, though we were right there in front of them, face down on the ground. We'd burrowed down into the loose shale and flicked dirt and rubble over our clothes so we blended into the grey landscape. A dozen lungfuls of dust later, the guys called off the search and went back inside. As we got back to our feet, gravel cascaded down our tunics.

"What a clever way to hide," I said. It had been Riley's idea. "Though a bit grubby." I spat out dirt clinging to my lips.

"Could you make out what they were saying in there?" Riley asked.

I sighed. "Unfortunately, yes."

On the walk back, I told him the guys were planning to rob a tomb—Nuru's tomb. It seemed my day as a mourner had made a big impression on Razi, who had paid close attention to my description of the riches within. He'd stored the info away for a time when he might need it. And, with Sahara facing a potential beating over a tax bill, he figured that time was now.

The guys were planning to break into the tomb tonight.

"If they're caught, they'll be beheaded," I said. "We have to talk him out of it."

"I think he's a bit beyond talking, don't you?" said Riley.

"Well, what can we do then?"

Riley sighed. "I'm thinking."

He was still thinking by the time we got ready for bed that night.

"Cutting it a bit fine, aren't we?" I said.

"The first part of the plan is this," he said. With a furtive look around, he opened a pouch on his belt and extracted a small amount of pale brown soil. "Put that in a drink and swig it down. When everyone goes to sleep, we'll have to pretend to sleep as well. This will help you stay awake. So we'll be alert and ready to follow Razi when he leaves."

"And do what?"

"Convince him to change his plans."

I slipped the powder into a mug of weak beer. It tasted disgusting, like river water, with crunchy bits in it.

"What if I doze off anyway?" I said.

"I'll wake you. As soon as Razi makes a move."

The next thing I knew it was morning. I was by myself in the room. My head was throbbing, my mouth super-dry. The sun was up, its rays painting glary stripes on the wall. Outside the house, a terrible howling began, like an animal somewhere close was in pain.

I staggered up and, fighting a wave of nausea, emerged into the blinding light of day to find that it was Sahara, Amunet and Layla making the sound. They were on their knees, hands clasped above their heads, begging for mercy from some beefed-up guards in white and gold. Through half-open eyes, I made out Razi, wrists chained. Riley was there, too, face blank with horror. And Sacmis. *What is she doing here?* Watching with concern? No, wait—there was a flicker of a smile. *Fake concern.*

"What's going on?" I asked.

"We are arresting this man on suspicion of tomb robbery," said the guard.

"Tomb robbery!" I said. "But that can't be right. He was here with us all night."

"We have a witness," said the guard. He turned to a man on his left, pudgy and mean-looking—Seth.

The guards stormed into the house, re-emerging minutes later with jewels and pottery I'd never seen before.

"I am sorry, mother," said Razi. "I have shamed you."

"Nooo! Please!" cried Sahara as the guards dragged Razi away.

"I am so sorry for your family, madam," said Sacmis. "If there is anything I can do to assist you in this sad time..."

"No, thank you," I said, speaking for the family who were unable to do so at the time. "You and your brother have helped us quite enough for one day."

Sacmis struggled to hold back a smile. Edging closer, so only I could hear her, she whispered: "You did me a favour, Madison. The vizier's son, Phoenix, might once have preferred you. But after this shame to your friends, he is certain to reconsider his good opinion. Your loss may be painful for him, but I will be there to ease his pain."

Sacmis had won. Game, set, the whole tournament.

CHAPTER 32

The morning passed in a blur of pain and self-recrimination. If only I had stayed awake, maybe I could have talked Razi out of going. Why did I have to sleep so soundly last night, of all nights? And why hadn't Riley woken me as he'd promised?

It was some time before I could get my friend aside to get the answers.

"What happened?" I demanded. "That drink was supposed to keep me awake! And why do I feel so bad?" Even now, my tongue felt too big for my mouth.

"The drink I gave you was actually a sleeping draught," said Riley.

"What?" I was spitty on the "t".

"I didn't want you to get caught up in the robbery," said Riley. "Without the time machine, I couldn't be sure of keeping you safe."

"You don't have to keep me safe, Riley. I can do that myself. But Razi needed us last night. And we weren't there for him."

"I was. I tried to talk him out of doing the robbery, but he was set on it to protect his mother. So I followed him."

"Well, that was stupid. What if something had happened to you? What would I have done then?"

"Err…"

He hadn't thought of that? He hadn't thought of a lot of

things, it seemed to me. But what was the point of being able to do super-clever stuff like build a time machine or make a sleeping draught if you didn't think through the whys and wherefores of the situation? If you asked me, being half a genius was worse than being none at all.

"I'm sorry," he said.

So you should be.

"Two of us together have got to be better than just one on our own," I said. "In future, no matter how dangerous things are, we work together. Agreed?"

"Okay."

"So, what happened?"

Riley explained that Razi had met Seth and Lisimba and gone to the tomb. "I followed them, but I didn't go in." That was something, at least.

The tomb was well-protected by booby traps, Razi told him later. Within minutes of entering, Lisimba was crushed to death by a boulder. As devastated as he was by his friend's death, Razi pushed on for Sahara's sake. In one room, he almost stumbled into a pit filled with sharp spikes but stopped himself just in time. Seth bailed out then, saying he was too scared to continue.

"Though now we know he was reporting back to the guards," said Riley, "setting Razi up to be captured if he made it out."

When Razi came upon a small outer chamber with a few bits of treasure in it, he grabbed those and headed back the way he'd come. Riley waited for him at the entrance with the reflective cloth.

"You mean the invisibility cloth you had over the bike?"

Riley nodded. "And lucky I did too. There were a lot of guards sneaking about in the dark."

"I suppose Seth had seen to that," I said. "The snake."

"Razi and I hid under the cloth and got past the guards and back home again."

"But you didn't hide the stolen things when you got back?" I said.

Riley shook his head. "We thought he was in the clear."

That was where they needed me. I wouldn't have trusted Seth and I would have hidden the booty, just in case.

"What will happen to Razi now?" I asked.

Riley paused that bit too long. "Whatever it is, it won't be good."

In the afternoon it seemed like everyone in the village trekked to the square where a *kenbet* had been convened to hear the charges against Razi.

Five old men in black cloth caps stood in a line with Razi on his knees before them, hands chained, flanked by guards. About fifty villagers formed a semi-circle around the men. Sahara, Amunet and Layla were in the centre and they were a mess—sobbing and clinging to each other. Riley and I stayed close by, trying to appear strong for their sake. Though I'd never felt less so.

The oldest official stepped forward. "The man before you is on trial for tomb robbery." Though his voice was rasping and weak, we heard every word. "It is alleged he and his friend broke into the tomb of the great Nuru, violating its sanctity and plundering its riches for personal gain. His evil accomplice perished inside. The survivor stands before you today. Thanks be to the gods, the thieves only managed to penetrate an outer chamber of the building, so Nuru's body was not disturbed and his chance of an afterlife remains intact."

A spark of hope ignited in me. Perhaps it wasn't so serious? Maybe Razi would get away with a beating today? The girls gulped up their tears, too, daring to hope.

"However," the official continued, "we are bound to consider not only what occurred but the robbers' intentions going in. We have it on good authority that they planned to do whatever was required—to desecrate every part of the tomb, defiling even the remains of the great man himself, if necessary—to satisfy their lust for riches."

Layla lost it at that point. "No! Mama. Please! Make them stop."

"Silence!" The heftiest guard took a threatening step towards the girl. Razi surged to his feet and tried to launch himself at the man, but two guards at his side held him back, then pummelled and kicked him till he was slumped on the ground, his face a mess of blood.

I turned away. It was too painful to watch.

"What say you, Honoured Ones?" the man said. "How do you think the Pharaoh, our immortal ruler who speaks directly to the gods, would answer the question of this crime?"

"Mercy!" shouted Sahara, throwing herself down onto the dirt, arms extended. Amunet and Layla did the same: "Mercy, Mercy!"

Several voices in the crowd began a whispered chant: "Mercy! Mercy!" Riley and I joined in.

The official conferred with each of his fellow judges, then stood before Razi, who was slumped on the ground. The guards hauled Razi up and yanked his head back by the hair so he was eye to eye with the man.

"You are guilty of tomb robbery," said the man. "The sentence is death. I call upon the Pharaoh's executioner to carry it out immediately."

"Nooo!" Sahara cried.

Faces flashed past, twisted in grief. I saw lips moving, spittle flying. But I couldn't make out individual words. It was all white noise and glare. Bile surged up into my throat, hot and sour. I was going to be sick.

I pushed through a wall of people and doubled over, taking slow breaths to calm myself. Riley staggered out after me, pale as vanilla. He bent over and hurled.

I kept low till the worst of the nausea had passed, then stood up. Everything was shifting around me, a blur of colour and movement. Too loud, too bright. Somehow, in the middle of it all, I sensed a stillness to my left. I turned and, on the other side of the square, one man seemed calm among the melee. He was tall and blond and wore an expression of concern.

"Riley," I said. "There's Peterson."

Riley got a brief look at him and started moving his way. And the guy took off. We chased him, dodging and weaving through the crowd. At the end of the road, Peterson turned back to us before rounding the corner. I hitched up my dress and charged after him, Riley bobbing along beside me.

We pursued him through the village streets without passing a single person—everyone was at Razi's hearing.

Peterson might have been old but the guy was fast. Each time he got to a corner, he made sure we'd seen him before he zoomed off again. It was like he wanted us to follow him. Like he was leading us somewhere.

"Where do you think he's taking us?" Riley said. "It could be a trap."

"I suppose."

I didn't care, I just wanted to keep running. It felt good to be moving fast, away from that awful scene.

"Should we be chasing him now?" Riley asked. "Shouldn't we stay with the family?"

"We have to catch him. He knows something important. I'm sure of it. That's the only way we'll help Razi right now."

Peterson led us through town and out the other end, into the fields, running right into a corn field where the stalks were as tall as my shoulder. I saw his blond head bobbing among the crops and heard the *crunch*, *crunch* as he shouldered plants aside to go in deeper. Then it went quiet.

We battled our way into the field as he had done, making for the scarecrow in the centre. I thought we might find him crouching there, ready to spring at us.

Riley reached the centre before I did and, over the stalks, I saw his face crease in confusion.

"What is it?" I called.

As I pushed that last stalk aside, I got my answer. Sitting in the middle of the crop, shiny as new, was our time machine.

CHAPTER 33

"He took our machine and then gave it back to us!" I said. "But why?"

"Let's get out of here and figure it out later," said Riley.

"No," I said. "Isn't that why we're in trouble now? Because you didn't think things through before creating the machine?"

"Okay, so let's think. Why would he give it back to us?"

It was hot and stuffy in the middle of the field; not much air was getting through the vegetation. After all that had happened, I could barely hold a thought in my head, let alone do the twisted thinking needed to figure out what Peterson's motivations might be.

"You're right, let's go," I said. "Where to?"

"Home."

"Home, to our own time, you mean?" Excitement surged through me at the thought. "But we can't leave Amunet's family to face this alone."

"There is nothing useful we can do here, Maddy," said Riley. "Maybe if we go home and think it through, we can work it out. With the distance of time and space. Besides, we don't have much time before the time portal shuts from the other side."

"Let's go, then."

I climbed into the time machine and got settled in the side car as Riley straddled the bike. He took a breath, then jammed his foot on the accelerator. I half expected the engine to splutter and cut out. But it purred, then roared to life, as if it had just been serviced.

"I've set the time dial for the same night we left," said Riley. "That way we won't have to explain to our families where we've been."

And we were off. Up, up, up. Moving super-fast. I clung on as the machine shot through the cloud. Riley tapped some keys on the control panel and we levelled out, sailing horizontally across the air and through time. The machine's noise dropped a semi-tone to more of a plane-like hum. Light flashed and pulsed around us as the years and millennia raced by.

Riley looked over, smiling. I beamed back. We'd see our families soon. And friends. I could hardly wait.

"What's the first thing you'll do when you get home?" I asked.

"I'll make some detailed notes about everything that's happened while it's still fresh in my mind."

Typical scientist.

"You?" he said.

"I'll just hang out."

I'd have a hot bath, call Lauren and listen to whatever she wanted to say—no judgements. I'd give Gran a big hug and coax Mum away from her work. And the three of us could watch one of our favourite shows and drink hot chocolate. We hadn't done that in a while. And when the time was right, I'd video call Dad.

My cheeks stretched into the biggest smile as I pictured it all. I'd put on my pink pyjamas and super-soft dressing gown—after my bath, of course, where I would wash weeks of Nile grime away.

Though, I wished I could as easily wash away the heartbreak of what Razi and his family were going through. A horror beyond anything I'd ever imagined.

"Brace yourself," said Riley. "We're going down."

Excited, I peered over the edge of the bike, looking for the familiar Sydney skyline—the high-rise buildings, the busy harbour with boats bobbing on the moonlit water, the arc of the Sydney Harbour Bridge flecked with lights as cars crossed back and forth.

What I saw was nothing like that.

The skyline was modern but unfamiliar. There was no Harbour Bridge, no Opera House. Instead, standing at the point of the harbour where the familiar white sails should have been, was a golden pyramid.

CHAPTER 34

This was *not* the Sydney I knew. The skyline was modern, with high-rise office and apartment buildings and busy traffic. But among the structures, I saw some pyramid-shaped buildings as well as the curved rooftops and towering minarets of a mosque. And wait—were those camels I could see in some of the streets?

"We've gone wrong," I said. "This isn't Sydney. We're in an Arab country."

Riley frowned at his control panel. "The co-ordinates are correct."

"Something must be wrong with your instruments because look down there. See for yourself. That's not Sydney."

But as I looked again, I found the shape of the harbour and its foreshore did look familiar. My mind sketched in the missing bits—the Opera House here, the Harbour Bridge there.

Oh no!

"This is Sydney," said Riley. "Just not the one we left. I guess our journey did have some impact on the world after all."

We tried to land the machine in what should have been Riley's backyard but now looked like a large stable. So Riley swung back up into the air to search for a quiet park where we could set down.

As he switched the engine off, the silence closed in on us. For the first few minutes, we just sat there, not speaking, not making a move to get out.

"What about our families?" I was the one who said it. "Where are they?"

"They could be living somewhere here in town. Or they might still be in England," said Riley.

"In England?"

"We'd need to do some research, but it looks like maybe the history of Australia is different now."

"You mean Captain Cook didn't come to Australia? No convicts, no First Fleet?"

"I'd say it's entirely possible the Egyptians got here before him this time around."

"But...I don't understand," I said. "How could anything we did in Ancient Egypt have changed that? We introduced toothpaste and scarecrows and that's all. Surely they couldn't have brought about this epic change?"

Riley pressed his lips together. "We'd need to go online—if there is such a thing—or to a library to research world history and find the answer to that."

Questions swirled around in my head, like sandstorms in my brain, each answer bringing five more questions with it. I walked around the park in a fury of disbelief and denial and found myself standing in front of a large statue. We used to have statues of famous historical figures in our parks. Perhaps it would be a clue as to what had gone on since we left.

This statue was badly cracked and striped with bird lime. It was of a woman who looked more than a little familiar.

"Riley," I said, "is that who I think it is?"

The petite chin, the self-satisfied sneer on the button lips? The engraving beneath it said: ISIS, THE GREAT PHARAOH.

"It does look a bit like Sacmis, if that's who you mean?" said Riley. "But it says Isis, a pharaoh."

"Have you ever heard of a pharaoh called Isis?" I asked.

Riley shook his head. "We need to find a library."

"Can we go and see my family first?"

Riley licked his lips and looked down. I thought he might argue, but he nodded. "Okay, let's go," he said.

We hid the time machine in the bushes and covered it with Riley's reflective cloth, then headed to the road.

The city was heaving—it must have been peak hour. Traffic was at a crawl. Brown clouds of pollution hung in the air like ghosts of the city's past. Around us a scent arose, of dirt and spice and, oh yes, dung.

Buildings crammed the skyline, though there seemed no plan to their placement. A dirt-coloured high-rise apartment block, with washing flapping on the balconies, stood next to a modern office block, all shiny surfaces and sharp angles. A high-rise department store was around the corner from a market where vendors sold goods from blankets on the ground, as in ancient times. I watched a woman in a well-cut business suit hurry past an old man in the kind of linen gear I was bashing against the rock thousands of years ago (well, just a few hours in my time!). Old and new sat side by side, as if two different time periods co-existed in one space.

The people all looked happy, though. They seemed to smile a lot. When I mentioned this to Riley, he shook his head. "I'm not sure they are smiling any more than normal, it's just that—"

"—their teeth are so white and sparkly." I finished his sentence.

He was right. Everyone had lovely teeth. Evenly spaced and shiny. This was one good thing we'd done. Well, Riley had done. Dental surgeries dotted the main road—one or two on each block, with names like THE SMILE STUDIO or GRINNERS ARE WINNERS.

"Hey, maybe that's how this all happened," I said. "Maybe someone in the past was supposed to die of tooth decay but, by using the toothpaste you introduced, they didn't die till years later. They lived long enough to have kids, and those kids had kids and so forth, bringing whole generations into the world that had never existed before. And somehow that brought all these changes about."

Riley stroked his chin. "But that doesn't explain how the Egyptians found Australia before the English this time around—if that is what happened."

A lone red car with Camel Driving Services on the door sat at a taxi rank. We jumped in the back seat.

"Where to?" the driver asked. He smiled and his mouth glinted with gold.

"Err, do you know Harris Road, Crows Nest?" I asked.

"Crows Nest? Where is that? East? West?"

"North," I said.

"I do not know it," said the driver. He gave us the once over, his eyebrows drawing together. "May I ask how you intend to pay for the ride?"

We must have looked like a fare risk in our dusty linen gear. I explained we were new in town and had lost our money "through an unfortunate encounter with a thief", but that we could trade a necklace in exchange for his driving services for an hour or so.

The gold in the guy's mouth retreated from view. He wasn't interested in jewellery. At least not until he saw the necklace Razi had made me—silver with a red stone called jasper. It was simple but beautiful.

"I am at your service for half an hour," he said.

"Great," I said. "Can you start by telling us what's the name of this city and country?"

The guy adjusted his rear-vision mirror to see if I was joking. Then shook his head in a *who-hooked-out-your-brain* kind of way.

"This is New Egypt and the city in which you find yourself is called Phoenix," he said.

Riley went pug-eyed at that. *Phoenix?* It had to be a coincidence. Surely?

"Where to?"

"Just drive," said Riley. "I'll direct you."

Everything had changed—the roads, the street names. There was a bridge across the harbour, though not as spectacular as the Sydney Harbour Bridge and in a different location. We arrived on the right side of the water but much further north and had to weave through unfamiliar suburbs to make our way home by feel. If it hadn't been for Riley's incredible sense of direction, I wouldn't have had a hope.

"I can't wait to see my folks," I said.

"You know, it's possible, Maddy, that..." he began, then he had a coughing fit.

"What's possible?"

"It's possible that…" He cleared his throat over and over. "Never mind."

We passed streets with row after row of the same dung-coloured high-rise apartment blocks. There wasn't much in the way of trees or gardens. Rubbish bins lined the curbs, like an invading army.

"Pull up," Riley said suddenly. The driver jammed on the brakes. Riley pointed to an apartment block, exactly the same as the others we had passed.

"That's the spot where your house used to be."

Arabic music spilled out of a first-floor window. A strong scent of cooking, more pungent than the usual Crows Nest scents, permeated the street. A white goat shot out from the car park, pursued by a barefoot boy who seized it by its goatee beard and dragged it back inside.

I got out of the cab, hoping Riley was wrong and this wasn't actually the place. Maybe he was a tad off, and we'd drive a bit further along or turn the corner and there would be my home, the only single-storey house on the block, just as I'd left it. With Gran and the folks inside.

I looked up. Despite the pollution, I could tell I was looking at the sky from exactly the same angle I used to as I lay in bed. This was the spot where my home should have been.

"Maybe they've got an apartment in the block?" I said.

I buzzed a few numbers and asked for Grant and Sarah Bryant—my parents—and Emily Porter—my Gran. But no one had heard of them. Riley watched me, growing stiller, as I grew louder and more frantic. He knew. He'd known since before we got in the cab.

My family wasn't here.

"They could be living somewhere else in the city," I said. "Maybe even somewhere close by. But how will we find them?"

"I'm not sure," said Riley. "If they have something like the internet here, we could look up their number. Or we could find a phone book. But that will only work if their names are still the same."

"Of course they're still the same," I snapped. "What else would they be?"

I felt like I was filling up with sadness. It started in my legs and rose up through my gut into my chest, climbing up to my throat and higher still, until it began spilling out through my eyes—a trickle of tears that built to a flood. Riley drew me into his arms and held me and I sobbed till his shoulder was sodden. He didn't say much. What could he say when my life and all the people I loved were not just gone but had been totally erased? As if they'd never existed at all.

It was the same for him. His life, his family.

All gone.

"Wait," I said, stopping suddenly. "They can't be gone. Because if they didn't exist, then I wouldn't either. I'm here, I'm their child, which means they must exist somewhere."

It was logic, pure and simple. And just like that, I was no longer sad but excited. My parents were alive, somewhere. I just had to find them. I looked over at Riley expecting to see him smiling and psyched too. But he wasn't. Instead, the divot between his brows deepened as we climbed back into the cab and he told the driver to take us back to the city to a large library. We watched the strange sights flash by in silence.

After a while, although I really didn't want to, I asked: "Riley, is there some way we could be here without our families existing?"

"Maybe," he said. "Our timeline might be different to everyone else's. Because of the time travelling."

"I don't understand," I said.

"It might be that in taking this temporal journey, we've created our own unique timeline that branches off from the general linear flow. If you think of a timeline as a tree, everyone else is moving along the main trunk, but we've moved onto a branch going off from that trunk."

"That…is just weird," I said.

"I'm only speculating at this stage but—"

"Well, speculate to yourself. This is our lives, the people we love you're talking about."

"But you asked me a question. I was just trying to—"

"Stop the car!" I shouted.

Our driver slammed to a halt. There was a squeal of brakes behind us and a crash a few cars back, followed by a succession of diminishing thuds. When the crunching stopped, a chorus of horns began.

I jumped out of the car and Riley slid out after me as our driver zoomed off, keen to get clear of the multi-car pile-up we'd caused. All traffic on the busy city roundabout had stopped, which made it easier to cross the road to the traffic island in the centre. Riley followed me, pink-cheeked.

"Where are you going, Maddy?" he asked.

"I want to look at that statue on the roundabout."

It was carved out of a rich red-brown stone, smoothed and polished to a shine, and the resemblance was staggering. The arm muscles looked stronger, more defined, there was a cruelty about the eyes, but there could be no mistake. This was a statue of me. It rested on a stone plinth with words engraved inside a chiselled heart: MADDEE, GODDESS OF UNREQUITED LOVE.

"What on earth does this mean?" I said.

"Unrequited love is a love that isn't returned by the other person, a one-sided love," said Riley.

"I know what the words mean, Riley! I just don't get how this happened. A statue of me? Seriously?"

A few cars managed to squeeze past the traffic mash-up and began circling around the roundabout. One driver going past glanced over at me, then his head snapped back for a second look. He drove right round the roundabout, honking and waving at me.

"There she is!" he shouted. "The goddess Maddee herself has come down to Earth!"

Others began honking, too, though whether it was at me or his erratic driving, I wasn't sure.

"Let's get out of here!" said Riley.

Riley grabbed my hand and we darted across the road, slipping into the crowd of pedestrians on the pavement.

"How did that happen?" I said, pointing back at the statue. "And don't say someone chiselled it out of stone."

"It had to be something to do with Phoenix," Riley said. "He must have risen to a position of power in Ancient Egypt. And I guess...you made an impression on him."

We spoke to a few people on the street and found out there was a library in the city, not far away. So we headed over.

The building was glass-fronted with a golden pyramid painted on the door. I watched people going in, flashing a library card at the heavily made-up girl on reception. We didn't have a pass. But that was no problem for me. I told the girl I was a visitor from the Institute of New Dental Technology doing research into the history of dentistry in Egypt.

"I believe it was a remarkable stranger from Nubia who introduced the concept of toothpaste to our great nation," I said, probably pushing it a bit. The woman raised her perfect eyebrows and shrugged—*whatever*—then pressed a button under the desk and let us in.

We passed the fiction section, where we saw a lot of stories on pharaohs' curses and mummies' revenges but no Shakespeare or Jane Austen or any of the classic British, American or Australian novels we'd studied at school. Following the signs to Egyptian history, we headed for the "ancient" section and found a shelf devoted to pharaonic history.

"Here's what we need!" Riley pulled out a heavy book with a smiling sphinx on the cover and flicked through the pages, stopping on the period we were interested in.

"After the murder of the chief vizier," he read aloud, "his son Phoenix rose to prominence in Egyptian society and was eventually proclaimed Pharaoh."

"Phoenix became Pharaoh?" I said. "Wow!" (And to think, he'd fancied me. I couldn't wait to tell Lauren. But, of course, I couldn't because Lauren probably didn't exist anymore.)

"But how did he become Pharaoh? He wasn't part of a royal family, was he?"

"As far as I understand it, you don't always have to be. Elders and elite citizens had a say in who their leader was. He must have done something really impressive after his father died to get to that position."

Riley continued reading: "His wife, Sacmis, was a strong presence by his side."

"He married Sacmis? Oh, that's not good."

"The Pharaoh Phoenix died early in his reign, when he was poisoned by a slave girl—" Riley looked up at me "—called Layla."

"What? Layla was a slave? And she murdered Phoenix?"

"Although some suspected his wife, Sacmis, was behind her husband's demise," Riley continued.

"Sacmis!" I said. "That makes more sense. So, she murdered Phoenix and Layla got the blame!"

I was so right about that girl! But I couldn't believe things had gone so screwy after we left to become the absolute worst version of history imaginable.

Though, as I watched Riley's eyes sweep back and forth across the page, and he fell silent, I wondered...was there even worse to hear?

"What is it?" I asked.

"Nothing, I...err..."

"Oh, move over!" I shoved him aside, found his place on the page and read on: "After Phoenix's death, his wife Sacmis succeeded him as Pharaoh, taking the name of Isis during her reign."

Sacmis had become Pharaoh? Now, neither of us could

speak. I wasn't sure I'd ever speak again! Riley continued reading but I had to sit down. The bad news didn't end there, though. Riley could find no reference to England or the US or any of the other countries on the world map. Everything had changed.

"But how? I just don't get it," I said.

Research gave us some, but not all, the answers. It seemed Phoenix had turned Egypt into a nation of explorers. It began when he persuaded the Pharaoh of the time to back his quest to find "the great land south of Nubia". The leader sanctioned a fleet of boats to explore the southern seas. While most returned empty-handed, or not at all, one crew made it to the land we called Australia and claimed it for Egypt thousands of years before Captain Cook's due date.

As a reward for initiating the Great Quest, Phoenix became Pharaoh. Under his rule, Egypt went from strength to strength.

"He led the nation in exploration and wars to gain still more land for his empire," Riley read. "In his second decade as ruler, he focused less on war and expansion, more on consolidating the gains already made.

"Following his murder—" Riley looked up at me in horror "—his wife, the new pharaoh, Isis, overturned her husband's peaceful rule and reintroduced an ambitious program of Egyptian expansion as part of her stated desire to 'rule all the lands on Earth'."

I goggled at the words on the page. "I knew Sacmis was ambitious, but...?"

Her hunger for power had meant my parents and Riley's and all our ancestors had probably never been born. And even if they had, their names would be something Egyptian that we had no way of ever discovering.

As we headed back out onto the streets, I felt unsteady on my feet and my head throbbed big time. Everywhere I looked, I saw Gran at the kitchen table with a chocolate moustache after her evening hot chocolate. Or Lauren laughing and throwing back her hair, which she'd dyed purple for a more "exotic" look.

Would I truly never see them again? I couldn't believe it. Or accept it. I wouldn't.

"Watch out!" Riley pulled me back just before I stepped in front of a car.

"Are you okay, Maddy?"

"No. I'm not." I had never been less *okay* in my life.

We sat on the cold stone ground by the harbour, legs swinging over the edge of what used to be Circular Quay, Sydney's ferry and cruise ship port. Beneath our feet, the ocean was the same inky black it had always been, reflections of gold, red and white city lights sliding across its surface. The harbour was thick with vessels, the scent of petrol blending with dead fish and salt water. As we watched, a sleek modern vessel cut across the path of an old-style sailboat, almost causing it to capsize.

And it all became clear to me.

"Everything is my fault," I said. "Every horrible thing that happened to our family in Egypt—to Razi, Amunet, Sahara and Layla—and the loss of our families and life here in Australia, and in England, is all down to me. For saving Phoenix's life and giving my name as Sacmis."

Riley didn't reply for a while. I guess he was thinking it through, trying to untangle the strands of cause and effect, guilt and blame from thousands of years ago to this moment.

"What you did was a single action," he said. "There were a lot of other things, a whole chain of actions, that had to happen to get to this point, which you're not responsible for. You can't blame yourself for this outcome, Maddy."

I could. And I did.

"There's one thing I don't understand, though," said Riley. "How did Phoenix come to be looking for a land south of Nubia in the first place?"

I thought for a while, then shuddered as a memory floated back. "I might have said something at the vizier's party that night. That I came from a land far south of Nubia. I didn't think he'd do anything about it though." *Well du-uh!*

"So Phoenix did like you?" said Riley. "He liked you so much that, when you disappeared, he sent people, literally, to the ends of the Earth to find you."

Riley was right. And I might have been flattered by that idea if my so-called charm hadn't led to the end of the world as we knew it.

If only I hadn't mentioned Australia to him. Or thrown Sacmis onto his path. And if I hadn't made such an enemy of her, maybe her family would never have stitched Razi up the way they did. Of course, if we'd never time travelled in the first place, Azizi—or whoever-the-hell he was—wouldn't have been trying to kill us that night, so the vizier might not have ended up dead in the first place.

A lot of *ifs* and *if onlys!*

This was a nightmare. It couldn't be happening! I wouldn't let it!

"Riley," I said, "we have to go back and put things right."

I thought Riley would argue, tell me it was impossible and give me all kinds of reasons, technical and temporal, for why it wasn't possible.

Instead, he nodded. "Okay."

CHAPTER 35

We decided to get some sleep before we began our next mission. Who knew when we'd get any again? It took a while to nod off, but eventually we did close our eyes for four or five hours.

I woke up to the sun rising over the harbour in a city that wasn't my home. I was starving and parched—we both were. We thought we'd better fix that before moving on to fix the world. Near the park was a local grocer's shop where we exchanged an hour of labour for food. Ahmed, the shopkeeper, got us to unload his truck and unpack boxes. For that, he paid us with a pack of dates, a tin of beans, some fresh pita bread and as many glasses of water as we could drink. We needed to be well fed and watered because today was set to be a big day for us. In fact, it wasn't overstating it to say it was going to be a huge day for the whole world.

"Wait," I said to Riley. "What about our clothes? When we got to Egypt last time, I was wearing track pants. I think that was part of why we got so much attention."

"You're right," said Riley. "Do you reckon they'd have track pants here?"

"I haven't seen any."

Ahmed pointed us to a charity supply outlet a few blocks away. There were no track pants but they did have business trousers and shirts—manky ones. Riley took some grey pants and a pale blue shirt, and I took some black striped trousers with a red top. That should get their attention.

"Ready?" said Riley.

"As I'll ever be."

We changed into our new gear then retrieved the time machine and took a last look around. I wished I had my phone to capture the moment because, if we were successful, this city would be nothing but a lost memory in time. Ahmed the grocer, who'd helped us, the taxi driver, their families and those they loved and everyone else alive in the world might cease to exist. I felt a stab of guilt at taking so much from so many.

How many others would lose out like this, how many worlds and people would exist one minute and not the next, if Riley released the time machine to the public?

As I settled into the sidecar and began psyching myself up for what was to come, I saw Riley frowning at the controls.

"Is there a problem?" I asked.

"No-oh," he said, in a way that was disturbing. "I was just thinking."

Hmmm. Weirdly, I didn't want to ask what.

"We're not going to land on that crocodile island like before, are we?" I said.

"No. I've recalculated the interface co-ordinates."

And we were off. There was the usual rocking and rolling. I didn't watch the modern Egyptian landscape change and disappear. I was too busy figuring out what our next move should be. We would pretty much have to replicate everything we did before, with a few small differences.

"Let's open the portal for a longer period this time, shall we?" I said. For who knew how long it would take to fix things.

"I'll leave it open-ended," he said.

"Good idea!" Why didn't he do that in the first place?

Almost as soon as we arrived in Egypt last time, I'd made an enemy of Sacmis. But given what we knew about how powerful she became on one timeline, and the extent of her ambition and spite, would it be wise to do that again?

On the other hand, if I was nice to her from the start, Amunet might not talk to us. As I recalled, it was the sharp way I'd handled Sacmis, her enemy, that made Amunet stick around after the performance and invite us back to her home. *Hmmm. Tricky.*

And while I was thinking about changes, I wondered whether there was anything I could do this time to stop her falling in love with Riley? That had brought her nothing but pain.

There was a lot to think about and not much time to do it because the wind was whirling, the sand swirling and...*boof*... we were down again.

Back in Ancient Egypt.

CHAPTER 36

We went to hide our machine in the reeds by the Nile River, as before, but something was already there. Something Riley could feel but not see. He moved his hand around a bit, and an invisibility cloth came off. Beneath it was an exact copy of our time machine.

"What the—?" I said.

Looking along the river, up into the fields, we saw *ourselves* being marched into town by locals, as we had been first time round.

"Riley," I said, "if we're here, how can we be there at the same time?"

"Ah, I must have got the timing a bit wrong. It looks as if more than one version of a person can exist in one time period. Interesting. I wonder how many versions a period can take."

"Well, that's a good question. But perhaps now is not the time?"

Something in my tone made Riley get with the programme.

"Right," he said. "We need to travel out of the period and re-enter at precisely the same time as before so we can overlay a new past onto the one that's already happened. And I need to think about an *OVERWRITE* button for future models in case I need to do a period over again." The last part he muttered as if to himself.

"Wait!" I said, settling back into my seat. "What if we just blast off and come back at the same time we did first time around and then do nothing? Just sit here for a few moments, then go home again. Have no interaction at all with anyone or anything from the period. Wouldn't that basically wipe out our last trip through time and all the consequences that flowed from it? So everything would go back to how it was before we time travelled?"

"Well, yes, I suppose."

"So, Sydney would return to how it was before? And our families and friends would reappear too?"

"In theory, yes." Riley scratched his head. "But then the Egyptians wouldn't have toothpaste. And Razi might still be beheaded."

"*Might*," I said quickly. "We don't know for sure that any of that would have happened if we hadn't been here in the first place."

"True. But we do know Sahara would probably have been beaten for non-payment of tax," Riley said. "And that Azizi would still be loose somewhere in the period to cause whatever problems he chose to."

By "cause problems", I guessed he meant the guy could do things, small or big, that would lead to Australia and England and the whole world as we knew it ceasing to exist. I shook my head. Leaving Azizi here unchecked was way too dangerous.

"Okay," I said. "We'll go back. And focus on fixing one thing at a time."

So that's what we did. A short trip beyond the clouds and we were down again. And this time, when we pushed the machine into the reeds, there was nothing else there.

As the sand settled, we found the same crowd watching us as before. The guy at the front with the map of Australia birthmark on his cheek stepped forward to confront us in the same angry way. But this time, Riley and I struggled to control our grins. This was great news. It meant that, though things had gone horribly awry in history since the point we first left Egypt, at least everything before that time might be the same.

In theory, it should mean that Sacmis and Amunet would be exactly where they were first time around. And that we might have a shot at pulling this off by keeping some things as they were while re-doing the bits that we thought had made the world go off course. Though, knowing which bits to change and which to leave was kind of tricky. And if we got it wrong, well, we would create a whole new world of trouble. Literally.

The first time we arrived, we hadn't yet taken Riley's language pill and so couldn't understood the birthmark guy's ranting. This time we did.

"Who are you? And where did you come from? And what are these strange vestments you are wearing?" he demanded. "Answer me now or it will be very bad for you."

I was tempted to reply this time but in the interests of keeping things the same, I stayed quiet. When Riley opened his mouth to speak, I gave a rapid head shake and he shut it again.

We got the same rough treatment as we had first time around. They led us through the fields and up to the main village square, though the old guy with the terror grip on my arm dragging me along probably wondered why I seemed so happy about it.

And so it went on, as expected.

I sang to the crowd assembled at the market. I knew what was coming afterwards, and then, there it was—Sacmis's rude comment about me.

"Look at the way the woman is dressed," she said. "Like her family disowned her and sent her out to the desert to die in shame."

I was so pleased to hear it, not just because it meant events were on track but because, for once, I'd had time to plan my comeback. "Oh, yes, the desert of shame," I said. "That's where you and I met, isn't it, sister? Your parents sent you there to search for your heart, which has been missing since birth."

It wasn't that good really. But it got a cackly laugh from Amunet, which was the point (mostly). Sacmis flounced off, radiating hate.

And we got the invite we needed from Amunet to stay at her house.

So far, so good.

This time, however, before Amunet could get too hung up on Riley's golden curls and lapis lazuli eyes, I told her my brother was betrothed. And that was that. She didn't fall in love. The simple lies were the best, as I'd told Riley.

Things mostly went along as before except for a few small but significant changes.

First, after I'd been there a few days, I made sure to run into Sacmis "accidentally" in the veggie patch, where I apologised for being rude at our first meeting.

"There's nothing I would like better than for us to be friends," I said. I had trouble getting the words out. My throat constricted, reluctant to release them. My pride didn't like it much either, but it was all part of a bigger plan.

At first, Amunet was hurt by my offer of friendship to Sacmis, given the bad vibes between their families and her broken engagement with Seth. But she wasn't a natural grudge-holder so she came round to the idea.

Now that we were all "friends", there was no sabotaging each other's dance routine on market day. Amunet and I had our troupe; Sacmis had hers. We smiled and wished each other good luck—like friendly sharks—as we headed to opposite ends of the market to do our thing.

While we did our show, my eyes scoured the crowd. There was Dalali, the vizier's servant. But no Azizi. That was different. And strange.

In our break, I asked Dalali about "a servant called Azizi who I believe works for the vizier". She'd never heard of him.

"But how could he have disappeared from history like that?" I asked Riley later. "When we first came back, we saw ourselves here like last time. Shouldn't he still be here too?"

"All I can think," said Riley, "is that he came back and overlaid a new history onto the old one—one that didn't include him. A bit like covering over his footprints in the sand so no one could follow him through time."

As usual, my brain blew apart trying to work that one out. And worrying about whether we should be covering our footprints, too, in case someone tried to mess with our timeline.

The good news was that, now Azizi was out of the picture, we didn't need to worry about him. Although that didn't stop me looking for him, constantly, and for Peterson and other potential time travellers. Though, unless they turned up in blue jeans, packing a mobile phone, how would you know?

The taxman, Babu, was just as vile second time around. Though knowing which stool he would sit on during his visit, I smeared squished dates and honey on the bottom to encourage ants. He squirmed the whole time he was in the house from ants in his pants. It wasn't much but it made me smile.

We got Razi to behave more meekly towards him this time, which helped. But as we didn't have any Aussie coins left to bribe him with, we ended up in pretty much the same situation as before—dependent on the sale of Razi's necklace at the vizier's party to make our payment.

Phoenix fell into the Nile again. I knew it was coming and watched as he toppled into the water. When the tide carried him past me, I considered staying put, dry on the river bank, and letting things play out. If I hadn't been here in the first place, he would have drowned anyway. Perhaps he was meant to.

But I couldn't stand by and do nothing. Phoenix wasn't a bad guy, really. So I swam out and rescued him again.

This time, though, when he asked for my name afterwards, I gave my real one. And, remembering how it was my mouthy attitude that had got his attention, I played it differently, bowing and smiling and pretending I was half in love with him, like any other Egyptian girl. So, naturally, he was not the least bit interested in me.

"Well, that's fixed that," said Riley.

I nodded and stretched my lips into a smile. Though, in truth, I was disappointed. A part of me—just a teeny part— did like Phoenix, with his brooding good looks and arrogant strength. If we'd been in my time, we could have hung out a bit, maybe gone to the beach or the movies together. But it wasn't to be.

Phoenix asked if there was anything we wanted as a reward for saving him. We asked for more time to pay the family's tax bill. But that didn't work as he said he had no influence over his father's tax advisers.

"Is there something else you might want?"

"May I request a few moment's conversation for my brother with the vizier on the night of his birthday celebration?"

Phoenix frowned, no doubt thinking this was a weird request, but agreed anyway.

As he went to leave, he turned and gave me a wry smile and just for a moment, I felt a connection between us stretching across thousands of miles and years, tinged with regret that we would never get to know each other.

Then he was gone.

CHAPTER 37

The vizier's party was one thing we really needed to change. Starting with the vizier not dying, Razi not losing the sale of the necklace and therefore not needing to rob Nuru's tomb to pay his family's tax bill. We also wanted to make sure Sacmis and Phoenix did not hook up during the evening to take over the world.

And this time round, I would keep my big mouth shut about the fantastic land down under so no Pharaoh-in-waiting could go all *world explorer* on us.

But as we approached the big night, some things were already different—the major change being that, on market day, Azizi was not around so Dalali chose Sacmis's dance group to perform for the vizier, not ours.

So, although Sacmis would no longer be sitting beside Phoenix as his date, she would be swirling and whirling and fluttering her eyes only a few feet away. A bit like placing a stick of dynamite close to a fire.

"What if Phoenix falls in love with her while she's dancing?" I said.

"How likely would it be?" said Riley. "He must see beautiful dancers all the time."

"True. But we need to make sure."

So we came up with a plan.

On the morning of the vizier's party, I slipped out while

the sky was still blue-black like a fresh bruise to knock on Sacmis's door.

"Good morning, Sacmis," I said. "I wanted to wish you good luck at the party tonight."

"Thank you, Maddy," she said. "Your words of encouragement are like the sunshine in a dark day."

Yeah, right.

"It would mean so much to me," I said, "if I could help you with your dress and makeup today. I want to do my part to ensure you get all the success you deserve."

She considered my request for a time, then gave a gracious nod of agreement. I was in!

It was a day of massaging oils into her skin, preparing her clothes and hair for the show and praising her beauty. And listening to her talk about her hopes and dreams for the evening and beyond.

"I pray to the gods I will find a strong and handsome man tonight who will allow me to be all that I can be."

Yeah—nah! That was not going to happen. Not if I could help it.

When no one was watching, I mixed a powder into her face cream. It was a mild but effective skin irritant Riley had concocted. By the time she hit the stage that night, her face was covered in angry red welts. Her dancing was impressive but whenever the steps took her close to Phoenix, he recoiled, as if afraid he might catch something.

And just like that it was goodbye to the Pharaoh Isis! And her plans to take over the world.

Amunet and I managed to get work at the party as servers.

And, as my reward for saving Phoenix this time around, Riley got his audience with the vizier. While he demonstrated his toothpaste, I hovered close by to keep watch for Azizi or Peterson or some other time traveller who might do something bad and create problems.

The toothpaste demonstration went well again. And the vizier called for wine to celebrate, which was my cue. I made sure I was positioned to watch the pouring of the drinks and I offered to carry them to the great man myself. Even so, as the vizier raised the cup to his lips, Riley and I leaned in slightly and held our breath, just in case.

But when the vizier put the empty vessel back down, he was still smiling and in good health. *Talk about relief!*

And it seemed to prove that Azizi had been the poisoner first time around. We knew he was a time traveller and that he'd targeted Riley that night. Why? We still weren't sure. Which was disturbing. Especially as we weren't too clear on why he wasn't here this time around or where he'd gone. Or when. We knew he was from the future, but how far into the future? It could be hundreds of years after Riley and I were born. Or close to our own time. He might even be from our own time. When it came down to it, we didn't know much at all about Azizi except that, right here and now, he wasn't around and we seemed to be in the clear. Back on track.

We relaxed a little after that. Sacmis fretted over her inflamed skin. I offered to help her apply more cream to "cool her face" (you couldn't be too careful with these things). Razi negotiated with the buyer of the necklace and flirted with the same girl as before. Maybe this time, they would have a chance to get to know each other.

At some point, I slowly released the breath I'd been holding all night. I thought I was safe, that we were all safe.

I was wrong.

There was that gagging sound again—a nightmarish echo from the past. I looked over and saw the vizier, once again, choking to death. It wasn't the wine this time. Some nuts he'd gobbled while he was talking had stuck in his throat.

Riley slipped behind him, grabbed him around the middle, squeezed, and—*whoosh*—the half-chewed nuts flew right back out of his mouth. A few seconds later, colour returned to the vizier's face and he beamed. He was okay! Riley had saved his life! The room burst into applause. Now Riley really was the man's best friend.

"You must be pleased with yourself," I said as Riley reappeared at my side. "You've launched toothpaste to the ancient world. And you saved the vizier's life."

"Yeah, that was...strange."

"So do you think the changes we've made here will bring our families back?"

Riley twisted his lips to the side as he considered it but I never got to hear his answer. Because the vizier's friends began shouting for help. Riley and I both rushed over, pushing through the crowd, to see the vizier on the ground, clutching his chest and gasping for air.

"Is he having a heart attack?" I asked.

Riley started to shove people aside but I pulled him back. "Wait," I whispered. "If you do CPR on him and he dies, these guys will think you killed him."

"I can't stand here and do nothing," he said. "I have to try."

Riley did his best to push through the wall of people around the man. But by the time he got through, it was too late.

Well, put me in a jet-black wig and call me Cleopatra! The vizier was dead—*again.* Razi's sale of the necklace was scuppered! *Again.* And the family was in dire straits with their tax agent. *Again!*

CHAPTER 38

As things stood, there was a good chance history would repeat itself, ending with Razi's death in the village square. But Riley and I were determined to change that if we could.

We tried to make sense of it all as we walked home after the party. It was dark and cooling down quickly, a scent of wet earth drifting on the breeze.

"What happened tonight?" I asked. "I just don't get it."

"Me, neither," said Riley.

There were heaps of times when I'd wanted Riley to say he was as clueless as the rest of us. Now was not one of them.

"Could it just be a coincidence that the vizier had a heart attack on the night he'd been poisoned the first time around?" I asked.

"I suppose."

"You suppose? Come on, Riley. What sort of answer is that from the brainbox who invented a time machine that brought us here and changed the world?"

"Well, I might have a theory," he said after a few minutes' brooding. "It's only a theory. I guess we're learning about time travel as we go." (Like a lion tamer learns their art one lost limb at time!)

"It could be that if you die, death is embedded in the flow of time," he continued. "So even if the circumstances change and new timelines branch out from old ones, death can cross timelines."

"Death can cross timelines? That's your theory?" I said, irritated beyond belief. I didn't fully understand what it meant but I was sure I didn't like it. "So, if Razi was beheaded last time, then he's destined to go this time too? One way or another?"

"Well, I don't know," he said. "Firstly, it's just a theory and a loose one based on an unscientific sample of one. And secondly, when we blasted out of this time zone, we weren't sure that Razi had been killed."

"So even if your theory does turn out to be right...?"

"We still might be able to avoid Razi's death this time around, because we are changing things from an earlier point in time, before the catastrophic event."

Oh.

"This time travel thing is...*complex*," I said. "Complex" wasn't the first word that sprang to mind. But *that* word wouldn't have helped things at this moment.

"Have we done the wrong thing again, Riley?" I asked.

"I don't see what else we could have done, what other choices we had."

The next day, we watched Razi as we'd done the first time through. His movements were pretty much the same as last time. After breakfast, he snuck out of the house, along the river and up the crumbly hill to the abandoned building to meet with Lisimba and Seth.

Tonight, he would lead them into Nuru's tomb. By morning, Lisimba would be dead and Razi would be in serious trouble. Unless we managed to change things this time.

Plan A was to talk Razi out of the robbery. But if we couldn't do that—and let's face it, he was stubborn when it came to Sahara's safety—there was only one other thing we could do. Go through the tomb with him and make sure he got out alive, with the goods he needed to pay the tax.

"What happens if we get caught?" I said.

"I think we know the answer to that," Riley said.

I nodded and touched my neck. "There's no going back from that."

"No."

"Do you think the changes we've made this time around will have fixed things back home?" I felt a little choked, just saying the words.

"Possibly," said Riley. "Although it may be that we have to return to the future to trigger the changes—the ripple of cause and effect—to put things right."

It took me a moment to wrap my brain around that. "So if we never make it out of the tomb," I clarified, "everything in the 21st century will stay Egyptian? Our parents and everyone we know will be gone for good?"

Riley nodded. "We could go home first and trigger the changes," he said. "Then I could return and help Razi through the tomb."

"*You* could come back?" I said. "On your own? Without me?"

"There's no need for us both to risk our lives."

"You've helped Razi once before on your own. That didn't end well. No, if we do decide to go home first, then we both come back afterwards to help Razi. Okay?"

Riley nodded. "Okay."

"So are we going home first?" *Please say yes.* I was getting excited now.

"We could," he said, in a way that implied the opposite, "except..."

"Except what?"

"Every time we travel in or out of a period," he said, "there's a risk something could go wrong."

To go home first? Or not to? On the one hand, I was desperate to see my family and friends again. Have a bath, spend a night in my own bed. On the other, how much could I really enjoy anything when I knew what Razi would face if we couldn't get back here?

What a choice! I paced, and glared. Glared and paced. (*This is all Riley's fault!*) And sighed.

"We're here now," I said. "Let's get Razi through the tomb safely, then go home. Together."

CHAPTER 39

That night, Razi snuck out of the house, just as he'd done before. But this time, Riley and I followed him.

"Razi," I said. "Don't do this. We'll think of something else. Some other way to make Babu back off, to buy more time to pay."

Razi shook his head. "I cannot take the chance my mother will be harmed. I am committed to doing this tonight."

"Well, if you're set on going," I said, "then Riley and I are coming with you."

He looked from me to Riley, who nodded.

"I would not ask this of you," said Razi. "It is too dangerous."

"We're coming and that's that," I said. "But are you sure we should take Seth? I know there has been bad blood between your families."

"Things have been difficult between us in the past," said Razi. "But we are now firm friends."

Seth was coming whether we liked it or not. I just hoped the changes we'd made to our relations with Sacmis had created enough goodwill between the families to make him less likely to betray us.

Unfortunately, though, there really was only one way to find out.

"Hold on a moment," said Riley. He opened a cloth bag tied to his belt and pulled out three cylindrical tubes, one for each of us. They were slightly longer and thicker than a marker pen, hard and cool to touch and composed of a murky substance with white specks inside.

Riley banged his stick on the ground and slowly it began to glow brighter and brighter until it was green and luminescent and giving out as much light as a torch.

"Wow," I said in awe. "You made a light."

"What is this? Magic?" Razi looked terrified.

"Not magic: chemiluminescence," Riley said. "The outer tube is composed of a transparent resin, while inside is a group of substances that, combined, become unstable and..." He paused and, seeing our utter non-comprehension, settled for: "We'll need them for light in the tomb."

Razi banged his torch on the ground and, as it began to glow, gave a high-pitched giggle. "I have a fire in my hands and it does not burn me!"

"Shhh." I put a finger to my lips.

"Sorry," said Razi.

We walked past the fields and along the river bank on our way to Nuru's tomb. It was cool out tonight. A breeze had carried off the staler smells of the day. The river was calm. The fields were so dark, they were like black holes where you could imagine pure evil lurking. I shone my torch at the darkness and gasped as I saw glassy eyes reflected back.

"What's out there?" I whispered.

"Hippos, probably," Riley said.

We walked faster after that. I scanned constantly—left for hippos on land, right for crocodiles in the river. And, of course, we needed to keep an eye out for guards around the tomb. It was a long, twitchy walk till Nuru's tomb appeared in the distance, like a high-security prison. It was bigger than I recalled, blocking out starlight, like a bully standing over us.

"Good evening." A deep rumbly voice made me literally jump as, out of the shadows, strode Razi's two friends. Lisimba had wavy hair like a lion's mane and muscular arms and legs. Seth was more like a brioche bun, soft and spongy, with no hair at all and a smile like a sneer.

"What is this pair doing here?" Seth glared at Riley and me. "Can we trust them?"

That's rich, coming from him.

"I trust them with my life," said Razi.

Awww.

"Very well," said Seth. "But if they do anything suspicious, I will cut out their tongues and hearts and feed them to the fish."

O-kay. So the team building had got off to a good start.

Riley gave the guys their own light sticks. They giggled and squealed over them till Razi told them to "Shhh", shaking his head in a "Not Cool, Dudes" kind of way, and we got down to the business of breaking and entering the tomb.

"If anything happens to me tonight," Riley whispered, "you make sure you get home, Maddy."

"If anything happens to you, Riley," I said, "I'll never get out of Egypt or this time zone. I don't know how to operate the time machine."

"You'll figure it out," he said.

"No, I won't. And then the world won't be put right. Our families and friends will never return to existence. You have to make it out of the tomb tonight. Even if I don't."

In the thin, spooky light, I saw shadows slipping into a vertical crease between his eyebrows. I'd got him worried now. *Well, good.* He should be worried.

He'd started all this with his way-too-smart invention. It was up to him to finish it.

CHAPTER 40

The tomb loomed over us. Its double stone doors, carved with hieroglyphics, seemed to dare us to break in.

"I wonder what the symbols mean," said Lisimba.

"Yeah, I wonder," I said, widening my eyes at Riley in warning to stay quiet. The pair of us could read the symbols on account of taking Riley's language pill. It said: *All who disturb the slumber of the great Nuru will die in despair and agony.* But there was no point in freaking the guys out.

The doors looked impossible to break through. Still, Lisimba clenched and flexed, preparing for the first challenge of the night.

"Stand back," he said. "I will get us inside."

"Wait," said Seth. "Before we begin, I have something to show you."

From within the folds of his tunic, he extracted a booklet containing maps of all the tombs in the area and a list of the treasures hidden inside. It was called *The Book of Buried Pearls.* "This may help us find a way in," said Seth.

"Where did you get that?" I asked.

"At the market," said Seth.

He got a book like this, which would surely be illegal, at a public market?

"And how much did you pay for it?" I asked.

"I gave twelve dung bricks for it."

Twelve dung bricks? When a fresh loaf cost three? That sounded too cheap. The whole story had a whiff of *you-know-what* about it. We crowded around to see the scrawls and symbols on the map. They meant zero to me and from the baffled looks on the guys' faces, they were just as clueless. Riley, however, peered intently at the pages and his eyes gleamed with intelligence.

"We'll enter from this side," he said, pointing to the left of the building. "I'm sure you all noticed the mismatch between the tomb map and the structure?"

We nodded as if it was obvious, wearing similar vacant expressions.

"My guess would be that this section—" Riley tapped the page "—was added on later. Which may give us our best chance to get inside."

As we rounded the corner, Riley raced up ahead, shouting about sand levels being artificially raised—whatever that meant. Like a kid on a beach holiday, he dropped to his knees and started digging beside the wall, flinging sand back in handfuls.

"So we will burrow underground, like worms of the earth?" said Razi.

"Most of the top layer is soft sand. It's easy to dig." Riley dropped back into the hole. "It was probably put here after *myaw myaw myaw*." That's what it sounded like.

"After what?" I said.

Riley bobbed up, sand sprinkled through his hair. "This part was built on later. And the sand was put here to hide something. Look."

I peered into the hole at dark, murky earth. *Nope! Nothing!* "What am I looking at?"

"The foundations of this wall are pretty shallow. If the floors inside are made of sand too, then—" he paused, waiting for one of us to leap in and finish his thought; we gaped back, not an idea between us "—then it shouldn't be too hard to dig our way in."

We dropped to our knees and scrabbled at the earth. All except for Seth, whose idea of helping was to watch and offer advice like "Dig faster!" and "Why are you resting? The hole won't dig itself!"

My hands were cold and I had wet sand clumped under my fingernails. But within half an hour, we had carved out a space big enough to squeeze through.

One by one, we went inside.

The first thing to hit us was the smell. Stale and musty. Like death. When something touched my shoulder, I shrieked. But as we brought our torches around, I saw it was just spider webs. The room was thick with them, especially one corner.

"Let's get this done, guys!" I said.

"Everyone be careful what you touch and where you step," Riley said.

Waving our torches about, we saw that we were in a good-sized room with a high ceiling. I glimpsed colour on the walls—greens and shiny gold—and some shadowy objects piled up at the end.

"Can I have a couple of torches over here?" I pointed to the long wall. We shone our lights on a painted mural with a colourful scene of Egyptian families picnicking and women dancing in a lush garden.

"Such beauty!" said Seth, running his hand across the hair of one of the women in the picture.

"Don't touch anything," Riley hissed.

I swung my light up to the ceiling. It was painted like a night sky with gold stars on a dark blue background.

While we checked out the painting, Riley headed over to the creepy insect corner to inspect the spider webs. In Australia, we had heaps of spiders. I once counted seventy-two strung between trees and power lines on the short walk to school. I was used to seeing big collections of webs. But that didn't mean I liked it. I went over to look.

"Eeoo. They're revolting," I said. "They look well fed though. What are they eating?"

"Scorpions," said Riley. I studied the silvery strands and saw a few part-wrapped scorpions—as long as my index finger and black as midnight—motionless in the middle.

"Errgh!" I said. "Aren't they deadly?"

"Yeah," said Riley. "But where are they coming from?" He looked up at the ceiling.

"Over here," called Seth from the end of the room. "I have found a doorway to take us deeper into the tomb."

"There may be no need for that!" shouted Razi, at the opposite end. "For I have found all we seek. Come, see for yourselves."

We hurried over to Razi, who had found a pile of goodies—vases and shiny platters, goblets and jewellery. The guys whooped and danced about.

"We have riches beyond our dreams!" said Lisimba.

"This night of tomb robbing was far easier than I

expected," said Seth.

And he was right. I thought we'd have to go through a few booby-trapped rooms at least. Yet here the goods were laid out like presents under a Christmas tree, in a room that was, actually, not that hard to break into.

I looked around for Riley. He was over at the painting now, frowning.

"That's odd," he said. "At first I thought the women in the painting were smiling, but, when I look closer, they're actually grimacing."

"You're right." Seth peered closely at the wall. "A scorpion hiding behind a blade of grass is biting this woman. She is in pain."

Taking a second look, I now saw that everyone in the picture was gritting their teeth, not smiling.

"And there are scorpions everywhere," I added. "In the pattern on this necklace, in the strands of this woman's hair. Even some of the leaves are scorpion-shaped."

"This painting is not at all what I thought it was," said Seth.

"Nor is this treasure pile," called Razi. "The jewellery is worthless. The goblets are chipped and the vases are fixed to the floor."

"Fixed to the floor?" said Lisimba. "Stand back. I will unfix them." Grasping the belly of the biggest vase, his arms and leg muscles trembling, he tried to lift it.

"No, Lisimba!" Riley shouted.

There was a loud click and a whirring sound.

In unison, we looked up at the ceiling. The image of the night sky was changing. The wooden slats it was painted on were turning.

"Quick everyone, under the spider webs," screamed Riley.

We raced over to huddle under the thickest part of the web as scorpions flew from the ceiling in a black mass. No, they weren't flying. They were falling. Like rain. Scorpion rain.

"What is this torment?" called Lisimba.

"It is Nuru's revenge!" said Razi.

"May the gods have mercy on us," said Seth.

Scorpions stuck in the webs' sticky threads, which began to sag, then tear. One web, with a least twelve scorpions in it, snagged on Seth. He shrieked as he flicked the creatures off his arms, face and body.

I shone my torch at the floor to find the sand alive with black wriggling things. As the scorpions came at us, we stomped on them and kicked them away. One fell on Riley's thigh. I flicked it off. Another crept onto Lisimba's knee; Seth whacked it with his torch.

"Behind you, Maddy," Riley shouted. Two scorpions reared up, ready to strike, until Razi kicked sand over them, burying them.

We shredded the air with our screams and ran on the spot, knees up, so none of the scorpions could give us a deadly nip. Eventually, most of the black specks were still. We slowed down to catch our breath.

"Thank the gods these spider webs were here to protect us," said Lisimba.

"And thank Riley, too," said Razi, "whose idea of sheltering under the webs may have saved our lives."

It was then I noticed the painting on the ceiling had changed, into one of a sneering, slavering scorpion. *Creepy.*

"When Lisimba tried to lift the vase," said Riley, "he must have triggered a booby trap that released the scorpions from the ceiling."

"Take more care in future, Lisimba," said Seth.

"It was not my fault," said Lisimba. "If you were not so weak, it might have been you lifting the vase."

"I would not have been so stupid," said Seth.

They pushed and shoved each other. Seth picked up a goblet and threw it at Lisimba's head. He ducked and crash-tackled Seth to the ground, where they rolled around on the floor as they fought.

"Stop this!" said Razi. "Remember why we are here."

"Quiet!" said Riley. In the silence, we heard that grinding sound again, like mechanical equipment starting up. I trembled with fear. No, wait. It wasn't me. The floor was shaking.

"What should we do?" shouted Seth.

We all turned to Riley.

"Run!" he said.

And we were off, crossing the floor super-fast, headed for the door Seth had found at the end of the room. I was at the back of the group and, as I approached the doorway, I glanced up. A mass of rocks was suspended over the doorframe behind one large boulder.

"Riley, watch out! There are rocks on top of the—"

A loud crack drowned out my words as the wooden support holding the stones split and the rocks cascaded down.

"Hurry!" Razi called as he leapt through the doorway.

Riley and Lisimba followed, small stones glancing off their skulls. Seth was about to leap forward when a large stone dropped in front of him. He paused, leapt over it and hurtled through.

The big stone, holding the rest back, rolled forward.

"Come, Maddy!" called Lisimba, beckoning me from the door. I tried to run but kept stumping my foot on fallen rocks. The boulder was coming straight for me. I crouched down and covered my head, expecting to feel it crush my head any second.

But I felt nothing. There was a deep groan beside me and I looked up to see Lisimba holding the massive boulder back, his arms shaking with the effort.

"Go!" he croaked.

I clambered to my feet and hurled myself through the doorway. *Just in time.* There was a deafening crash. *Oh no! Lisimba!* But when I looked around, he was on the ground beside me. Somehow, he'd managed to slip out from under the load and dive to safety before the whole lot came crashing down.

Dust rose in the air around us, like smoke, catching in our throats, making us cough. A thin layer settled into the corner of my eyes and the cracks of my dry lips. As the cloud cleared, we saw that the exit we'd come through was now completely blocked off. For a moment, we stood, stunned, taking in what that meant—we couldn't return that way even if we wanted to.

Fear gripped my chest and drained the strength from my legs. It was an effort to stay upright. From the tortured looks of the others, they felt the same. We wondered if there was any other way out or whether this cramped, airless space would become our tomb too.

CHAPTER 41

"Are you okay, Maddy?" Riley's blue eyes looked especially bright in his dust-caked face.

"Yeah, fine," I lied. "Thanks to Lisimba. Is there any way out of here, do you think?"

As Riley pulled out the map and studied it, everyone held their breath. "Should be," he said, pointing along a tunnel on the left. "This way."

We were in a narrow corridor. Long and dark, with no markings on the walls and not nearly enough air. What little there was had a mustiness about it, like an invisible hand around your throat, squeezing.

Riley, in the lead, stopped and signalled for us to do the same, tilting his head to listen to something.

"I thought I heard heavy breathing or something," he said.

"I'm pretty sure that was us," I said.

The creep factor, already high, climbed up a notch. The sickly green light from our glow sticks, combined with the hulking shadows we cast, was enough to make anyone jumpy. But even worse was the thick blackness ahead, like a curtain drawn to conceal who-knew-what lurking in the dark.

Riley knelt down, then crawled a few feet along the corridor. Keeping low, he pulled out three stones from the pouch on his belt and began juggling them. I had some idea what he was up to as he threw the stones higher and higher.

Eventually—*whoosh*—a volley of a dozen sharpened sticks shot out from above, bouncing off the stone walls with a *ping, ping, ping*. If Riley had been standing up, they would have hit him around chest height. Riley picked up one of the sticks and held it to the light. Something shiny was visible on the tip.

He sniffed it. "Poison," he said. "But we should be safe now. The trap's been sprung. I don't think anyone comes back to reload." He stood up slowly.

"Are you sure?"

"Pretty sure," he said, then dropped back to his knees. "But just in case..."

He crab-walked along the dark corridor and we followed likewise. I knelt on my linen tunic to protect my knees and collected thick, black grime as we went. The corridor was only about twenty feet or so but it took forever to crawl through as we had to keep stopping while Riley juggled the stones to check for more traps.

I only just kept a grip on the terror rampaging through me by focusing on what we'd do next—not *if* but *when* we made it out of this time zone. First, we'd inhale lungfuls of air. Never again would I take fresh or even dung-scented air for granted. Second, Riley and I would leave Egypt, triggering the cascade of changes we needed to bring our world and the people we loved back into being. And this time we could really enjoy being home because we'd know Razi and his family were safe back here.

If we managed to get that result, this terror would have been worth it.

As we reached the end of the corridor, the relief I felt was epic. It was the same for the others. We all took a moment to breathe. The guys muttered prayers of thanks to various gods before steeling themselves for the next challenge.

We were at the doorway to a much larger space. Shining our torches around, the room seemed empty. There were hieroglyphics, like graffiti, on the walls opposite that read: *Welcome Thieves and Goodbye.*

"I wonder what that says," said Razi.

Riley and I shrugged.

Across the room was a wooden door. We stared at it with longing and fear. "It could lead to treasure. Real treasure," said Razi.

"Or it might be a way out of the tomb," said Lisimba.

"Or to a slow and torturous death," said Seth.

Whatever was behind it, no one seemed in a hurry to find out.

"Lisimba used his strength in the first room to save us," said Razi. "Riley used his skill in the corridor to get us through. I will do what I can in this room to ensure it is safe for all."

"No, Razi," I said.

But he was already backing into the room, a forced smile on his face. A few steps in, he dropped to his haunches and looked around, like an animal sensing a predator. He took a small step sideways and paused. Then another. And another. We strained our eyes and ears and every other sense for a sign that a trap was about to be sprung.

"It seems safe so far," said Razi, his voice cracking. After a few breaths to psych himself up, he leapt into the air, arms up, before dropping back into a crouch.

"What are you doing?" said Lisimba.

"We need to know whether the room is safe," said Razi, side-stepping a short distance before leaping again.

He was tempting poison darts to fly towards him.

Now a tad high on his success, and perhaps a lot short of oxygen, he tried something more daring. He did a cartwheel then went back into a crouch.

"Don't get over-confident," I said.

He looked around the room, eyes insanely big. When no darts came his way, he laughed hysterically.

"Stop this now! I beg you," said Lisimba.

But he cartwheeled again and, without pausing, went straight into a second spin. Till he reached the door on the opposite side.

"Do NOT touch the door," said Riley.

"Razi, no!" said Seth.

He grasped the door handle.

"Stop!" I shouted. Everyone stopped and turned to me. "The hieroglyphs on the wall are a warning. They say: 'Welcome Thieves and Goodbye'. The door could be a trap!"

Razi licked his lips. "But how else can we discover what lies behind it?"

I couldn't think of any other way. Neither could anyone else.

"Well then," he said. A protest of rusty metal resounded through the room as he turned the handle, then jerked his arm back in an attempt to open it. Once. Twice. Several more times. But the door didn't budge. He tried again and again, yanking harder each time. Straining, pulling with all his might. He roared with frustration.

"It does not open!" Razi glowered. "It is not a door at all. Just a trick to raise our hopes, then destroy them."

"A false door," said Riley. "I've heard of them. They're supposed to be a threshold between the worlds of the living and the dead."

Razi slapped the handle in irritation. "No treasure lies there—not for us anyway."

He did another cartwheel. Then a second, moving towards us, growing reckless. "There do not seem to be any traps in this room," he said, as he launched into a third twirl. "I believe it is saaaaaffe…"

And he vanished. We heard the sound of his screams getting further away and flashed our torches around the room.

But Razi was gone.

CHAPTER 42

"Where did he go?" said Lisimba.

"There are demons here who devour mortal men to stay strong," Seth stammered.

"Razi!" Lisimba called, rushing forward, no longer concerned about his own safety. Riley rushed after him and grabbed him—before he fell into a dark pit in the middle of the room, which none of us had seen.

The guys shone their torches into the hole. I winced, expecting to hear that Razi had been impaled on sharpened sticks or something grotesque. But they couldn't make anything out in the blackness.

"Razi, are you okay?" Riley shouted into the hole.

There was a tense silence, then a distant reply. "Yes, I'm alive."

"Hold on there!" said Riley. "We'll find a way to get you out."

Riley pulled out a rope from his handy cloth bag and dangled it down the hole.

"Can you see the rope, Razi?" Riley shouted.

"No," Razi called.

It wasn't long enough. He pulled it back up.

"So the only way out is down?" I said.

Riley nodded. "Razi, is it safe for us to go down there with you?"

"Yes, there is water here to soften your landing. But it is a long fall. You must brace yourselves."

We had to go into that dark hole? *Seriously?*

Lisimba stepped up to the hole first. He took a deep breath, then closed his eyes and went super-still. Then *snap!* He opened his eyes and jumped.

There was a long, tense silence. Too long.

"Lisimba!" shouted Seth, verging on hysterical.

"I made it. I am alive," Lisimba called. "My friends, the fall is nothing to worry about. Come down."

Nothing to worry about? Apart from the fact we were going deeper into an ancient tomb with a creepy mummy somewhere and who knew what traps lurking inside. Or that when we got down, we might find it was a dead end and we couldn't get back up here again. Apart from that, though, no worries at all!

Riley moved forward, glanced back and gave me a small smile, before leaping into the hole, as casually as if he was diving into the local pool. Those few seconds between him disappearing and shouting that he was okay were among the longest of my life.

Then it was my turn. I peered down, straining through the blackness. But I couldn't see a thing. I did not want to jump down there, but I couldn't stay up here. Not with Seth, who was sniffly and starting to hyperventilate, making me lose what little nerve I had.

"Maddy, it's okay," Riley called. "Come down!"

I took a deep breath. Then jumped. Into the scary black tunnel.

I gripped my stick light and didn't touch the sides, which meant I went down super-fast. I'm sure I screamed all the way down and—*whoosh*—plunged into a freezing body of dark water before bursting out to see Riley, Razi and Lisimba beaming at me.

"Well done, Maddy," said Riley.

"You are a brave girl," said Razi.

"You now, Seth!" Lisimba shouted. "Seth?"

I looked up towards the ceiling but couldn't see the hole we'd just come through or hear a single sound emanating from it.

"Seth!" called Razi.

"What will we do if he does not jump?" asked Lisimba.

"There is nothing we can do," said Riley.

"I should have gone last and assisted him with the descent," said Lisimba.

Assisted him with a boot in the butt perhaps.

Riley glanced over at me, frowning slightly. I knew why. He, like me, wondered whether this was the point where Seth would double-cross us. Did he know a secret way out of the tomb—one we'd missed? Was he meeting with the guards outside right now plotting for our arrest and grisly deaths as he had done before?

One of the main things Riley and I had changed this time around was relations between Amunet's family and Sacmis and Seth's. We wanted to make sure that if they rose to power, our friends were on the right side of them. But would the better vibes between us all now be enough to stop Seth dobbing Razi into the authorities? Or was betrayal just part of the guy's nature?

Or, worse, were there certain things on the timeline you couldn't change no matter what? Destiny? Immovable, fixed points that time had to flow around, like water skirting a rock in a river.

All this was in my mind as the room filled with an ear-splitting scream and Seth plummeted down. As he hit the water, a wave rose up and descended back on us like rain. Seth resurfaced with a great gulp of air and a cry of exquisite joy.

In that moment, even I was glad to see him. He hadn't betrayed us...yet. Though he still might before the evening was done.

We were up to our chests in water, which was grey-green and murky in the torchlight. It gave off a scent of dead things—not fish but something bigger. Something deader. The walls were black, the ceiling high—too high to even think about climbing back up. The *drip, drip* echoing around the room rapidly doused our happy moods.

We spread out to search for an exit. There didn't seem to be one.

"Is it a dead end?" I asked Riley.

"There's no exit I can see above water," said Riley. "But there might be one below."

"Below the water?" I said. *Oh, please no!*

Riley took a deep breath, then dived.

Drip, drip, drip.

"Do you think he will find anything?" Fear gave Lisimba's voice a higher pitch.

"Oh, yes," I said. "The water got in here somehow. There has to be a way for it to get out." It sounded logical enough, but I'd just made it up to keep everyone calm. To keep myself calm, mainly.

Drip, drip, drip.

Like a clock ticking away the seconds remaining in Riley's life. And ours. What would we do if he came back with bad news, that there was no way out? Or if he never came back at all?

Just when I was sure something bad had happened, he resurfaced.

"We are glad to see you, my friend," said Razi. "And what did you find?"

"There's a tunnel to another room," Riley said. *That was the good news.* "But it's quite long and we'll have to hold our breath for a while to get there." *That was the bad.*

"A while?" I said.

"Maybe we could look around once more," said Lisimba, "to see if there is any other way out?"

"Good idea," said Seth.

For the next ten minutes, we scoured that room, shining our torches into dark corners, tapping and pressing the walls, hoping to unlock a secret door or passage. All we found was scum, mould and dead rats.

The only way out was down, under the water.

Everyone grew still and quiet as Riley brought out six round stones from his pouch. They were made of the same material as our torches. A bash on the wall and they began to glow. "It's quite dark down there," said Riley. "These stones will help light the way to the next chamber."

"Oh, gods spare me!" Seth moaned. "I am not good in the water."

"You made it to the next chamber then?" I whispered softly to Riley.

He gave a small nod.

"And what was it like?"

A beat. "Bigger than this."

His eyes met mine for a second then slid away super-fast.

"Riley, what is it you're not telling me?"

"Nothing."

"Is there any way out from the next chamber?" I whispered.

He pressed his lips together. "There has to be."

CHAPTER 43

"The most important thing to remember is to stay calm when you're down there," said Riley as we prepared to dive. "If you can't hold your breath any longer, let the air out a little at a time. Not all at once. And try to keep movements to a minimum to conserve oxygen."

"To conserve what?" said Lisimba.

"Err...air," said Riley.

"Is it very far through the tunnel?" I whispered when the others weren't listening. "Are we going to make it?"

"You and I should be okay," Riley said. "The others..." He gave a quick head shake—he didn't like their chances. *Oh no.* This was really bad.

The guys each prepared for the swim in their own ways. Lisimba clenched and flexed his muscles like a strong man. Razi swung his arm about and ran on the spot, while Seth pummelled his arms and legs with his pudgy fists. Though they were all mega-nervous, no-one said anything mean to Razi about what a mess he'd got them into, which I thought was pretty cool.

I could have gone on my usual rant to Riley about how he was to blame for all this—for inventing the time machine. But I didn't feel like saying it just then. Perhaps, when we'd got safely through, I could lay that on him once again. For now, though, I just gave him a corny smile. He gave me one back.

"Maddy?"

"Yes, Riley?"

He held my gaze in this intense way, and I got the feeling he was about to say something important.

"Be careful, won't you?" he said.

"Sure," I said.

That wasn't it.

I tried to calm myself. Slow breaths in, even slower ones out. Till it was time. We each took a last lungful of air and dived down. Riley went first, then Razi and Lisimba, then Seth. I went last so I could push the slow swimmers along.

The water was concrete grey and cold in that *gets-into-your-bones, gets-into-your-soul* kind of way. Thankfully, Riley's glow stones kept it from feeling too claustrophobic. Though the sense of horror closing in was high.

The tunnel was just below the surface and wide enough for two people to swim side by side. But entering it was terrifying as you couldn't see the end. Already, I felt the pressure building in my lungs.

The guys kicked a little slowly for my liking so I swam up beside Seth and took his arm to speed him along. His eyes had a bulbous, terrified quality. When he started clutching his throat and twisting, I pointed to his mouth, signalling that he should let out some air. Bubbles gushed out, like a watery hurl. *Oh no!* He was only meant to let out a bit!

Up ahead, the guys kicked wildly but weren't moving that fast. So much for conserving energy.

When Seth began making high-pitched squeaks of panic, I did the only thing I could. I grabbed his head, tilted it back and covered his mouth with mine. Then I gently blew almost all the air I had into his mouth.

He sucked up my meagre offering and calmed down for a few seconds. Long enough for me to grab his hand and kick forward fast. My chest felt like it was being crushed slowly, but just ahead I could see a pale light.

I blew out my last puff of air and rose up, up, a bit more, just a tiny bit more. And broke the surface with not a second to spare. Seth and I sucked air down in great glorious gulps. Stale as it was, with a hint of damp and mould and something sour, air had never tasted better. Razi and Lisimba whooped, wild with relief that they'd made it through.

When his breathing calmed, Seth turned to me, hand on chest. "Madison, I owe you my life," he said. "And an apology. For ever doubting your intentions."

"It's okay," I said.

"If there is any way I can repay you, I will."

Razi splashed through the water and hugged me. "I am so glad you made it, Maddy. We all made it. Without you and Riley here, we would not have got so far."

I couldn't argue with that. But was it far enough? How much further did we have to go?

I looked around. We were in a room twice the size of the last one, with a really high ceiling and a wide sandy bank. Much better. And Riley? Where was he? He was behind me, striding towards the sand with purpose. Had he spotted an exit?

Oh.

Not an exit.

A croc.

A giant one. Half in, half out of the water, its open jaws revealing a set of jagged teeth and a bite diameter that could take us two at a time.

The joyous splashing and squealing stopped as the guys saw it too. I did a quick scan of the room to see where we could run if the creature came at us. There was no safe place. I'd been to Australian zoos often enough to know crocs could outrun humans on land and in water.

Riley stood still, about six feet from the creature. Way too close.

"What are you doing, Riley?" I said, trying not to move my lips. "Get away from the croc."

He just stayed there, watching it.

"The creature is my problem, Riley," said Razi, splashing through the water. "Back away and I will take care of it. If I fall, Maddy, you and Riley must find some treasure to take back to my mother before Babu returns. Will you promise me?"

"Razi, no! You're not doing this," I said.

"Promise me you will do as I say. That my death will not be in vain."

"Stand back, Razi," said Lisimba, grabbing his friend's arm. "I am stronger, I will fight the croc."

Razi and Lisimba jostled a bit for lead position until Riley shouted. "No one's going to fight the croc. We're going to rescue it."

Rescue it? It wasn't a lost puppy. IT WAS A CROCODILE!

What he did next made me think I was hallucinating, or at least, hope that I was. He went right up the creature, knelt down and leaned in closer to its mouth.

"What are you doing?" I shouted.

"This animal is sick," he said. "We need to get it out of here."

"What's wrong with it?" Seth asked.

"I'm not a vet," said Riley. (They scratched their heads, not knowing what that was.) "But from the lack of movement and the shallow breathing, I'd say it's seriously in need of light and warmth. If we don't take it out with us, it may die."

"But that is good, is it not?" said Razi. "It will save us the trouble of killing it."

This was where Riley and I were from different worlds to the guys. We'd been taught since we were small to respect wildlife. All wildlife. Even deadly creatures, like snakes, sharks and crocs.

"It will bring us good luck if we save it," I said. That should get them onside. And just now, good luck seemed in short supply.

"Maddy, can I have your belt?" said Riley. He took the white linen strip and looped it around the croc's neck to make a kind of lead. *A lead FOR A CROC!* The creature's olive-green eyes did not blink or flicker once as he did this—and believe me, I watched super-closely for any movement.

"Don't you think you should tie up the mouth as well?" I said. "Just in case?" The croc's teeth were caramel coloured with large pointy canines at the tip of the snout and around the mid-jaw, just right for chomping through human muscle and bone.

Riley tried to coax the croc's mouth shut, but in the end he had to force it down before looping Seth's belt around the tip to secure it. I wasn't confident it would hold if the croc felt like yawning or snapping one of us in two. But it was something.

"All right, so the croc's like our pet now?" I said. "What next? I'm looking around and I don't see any obvious places to—"

But as I spoke, I did see something—a shadow on the wall that wasn't quite right. I waved my light stick in that direction and found a staircase, built next to the wall, leading up to a door.

"How long have you known about that door, Riley?"

"I noticed it just when you did," he said.

Getting the weakened croc up the narrow steps was a challenge. It moved really slowly, so we got Lisimba to push it from behind while Riley made sure it didn't slide off the side.

I was a little nervous, being so close to such a dangerous creature, but I felt sorry for it too. It had been locked into the tomb as one of the booby traps. But no one had given any thought to its need for food or light.

Razi, in the lead, got to the top of the stairs first and paused at the door, licking his lips nervously. This was our moment of truth. When we learned whether we would ever get out of here or we would be keeping the croc company for eternity.

He pulled on the handle. And pulled again. There was a scraping sound as the door shifted slightly. "It opens," he said, smiling.

"I will take over now, friend," said Lisimba, squeezing past the croc on the stairs. His arm and neck muscles bulged as he pulled the door with all his strength. Then pulled some more.

Bit by bit, it gave way.

CHAPTER 44

In the next room, we hit pay dirt—the treasure chamber. And it was everything I'd expected of an Egyptian tomb.

The walls were painted in bright colours with scenes from Nuru's life—as a boy learning, as a father and husband, as a servant of the vizier. A panel above told stories of Egyptian gods. Flames burned in metal sconces around the walls. A shiny golden sarcophagus sat on a raised platform in the centre of the room. The reflection of the flickering flame made it seem eerily alive. On either side were piles of treasure—jewels, vases, goblets, platters and elaborate headpieces. Razi confirmed that this time they were the real deal.

"This room is the answer to all my family's prayers," he said. "Here we will find a way to rid ourselves of the nightmare of the taxman."

Seth put on a golden wig and a ring on every finger, Razi took several necklaces and some goblets, Lisimba picked up a bulky vase.

Typically, Riley's interest was elsewhere—on the candles burning on the wall. He raised his chin and sniffed the flames.

"It's funny, they look like they've just been lit," I said. "But they couldn't have been. Could they?" He shook his head but kept staring at the flames.

However it was they came to be there, I was glad to be out of the creepy darkness of the tomb.

"Don't touch the sarcophagus," said Razi. "We do not wish to disturb Nuru's journey to the afterlife. We will take only enough to pay the tax debt."

"After such a night as we've had," said Lisimba, "surely we can take an extra month's payment, at least."

"Very well," Razi agreed. "But that's all."

I grabbed a few bits of jewellery and an armband shaped like a snake. "Riley, come over here and help us carry a few things," I said.

My friend emerged from the shadowy end of the room.

"There's a door back there," he said, scooping up a few items from the pile.

"Do you think it could be a way out?"

"With a bit of luck," he said. "The air in here doesn't smell as stale as in the rest of the tomb."

Now I was excited. To think, we might actually make it out of here.

"I believe we have collected enough for the tax payment," said Razi. "So shall we go?"

"Yes!" we all chorused.

The vase Lisimba carried was useful for transporting loose bits and pieces. Grabbing a few final things, we began making our way to the back door when a low growl filled the room.

"What's that?" Razi froze, eyes as big as golf balls, looking about the room with dread.

In unison, we turned our terrified gaze to the croc, who was as passive as ever. The noise wasn't coming from him.

Then came a second growl, louder than the first. Resonant and deep, it made the candles flicker and the treasure rattle on the pile.

"It is the god Osiris, coming to take revenge on us for plundering Nuru's tomb," said Seth.

"No, it isn't," I said. "Everybody stay calm."

As the sound boomed out again, louder and a bit distorted, a few ceramic cups fell off the pile and smashed to bits. And our nerves shattered along with it. The Egyptian boys fell to their knees, whimpering. "Forgive, forgive!"

I looked over to see Riley's reaction. His eyes swept left and right as he tried to track the source of the sound.

Then came a dull knocking. We all heard it, though we wished we hadn't. A second knock confirmed our fears—that it was coming from *inside* the sarcophagus! The guys totally lost it now, throwing themselves face down on the ground, turning to total blubbering wrecks. I didn't blame them. This was the stuff of nightmares.

Next came an unearthly creaking and the sarcophagus lid began to open. I knew it was impossible, even as I watched it happening.

"Riley, what's going on?"

"Not sure, exactly," he said. Though he didn't seem nearly as freaked out as the rest of us.

Slowly, the sarcophagus lid fell back and the mummy within began to rise. Arms outstretched, groaning as if in ancient pain, it tried to sit up. I think Seth fainted at that point, Razi clutched his skull and shrieked as Lisimba bashed his head over and over on the floor.

"This can't be happening," I said.

"It isn't." Riley turned to me. "It's not what it seems."

Epic relief! "What is it then?"

The mummy was fully upright now. The moaning continued but there was another sound too—a scurrying that echoed around the room.

I looked up. More than a hundred scarab beetles, their shells shiny blue in the candlelight, moved in formation up the walls. It was like the whole room was alive, seething with bugs. *Totally gross!* They halted suddenly on the ceiling, evenly spaced, like an army awaiting commands.

"Oh mighty sire!" Razi cried, his voice shaky. "Ask of me anything and I shall obey. But please, spare my friends who have only come here this night to help my family with an onerous tax burden."

"You may leave," the mummy said. Its voice boomed out. "But the boy Riley and the girl Madison must stay."

What the—? An Ancient Egyptian mummy knew our names?

"We hear and obey," said Seth. He jumped up and started for the rear door.

Razi and Lisimba stood up too, but didn't move. "We wish to obey you, mighty one," said Razi. "But whatever it is you want with Riley and Maddy, please allow us to take their place. They are honoured guests of my family and only accompanied me here as a favour. If there is any evil to be punished, it is mine."

"LEAVE NOW!" the mummy commanded. "Or prepare to stay here, with me. FOREVER!" Everything and everyone in the room trembled at this last word.

Though, weirdly, in the middle of this mind-melting scene, a cool memory surfaced. "Riley, I saw Nuru's sarcophagus being carried into the tomb. That's not it."

"Are you sure?" he asked.

I nodded. Nuru's coffin was plainer, not so much bling to it.

"So if that's not Nuru, who is it?"

As Razi pleaded for our release, the bug army moved left, then right, then back to attention. Their shiny shells looked alive in the flickering light. *So creepy.*

Meanwhile, Riley crouched down and slid the rope off the croc's mouth. Slowly, the creature's jaws opened.

"Sobek, be free!" Riley spoke loudly, like he was on stage. "And greet this spirit from the underworld, your brother."

As the mummy got its first look at the croc, it gasped. But why would a mummy be scared of a croc? Or anything, come to that? It had to be the scariest thing in this room, or any room, by a long way. While the mummy focused on the croc, Riley crept up behind it, then snatched something small and black from inside the sarcophagus.

"Hey! That's mine!" The mummy grabbed at Riley's arm. In my friend's hand, I saw something like a remote control. Riley pressed a button and the bugs moved left; he pressed again and they moved right. When he hit a third button, they all fell to the floor, deactivated.

"Give me that!" The mummy clambered out of the sarcophagus with little grace. "Or prepare to die a death so painful people will speak of it for a thousand years."

The mummy chased Riley with loping steps. I followed and, hardly believing what I was about to do, tried to snatch at its bandages. I expected to feel the ridges of hardened strips of linen. Instead, it was one smooth piece, like a mould.

So, I knocked on the mummy. The knock resonated as if it was hollow inside.

"What the—?" it said.

I grabbed it from behind with both hands and pulled upwards.

"Let me go now! Or you die!" it screamed.

"What are you doing, Maddy?" Razi's voice trembled.

"Osiris, save us!" Seth gasped.

Riley hurried over to help me and the upper half of the mummy began sliding upwards. It was a body mould in two parts. Between us, we lifted the top half right off.

Standing in the mummy's trousers, so to speak, was someone I did not expect to see.

"Azizi," I said. "What are you doing here?" (The silliest question ever!)

"Making sure you two never make it back to the future," he said.

"Azizi?" said Razi. "I thought this was Nuru's tomb? Who is Azizi?"

"He doesn't look dead to me," said Seth.

"Why are you doing this?" I asked.

"History will record only one name as the inventor of the time machine," said Azizi. "And that is going to be mine."

Razi and the guys finally twigged that they weren't dealing with an underworld god but a human pretending to be one.

"Prepare to die, imposter!" Lisimba squared his shoulders as he moved forward.

Razi and Seth threw treasures at Azizi—small jewel boxes and goblets—until he dived back into the sarcophagus and pulled shut the lid.

That stopped us briefly. We drank that one in for a few seconds, then rushed over and yanked the lid back open.

To find the sarcophagus was empty.

"Ahhh!" The Egyptians lost it again, staggering about, hands on their heads to stop their brains bursting out, unable to begin processing what they had just seen. I couldn't figure it out either.

"Riley, what just happened?" I asked.

"He has a time machine. Not one like ours. Much more compact. Somehow he transported himself directly into the sarcophagus. Interesting."

In the meantime, something else was bothering me. It had been since the vizier's party, first time around.

"Did you feel like you knew the guy?" I said. "I mean, I know it was Azizi, but I feel like I've met him somewhere else. Before Egypt. He seemed familiar to me."

"He's almost certainly from the future," said Riley. "He'd have to be with that technology. Though, I can't say how far into the future."

"Could we have met him somewhere in Sydney, in our own time, do you think?"

"Perhaps."

"Of course, he wouldn't have called himself Azizi there," I said. "That's probably made up."

The more I thought about it, the more convinced I was I'd met him before. It was something about a scent, on his clothes, in his hair. A sour smell I knew well but couldn't quite name.

The guys were a mess. Naturally, we couldn't tell them the truth about what had happened. So I came up with a cover story, the best I could dream up at the end of a long night. They listened, sceptical at first.

"So the mummy wasn't real?" said Razi. "It was just a waking dream?"

"It is strange we all had the same dream," said Lisimba.

"Very strange indeed," said Seth.

"In Nubia, where I come from," I said, "tomb workers who spend too long inside airless rooms often have dreams about mummies rising from coffins. It's well documented."

"Documented?" said Razi.

Oops.

It wasn't my best story. But the guys bought it. They were so desperate for some kind of rational answer to the unearthly scene we'd witnessed, they would have accepted any half-decent or even quarter-decent explanation.

And when you thought about it, was a mummy rising from the dead really any freakier than travelling through time? At least the mummy would only affect the few that saw it in the tomb. Whereas time travel had the potential to affect the lives of everyone in the world, in every corner—past, present and future.

Letting that one out of its box was far, far scarier, I now realised.

CHAPTER 45

With just a little sweat, Lisimba managed to force open the door at the end of the treasure room. One more creepy corridor, a couple of breathless turns and we found ourselves outside another quite ordinary-looking door. Would it lead to doom? Or freedom? None of us said it, though we all thought it. With a surge of energy, Razi put his shoulder to the door and pushed.

And we were out of the tomb! Back in the desert, beneath a vast night sky alive with starlight. For the first few minutes, we just looked up in awe and breathed in the cool night air—in, out, in, out—savouring the scents of the river, the sand. Even the dung. It was sublime.

I was a little worried the first whiff of oxygen would awaken the croc's predatory instincts, that he'd snap the limp linen ropes binding his jaw and start dining on his rescue team. But he remained docile. Riley and I led him to the river's edge. The water was murky and dark. I wouldn't have wanted to go in there. I was a little afraid for him, but there was really nothing beneath that surface scarier than him.

"Time to say goodbye, Mr Crocodile," I said. "But if you ever meet us floating about in future, remember—you owe us."

"Just don't expect him to cry," said Riley. "The crocodile has no tear ducts."

Seriously! The guy was such a scientist.

"He's probably crying on the inside, though," he added, with a cheeky grin. *Wow, Riley made a joke.* He was human after all.

It was a tense moment when we slipped the binding off the crocodile's jaw and stepped back, waiting to see what he'd do. After a minute or so, he pumped forward on his stumpy legs, glided into the water and disappeared. We watched for a few minutes. I thought I saw his eyes pop up above the black water to take one last look at us before he disappeared for good.

"There's one future we've changed right there," I said. "A whole generation of crocs will be born now that might not have existed before. And if any of them kill someone they weren't meant to?"

"The changes continue on and on, branching out and expanding the consequences exponentially along the time continuum." Riley said it almost to himself, as though he was just figuring it out.

"How come we never thought of it before?" I said. Meaning, how come *he* never thought of it.

"I guess I was mostly focused on how to do it. Not whether I should."

Big mistake. As we now knew. But was it too late to undo it, I wondered.

"Do you think it's possible to travel through time without making a huge impact in the long term?" I asked.

"It's possible," said Riley, "but you'd have to be really careful and just observe and not interact meaningfully with anyone. I'm not sure that's something you can do, Maddy."

"Really? Not something *I* can do?" I said. "Tell me, by 'meaningfully', are you saying we shouldn't help people in trouble? Like people choking at parties or going through dangerous tombs? And we definitely should *not* create anything like toothpaste, which might help a whole society and change the future for generations to come. You're right, Riley, that's not something *I* can do."

This time, I think he got the sarcasm.

He grinned. "Maybe I was too proactive."

"You think we should have stood back and just watched when people were in trouble?" I asked. "Done nothing?"

"Technically, even being an observer isn't that safe because seeing things can change the decisions you would otherwise make," he said.

"So really, there's no way to stop the consequences when you time travel. No matter what."

"Probably not."

"Oh well," I said. "Maybe some things needed changing."

Once over the excitement of getting out of the tomb alive, we had to calm right down and take care in case any guards were lurking nearby, waiting to arrest us.

We were at the rear of the tomb and would need to get back to the front to start the journey home. But which way to go? The field side on the right or along the river to the left? If there were any tomb guards on patrol tonight, we had to be extremely cautious. Discovery could mean death.

In single file, our backs against the cool stone wall, we crept towards the corner closest to the fields. Razi was in the lead and we trod extra lightly, trying not to crunch stones or make a sound, the glow of our torches dulled beneath our clothing. Razi signalled for us to stop and we listened hard for any sounds around the corner. I heard the crackle of a night breeze in the palm trees, the soft *shoosh* of the water on the river bank. And...something else—I was almost sure of it.

Razi pointed at the corner, asking whether we thought it was safe for him to peek around.

Three heads in front of me nodded, *yes*.

I shook my head and gestured that he should get down low to the ground, on his knees. I figured those watching the tomb would be looking for people at head height rather than ground level. Razi knelt down and psyched himself up, once again, to look around the corner.

Behind him, we held our breath.

A tap on my shoulder made me gasp. Sacmis was there.

"Don't go that way," she whispered. "There are guards there. You have to go round by the river side."

"Wait!" I hissed. Word went along the line again like a game of whispers catching up with Razi just before he leaned out.

He looked back at me and I gave him a big headshake. I saw his chest deflate and he wiped sweat from his brow. He tiptoed over to see what was up.

"There are guards over that side," Sacmis repeated for him.

"You managed to sneak past them?" I asked her. "That was skilful."

Was it skill? Or something more like treachery? Had she come all the way out here to help us? Or lead us into a trap? I glanced at Riley. He'd heard her story but he shrugged—he didn't know whether to believe her or not.

It was up to me. The success of our mission, and all our

lives, depended on me reading Sacmis right. Was she lying and trying to get us caught and killed for reasons of her own? Or was she genuinely trying to help?

I stared into her eyes. They were watery and wild tonight. I studied her face and considered all I knew about her from the first and second times through the period. I tried to call up everything Gran had taught me about reading faces, detecting lies hidden behind a mask of truth and the little "tells" and muscle twitches that revealed what people tried to hide.

Was Sacmis an angel of mercy or a devil in a white dress?

"Maddy?" said Razi, his brow crinkled. "Shall we go river side, as Sacmis says?"

I paused, then nodded. "Of course." I smiled at her. "Thank you for your help."

So we reversed direction.

And got safely away.

CHAPTER 46

Back at the house, Razi tiptoed across the sleeping forms of his sisters and mother and slipped into bed. As far as they were concerned, he'd been there all night. We all had.

But before we went back in, Riley and I took a moment outside. The sun was about to rise. The sky was a deep blue with the last stubborn specks of starlight refusing to be extinguished.

"Wow," I said, sinking onto a rock. "What a night! It was a miracle we made it out safely. I have to admit, there were times I didn't think we would."

"It was a good idea of yours to hide the stolen goods," said Riley.

"I didn't want Razi to make the same mistake twice."

We'd buried all our booty in the sand somewhere Razi could easily get it when he needed to. Whether the guards would come knocking in the morning, as they had last time, was an interesting question. Would Seth follow his path of betrayal this time and dob us in to the authorities? I wasn't taking any chances.

"How did you know Sacmis was telling the truth about which way to go?" he asked.

"I looked into her eyes," I said. "I couldn't find a lie."

"Well, that was impressive," he said. "And to think she went out of her way like that to help you, just because you were friends this time."

"Yeah," I said. "Oh, and some of what you did inside the tomb wasn't too unimpressive either."

He gave me this half grin, which was kind of a new look for him—one I liked—before slipping into the house to sleep.

Lying on the hard ground between the girls, I smiled up at the darkness as I thought about how big-brained Riley had been impressed by *my* skill. Though he'd had only half the facts. I hadn't bet all our lives on what I saw or didn't see in Sacmis's eyes. Not completely. Rather, it was more to do with what I knew of her nature.

It was true because we were "friends" now, Sacmis hadn't gone out of her way to bring me or Amunet's family down. But the "friendship" would hardly have induced her to risk her life for us. For that, she needed something more tangible. Like a magic necklace, which I'd told her was in Nuru's tomb. One that could grant the wearer their deepest desire.

"I know what I would wish for," said Sacmis when I told her about it. "A husband who will allow me to be all I can be."

"I will search for the necklace," I said, "and if I find it, I will give it to you, my friend." That was a double lie, because (a) she was not my friend, and, (b) I would rather cut my arm off than give her something like that, knowing all about her "deepest desires". The lure of the magic necklace had been the right motivation to draw her from her bed to help us get out alive this time.

Elementary, really. Though, as I handed her a necklace— any old one I'd picked up in the tomb on the way out—and she looked up at me with big liquid eyes of gratitude, well, it wasn't my proudest moment.

CHAPTER 47

Babu arrived to collect the tax payment the next day. As Razi carried out the goods for him, Amunet and Sahara's eyes grew big, wondering where he'd got the stuff. I saw something in Babu's eyes too—disappointment that we were able to pay. *Hah!*

Amunet's father was due back from the pyramids in a few days, so next month's instalment should be less of a drama. And, anyway, Razi still had a few things stashed under the sand in case they came up short.

"Good to have some insurance," I said.

"Some what?" Razi asked.

Riley and I had done all we could to help the family so now it was time to go home—presuming there was a home to go to, that was. I was scared and excited. Though saying goodbye to our Egyptian friends was one of the hardest things I'd ever had to do.

"I had got so used to you being here," said Amunet. "I didn't think the time would ever come when you would leave." *That makes two of us.*

"Are you sure you can't remain longer?" asked Sahara. "You are welcome to stay as long as you wish."

"We really have to go," I said.

"But you will come back and visit, won't you?" said Layla.

"Of course, we will," I said, nodding and smiling. Though it was a lie. Unless something went badly wrong in the future, compelling our return, we would never see them again. Time travel wasn't like a train you took for weekends and holidays away. It was far too dangerous, too unstable. We'd learnt that the hard way.

On our first trip, Razi had been beheaded and, when Phoenix and Sacmis were thrown together, they changed the world, causing our home and everyone we loved to be erased in the process. If by some miracle we'd put things right again, we couldn't risk undoing it all with a visit back to this period, no matter how lightly we intended to tread.

"Farewell, my friends," said Razi, smiling broadly and clasping our hands in both of his. "Thank you for all you have done for my family." He leaned in to whisper, "You are my brother and sister now. It is a bond that nothing will ever break. You are welcome here anytime."

My cheeks were damp with tears as we headed back through the fields for the last time. The sun was sliding down the pale blue sky as kids played tip-chase and the girls of the village collected vegetables for the evening meal. Business as usual in Ancient Egypt.

When we got to the reeds by the river, we made sure nobody was watching before Riley pulled out the time machine.

"Are you ready to go?" Riley asked.

"Yes. And no," I said. "You?"

He nodded. "I suppose it depends what's waiting for us."

With a strong kick, he started the bike revving. Lights flickered on the screen in front of him.

And we were off.

CHAPTER 48

We were both pretty quiet on the trip back. I swung wildly between fizzing excitement and racking terror.

"Riley?"

"Yeah?"

"What do we do if things aren't back to normal at home?"

He paused before answering. "We work out how they're not normal and find some way to fix them."

Typical scientist. So calm and matter-of-fact about it all. My first reaction would be to scream and pound the ground, tear at my hair, shout about how unfair it was to the sky and sea and everything in between. Then break into a flood of tears that could drown the whole world. Or something like that.

I watched Riley work the controls with cool efficiency, his expression blank. He didn't seem to feel things as intensely as me. On the other hand, it was good to know that, if the worst did happen, at least one of us wouldn't fall into a heap.

About twenty minutes in, I saw him frowning at the controls and taking slow breaths in and out. *Oh no!*

"Riley? What's wrong?" I so didn't want to hear his answer.

"According to the co-ordinates on the screen, Sydney should be right beneath us."

"Should be?"

He nodded. "All we have to do is look down."

"Down there?" I pointed at my feet.

He nodded.

"What's the problem?"

A pause. "I can't look," he said.

"Okay," I said. "We'll look together, shall we? On three? One...two..."

We both peered over the side...into oblivion. We saw nothing but murky white. A wisp of cloud blocked our view below. Quite quickly, though, it began to break up. I glimpsed blues and greys and snatches of colour behind the white.

"Is that water I can see down there?" I said.

"Yes. And boats. Or no. Maybe not. Those sails look too big."

"And fixed. They're not moving in the breeze."

We smiled at each other, hopeful about what it meant.

As the last of the clouds blew away, we saw...the Sydney Opera House. Back on the point of the harbour, where it should be. Our city was back.

We were home.

CHAPTER 49

"We did it! We changed time back!" I shouted.

"I wonder if everything is exactly the same," said Riley. "Or maybe some things will still be a little different? Perhaps for the better?" He was oddly big-eyed and smiley at that thought.

"Well, I guess there's only one way to find out." So now it was me voicing that annoying phrase, but oddly I didn't feel the least bit irritated with myself.

Riley set us down in his backyard on the same night we had originally left. By the clocks here, barely minutes had passed since we first flew off on our travels, but in our time we had been away for almost six weeks.

The herb garden in Riley's backyard still looked the same. And there was Riley's dad's house. And the garage with the red door to the home lab. *So far, so good.*

As soon as the bike stopped, Riley jumped off and ran up to the back porch, pressing his face to the window.

"Dad's there, just where we left him." He seemed a tad disappointed.

"Yes, and...?"

"I just thought maybe Mum might be, too."

"Didn't they break up a while back?"

"Yeah, but..." he said.

"Is this why you took the trip through time? So your parents might get back together?"

"No," he said brushing his fingers through his hair. "I just thought, you know, when you change something in the past, even something small, the cascade of events means all kinds of things may be different as a result. And you never know your luck."

Luck? That sounded strangely unscientific, especially coming from Riley.

"Luck can be bad as well as good," I said. Which got me thinking—and fretting—about my own home. "I wonder if everything's okay back at mine."

"Do you want me to come with you and see?" Riley asked.

"No, I'll be fine." I could see Riley was dying to go inside. "Go say hi to your dad."

He grinned. "Well, if there are any problems, come back."

"There won't be," I said. "I can feel it. Everything's back to normal."

I was excited now. The thought of seeing my family was thrilling. But then, it felt kind of weird to be leaving Riley after spending so much time with him.

"Well, err...I guess I'll see you at school, then," I said.

"Yeah, see you round. Oh, one more thing?"

"Yes?"

"If I had to be lost in time, I can't think of anyone I'd rather have been with."

I expected him to look away or at the ground after saying something as embarrassing as that, but he kept looking right into my eyes.

"I can't think of too many other people I'd rather have gone with either," I said.

And there was this vibe. Strange and awkward and sort of exciting. He stepped forward and pulled me into a tight hug. I so was not expecting that. It was warm in his embrace and his hair smelt of Ancient Egyptian spice. With a hint of tomb.

I thought he'd give me a quick hug and step back quickly. But he kept hold of me and then his lips were on mine in a kiss that was soft and sweet. And unexpected.

"I'll see you at school tomorrow," he said.

I nodded. "Yeah."

He walked towards his back door. "Oh, and Maddy?"

"Yeah?"

"We can't tell anyone about this trip."

"Of course not," I said. *But can I tell anyone about the kiss?* Which was somehow even more amazing.

"We'll talk more in a day or so," he said.

"Cool."

Cool? Seriously? I never said cool.

I ran home as fast as I could in a long white dress and reed sandals. I had a few funny looks from fellow joggers I passed, but I didn't care. I was so happy to see the neighbourhood just as it was before. The same terrace houses and cute little cottages with electric lights and gardens and mail boxes. *Hang on!* Number 32 was different. It was a double-storey brick house now. I could have sworn it was a small blue cottage before, with a mermaid statue in the garden? *Hmmm.* Perhaps not everything was the same?

Would my home be the same?

A block away, I sped up. I was three houses away...two— both were gloriously familiar. Up ahead were the agapanthus flowers outside our brick fence, their purple heads strewn on the ground, snapped off by passing kids on their way home from school. *All as it should be!*

Hope surged into my throat, an achy lump threatening to burst forth in sobs as I first spotted our house. The lights were on inside and shadows moved about behind the curtains. Someone was home. I was *so* happy about that.

I knocked on the front door. It was the same wonderful door I knew so well, with a bit of old sticky tape on the door knocker left there from last year's Christmas wreath.

I waited. No one came. I knocked more insistently.

Gran opened the door, frowning. "Would it kill you to take your key once in a while? Save my poor old legs?"

I launched myself at her in the biggest hug ever. She couldn't understand why I seemed so pleased to see her when I'd only left home a short time before. Or why I was dressed in a white linen gown, edged with Ancient Egyptian sand. I babbled something about rehearsing for a school play—I barely knew what I was saying. I was just so happy and relieved that everything was back to the way I'd left it.

"Hi sweetie," said Mum, emerging from the kitchen. "I'm too tired to work tonight. Gran and I thought we'd watch *Girls in the City* and have hot chocolate. Want to join us?"

Did I ever!

CHAPTER 50

At school the next day, I was so happy to see my friends Lauren, Courtney and Chi that I let Lauren go on at length about a new website she'd found with "cool hair extensions".

"What, no snarky comments or eye rolls?" she said.

"Me? Never!"

Nothing could dampen my spirits. Not even my science teacher, Mr Johnson, who seemed unusually grumpy and snapped at me several times in class for no reason. He'd be even crankier after break time, I knew, when Riley broke the bad news to him.

I can't remember whether I went looking for him or he came for me, but Riley and I found each other under the fig tree by the library. We tried to pretend everything was normal, but we were both smiling too much and super self-conscious after that kiss.

"Shall we go and see him now?" I said. I didn't need to explain who the "him" was.

Riley nodded, though he looked less keen.

Johnno was in the science staff room and, thankfully, he was alone.

"I...err...am going to have to withdraw my project for the science fair this year," Riley said. "It's not ready."

Johnno folded his arms and wrinkled his brow. "You still have a couple of weeks. We could put in an interim plan and submit the revised spec later."

"It won't be ready even then. I'm sorry."

Johnno wasn't happy. He'd got his acceptance speech word perfect by now, I reckoned, and had already spent quite a bit of time imagining the looks on other teachers' faces when his student won the trophy for the fourth year running.

"You should have told me earlier." He sounded snippy as he gathered up his files and crammed them into a battered briefcase. "Maybe I could have helped you get it over the line. What is the project anyway? Perhaps there's still time to fix it?"

"No, it's...err...not working. And it won't be ready for a long time."

"Can you tell me what the gist was?"

Riley hesitated. "I'd rather not say."

And that was why I was here. I couldn't let Riley hint at the truth, no matter how much pressure Johnno put on him.

Our science teacher sat on his desk and gnawed at the skin around his thumb, laser staring at Riley, who couldn't meet his eye.

"Have you got anything else you're working on we can submit?" Johnno asked.

Riley shook his head.

"Well, it's disappointing," Johnno said.

"For you and Riley both, Mr Johnson," I added sadly-not-sadly.

Our teacher shifted his focus to me. I didn't look away, challenging him to say more.

Back in the playground, Riley kicked the silver seats, hard—a show of temper I'd rarely seen from him, even with all we'd been through.

"It's for the best," I said.

"Yeah, I know." He sounded almost aggressive.

"This is a new experience for you, isn't it?" I said. "Not winning."

"It doesn't feel great."

"Welcome to the world of humans."

It couldn't have been easy. His invention deserved heaps of scientific recognition, which he would never get—not without risking the future of the entire world. So the least I could do was give him some validation now.

"The time machine was amazing, Riley," I said. "I know that holding it back from Johnno and everyone else took a lot of strength. So, in honour of your great achievement by NOT releasing said brilliant creation, possibly THE most brilliant creation in the history of brilliant creations, I present you, Riley Sinclair—" I plucked a yellow weed from the grass and offered it to him "—with the Service to Humanity award."

He grinned and his cheeks pinked up.

"Thank you for that eminent award," he said, playing along. "But I think this year it's only right it should be a joint award, shared with Madison Bryant, without whose courage and strength, smart mind and mouth, things would have turned out quite differently."

As he tore another weed out and handed it to me, I felt my cheeks burning too.

Riley looked into my eyes, and I looked into his. And I had this feeling like something was about to happen. A thrill shot through me as he reached behind my head and...

The school bell rang. *What the—?* He whipped his hand back as if it had been burnt, awkwardness returning. "Thanks for that award, Maddy. I know it's best for everyone if the time machine doesn't get any other awards."

I hoped he would still think so as he watched some other kid step up to claim the title of Young Scientist of the Year this time. Or when the science department shifted the trophies in the cabinet back to fill the empty space they'd made for the trophy he wouldn't be winning.

"Now that you aren't releasing your creation to the world, I guess people in the future, like Azizi, won't find out about it. And so he won't be able to come back in a machine based on your model?"

"In theory," said Riley. "Although, that depends on how he found out about it in the first place."

"Only you and I know about it," I said. "And I'm not going to tell anyone. Are you?"

He shook his head. "No."

"So we should be safe?"

I intended it as a statement of fact, but it sounded more like a question.

It was weird being close to Riley now. My lips tingled with the memory of our kiss.

But he didn't make any more moves to repeat it. I thought about launching myself at him, but somehow I never did. We slipped back to being friends again. Like it had never happened.

I put the kiss down to a weird moment between us, like a scientific glitch, due to the emotional overload of being home.

CHAPTER 51

During the first days after our return, I kept looking for things that had changed. And there were a few small things. A new garden bed in full bloom popped up in the playground—I couldn't explain that. Some people looked a bit different. A few kids I'd never seen before turned up in our classes, and we had a new Phys Ed master. But everything else was the same, as far as I could tell.

"How have these changes happened?" I asked Riley.

He opened his mouth to answer, but I put a hand up to stop him and jumped in myself. "Is it because of the toothpaste? People who would have died of tooth decay got to have kids, who in turn had kids, who would never have been in the world before. And they had kids, and so on and so on."

"The ripple effect going on and on...yeah, I guess so," Riley said. "Or there could have been corruptions on the timeline somewhere along the way."

Corruptions? I'd never heard him mention those before. They didn't sound good.

"What 'corruptions'?" I asked.

"I mean someone deliberately changing something on a past timeline to bring about a particular outcome in the future. Like we did on our second time through the Egyptian time period to bring Australia back."

"So, manipulating future events through changes in the past."

Something about that idea brought about a fluttering in my chest. This was seriously bad news.

"But hopefully that's not the case here," he said.

One thing had changed for the worse for me. Ms Braithwaite, our year adviser, was now friends with Johnno. Before our trip, I'd lied to her about why I was late for class, knowing she wouldn't check the facts with Mr Johnson because they didn't get along. But in this present, they were friends and she did mention it to him. So I copped it.

"The school takes a dim view of students lying to teachers, Maddy," Ms Braithwaite said. "You can't lie your way out of problems in life. You have to do better than that."

I got a week of afternoon detention. Which sucked. And because I was kept late at school, I missed some key choir rehearsals at the Opera House so Mr Franklin replaced me in the a cappella. It was a heavy blow.

"Sorry, Maddy," he said. "These final rehearsals are too important to miss. Maybe next year you can be part of it."

I'd put the world to rights, but my own life was another story.

When Lauren asked Riley to come watch us sing with the choir at the Opera House, I tried to be happy about it. My two good friends getting together—what was not to like about that? Riley and I had shared a single kiss, but we were still just friends. That was all we were meant to be, it seemed.

The concert was awesome. A thousand kids from the state's schools singing harmonies in the main Opera House recital hall produced a sound that was seriously other-worldly. As

I sang, in the middle of them all, I could hardly tell whether the music came from my throat or my soul.

Mum, Dad and Gran watched from seats high up at the back of the hall. Mum had tears in her eyes all night, Gran said. Dad had come back from his overseas job specially to see it. At the interval, I saw him up there waving a pirate flag to get my attention. *So embarrassing. He still thinks I'm ten!*

Afterwards, the choir and all our friends and family gathered on the Opera House forecourt for a debrief. While they enthused about the performances—especially the a cappella I wasn't in, which got a roar from the audience—I found myself alone with Riley, looking out at Sydney Harbour, liquorice black and glossy with colourful lights bobbing on the surface.

"It was a bit different last time we were here," I said.

"Yeah," he said. "Good to see the Harbour Bridge back."

There were heaps of stars tonight but more twinkle from traffic flowing across the bridge.

"What do you think our Egyptian friends would make of all this?" I said.

Riley chuckled and shook his blond curls, which looked silvery in this light. "You were really something, Maddy."

"Thanks. We've been rehearsing for that concert for about six months."

"I don't mean the music," he said. "Though that was good too. In Egypt, you were...spectacular."

Wow! And I had this weird sense he was about to make some kind of move. I was surprised how much I wanted him to.

"Maddy?"

"Yes, Riley?"

"I was wondering—" he licked his lips and looked down, studying the concrete "—whether you wanted to..."

"Yes?"

"There you are, guys!" Lauren burst in, throwing an arm around my shoulders. "That was a-mazing!"

The three of us discussed the concert and laughed together, and the moment passed.

What had Riley been about to ask me? Was it to go out on an actual date with him? To be a thing, the two of us, like boyfriend-girlfriend? Or was he going to ask if I knew what the seating capacity was in the recital hall?

Watching Riley and Lauren talking—her mouth moving, him nodding—I had to fight the urge to squeeze between them. He met my eye briefly and smiled but then turned back to her. She was laying it on thick—like Egyptian honey on dates—really going for it, as she'd said she would, to try to get Riley for herself.

All I could do was stand by and watch—like watching the Sydney skyline melting all over again—and smile lamely. Lauren was my best friend. Interrupting her now to spoil her chances with Riley would be seriously uncool.

But Riley didn't have to keep standing there, smiling and twinkling at her like that. Not if he wanted to be with me. He could step away. Any time.

He's still there...still...there...

Now the two of them were laughing at something I really didn't find funny at all. And Jamie Fletcher popped into my head.

Jamie, with the mystic green eyes and over-confident smile. Before I went to Egypt, I had kind of a crush on him.

Lauren said if I wanted any chance with him, I'd have to dress and act differently—be a completely different person. I couldn't do that. I would have felt ridiculous, like I'd dressed up for Halloween. And then to go to all that effort, only to have him dump me—like he dumped everyone—and make me look like a love fool in front of all the kids at school! In front of Riley! *No way.* I didn't have the confidence to even try.

Now, though, I felt differently. Why shouldn't I consider Jamie as a potential date? Forget the hairdo and cute outfit to accentuate my best features! I would go as myself. He could take it or leave it. I'd been totally myself with Phoenix and, when I disappeared, he sent boats to all corners of the map looking for me. If I was good enough for the ruler of Egypt and of all lands on Earth on one timeline, I should be good enough for Jamie.

If he didn't like the real me, well...*whatever! No big deal!* But I was happy to give it a go.

"I wonder what Jamie Fletcher's up to tonight," I blurted out, mid conversation.

Riley's smile vanished.

"Jamie who?" asked Lauren.

She was reminding me of my emphatic words before we left for Egypt—that Jamie meant nothing to me. And rightly so. He passed from girl to girl quicker than the latest gossip. In the museum, he hadn't exactly been friendly. Well, not to start with, anyway. I couldn't help smiling as I recalled how he'd pretended to be an expert on Egyptology to get my attention.

CHAPTER 52

The next day at school, I found myself looking for Jamie in English and Science and around the corridors. But he was a no-show.

"I can't see Jamie Fletcher around anywhere," I said to Courtney as we packed up for recess. "He must be sick or on holiday."

"Who?" Courtney asked.

I chuckled. "Yeah, funny."

"No, seriously. Who is Jamie...Fletcher?"

Oh.

He was one of the things that hadn't been put right in our travels. But was it because of toothpaste and the ripple effect? Or was it a "corruption" of the timeline, with someone interfering with his past to change his future? Riley shrugged when I asked him.

That evening, the two of us were on shift at the soup kitchen when someone I wasn't expecting appeared in the queue with a tray. Peterson.

"Soup or stew?" I said.

"Soup please, Madison."

I slopped the food into his bowl and gave him a side serve of dirty look. "Would you like some Egyptian spice with that?" I said.

He grinned, then took his tray and sat down to eat with the others, laughing and talking with them as though this was exactly where, and when, he belonged. I was super-distracted as I served the rest of our clients. As soon as he finished his meal, I caught his eye and gave him an unsubtle head-jerk towards the front door, signalling we should go outside.

"I need to take a break," I told our shift manager. She stepped in to cover for me.

"Riley!" I called to my friend, washing up in the kitchen. He took off his apron and came too.

When Peterson entered the alleyway, we were waiting.

"Who are you and what are you up to?" I demanded.

"My name is Peterson," he said. "And I'm here to ask if everything is as it should be."

"Mostly," said Riley.

"Some things have changed," I said. "A boy at school disappeared. Jamie Fletcher."

He nodded slowly, taking that in. For some reason, I had a feeling it wasn't news to him.

"And how do you feel about that?" he asked. *A weird question.*

"Well, not good. To think a fellow student has been erased from existence because of our trip through time."

"Is he just a fellow student, or someone special to you?" he persisted.

I was oddly aware of two pairs of eyes—Riley's and Peterson's—waiting on my answer.

"No more special than any other student," I said. "The guy's not my favourite person, but it hardly seems fair he lost his chance at a life because of what we did."

But, hang on, weren't we the ones meant to be asking the questions here?

I turned the interrogation back on Peterson, asking what he'd been up to in Egypt, how he'd got there, why he hadn't told us the truth when we first met him.

He was "a friend", he said, with "an interest in time travel". As far as I was concerned those answers told me nothing and only raised more questions.

"How did you come to have our time machine?" I demanded to know. We'd been chasing him when we found it in the fields. "Did you get it back off Azizi?"

"No, I was the one who took it."

Riley looked as shocked as me at that answer.

"Why would you do that?" I was furious now. "Do you have any idea what you put us through, worrying about where it was and whether we'd ever get home again?"

He paced, considering his words. "I did it so Azizi wouldn't take it."

"So you knew Azizi wanted it?" asked Riley. "How?"

"That's beside the point," he said.

"No, that *is* the point," I said. "Can we trust you or can we not?"

"You can absolutely trust me. I was protecting you. I knew he'd come after the machine."

"How?" Riley asked. "Was this not your first time through?"

What the—? What exactly did that question mean? The two of them seemed tuned into something I wasn't getting.

"Let's just say, I had an idea of what he was up to," said Peterson.

"And do you have an idea who he is?" I asked. "Because I had this weird feeling I knew him."

I tried to recall the sour smell around him. It was so familiar but I just couldn't place it.

"No, I don't know who he is," said Peterson. That was a lie—one hundred per cent. I could tell. But why would he lie?

I shot more questions at the guy. Occasionally, Riley chimed in with a question of his own. His were mostly technical about time travel. Peterson side-stepped them all.

"You want to get Jamie Fletcher back?" he asked, boomeranging back to the original subject.

I nodded. "Do you know how we can do that?"

"I might have an idea. But it will involve another trip through time to fix the Fletchers' timeline, which has been corrupted."

Corrupted? That was the second time I'd heard that phrase in relation to time travel. I didn't like it any better this time.

"No way!" I said firmly. "Riley and I are not going anywhere near the time machine again. Ever! Are we, Riley?"

Riley didn't answer. He just stood there, eyes locked on Peterson.

"Riley!" I snapped.

"No, we shouldn't time travel again," he said. "It's too risky."

It was the right answer, but nowhere near the right tone. Especially when you considered that our first trip through time had almost destroyed the world as we knew it.

Peterson chewed on that for a moment. I thought he might try to persuade us to change our minds and take the trip. But he nodded, then said: "Okay, fine."

Shouting and loud metallic clangs came from the kitchen. Then a crash. We rushed back inside to help break up a fight between some of our clients. By the time we'd sorted it out, Peterson was gone.

"Son of a jackal!" I borrowed one of Razi's phrases. "Where did he go?" Or *when* might have been a better question.

We got our answer when we cleaned up later. Riley found a paper serviette with a message written on it from Peterson.

"If you change your minds, and want Jamie back, you must travel to the place where the desert horse sweats and the king draws more than water from a stone."

"What does that mean?" I said.

"I think it's a clue to where we need to go next if we want to bring Jamie Fletcher back."

"So the guy drops a riddle in our laps and leaves," I said, annoyed. "Does he think this is some kind of game? That erasing a person from existence is just an amusing conundrum to be solved?"

"I guess we might as well try to figure out the answer," said Riley. "Where the desert horse sweats and the king draws more than water from a stone."

"Hang on," I said. "A desert horse is a camel. We should know that after being in Egypt for so long." (Though, oddly, I hadn't seen any camels while I was there.)

Riley smiled and nodded.

"Is he saying we have to go back to Ancient Egypt again?" I asked.

"I don't think so."

"Riley, do you know what the answer is?"

"Maybe," he said.

"Well, just tell me. This is someone's life we're talking about. It's not a game!"

"All right," he said, "well, it's—"

"No, wait, don't. I can do this."

I took a breath and tried to think. Where the camel sweats and the king draws more than water from a stone. Hmmm.

Could you draw water from a stone? Not without some pretty heavy-duty mining equipment, I reckoned. So...so...?

"Hey, what was that story about someone drawing a sword from a stone—the one true king?" I said.

The answer came to me as I spoke the words. It was King Arthur and his knights of Camelot. I'd played my own version of it when I was young, with a plastic sword shoved into a pile of cushions.

"Desert horse sweats...camel...hot," I said. "Camelot. Is that the answer?"

Riley nodded, with a big smile.

"But what does it mean?" I said. "Camelot's not a real place, is it?"

"I think it means we have to time travel again to medieval England, to the site of the mythical Camelot."

I shook my head. "No, I'm not stepping into that machine ever again and neither should you," I said.

"You're right."

"We should destroy it, bury the parts in separate places a long way from each other, along with any plans you've written down for how to build it, so it can never ever be reassembled."

"Yeah, we can do that," said Riley. "But then we won't get

Jamie Fletcher back. Can you live with that?"

I had the feeling Riley would have no problem living in a Jamie Fletcher-free world. But would I?

The house was quiet when I got home. Gran was in bed, Mum was in her office working, Dad had gone back to Dubai again, way too soon. There was half a boiled egg on a bread board on the kitchen bench. Gran had probably left it there for me in case I wanted a snack when I got home. I wasn't as big a fan of boiled eggs as her, especially when they looked grey, slimy and gross, as this one did. I threw it in the bin and washed the bread board.

Then, I switched off the lamp in the hallway and went to my room. Lying on my bed in the dark, I thought about eggs and how they didn't have much scent, unless they were rotten. That scent—rotten egg gas...

I sat up. That was the sour scent I could smell on Azizi— rotten eggs. The school science lab smelled like that most of the time. It was part of the reason I wasn't keen on science.

But what did it mean?

I was too tired to figure it out.

A noise on the street outside made me peer through a gap in the curtains. A possum darted along our fence, backlit by moonlight. I sighed and leaned over to close the curtain completely. As I did, my eye caught movement on the street outside.

Was someone out there, watching the house? I was almost sure I'd seen a man in dark clothes peering this way. A burglar, perhaps? No. More than likely, it was just someone walking home.

But I couldn't shake the feeling—call it paranoia, or intuition—that whoever it was, they were connected with our trip, the full consequences of which had yet to be revealed. And in that moment, I knew—as clearly as I'd ever known anything—that the time to enjoy my home, my friends and family, my bubble baths and hot chocolate, was now.

Because although I was desperate to be finished with time travel, I sensed that time travel was not yet done with me.

❊ ❊ ❊

Cloaked by darkness on the street, he watched the light go out in the upstairs room.

"Good night, Madison," he whispered. "We'll meet again. I know exactly where and when."

ᴀCKNOWLEDGEMENTS

A book is never truly a solo project. Although there's only one name on the cover, I couldn't have completed this without a lot of help from my family, colleagues and friends.

First thanks go to Andy Cohen, my partner, for being my sounding board in the early stages, one of my first readers and an eagle-eyed sub-editor. As a writer working through a series for over a decade—perhaps closer to fifteen years—I've had a lot of ups and downs, which Andy has seen me through. The last book took five years to write with a lot of prompting from him. Thankfully, when I wrote those two glorious words, THE END, I realised I'd written not one, but two books. So The Time Travel Chronicles became a six-book series.

Thanks to my daughters, Alex and Tash, whose love of stories as young children inspired me to write something they'd enjoy. As they've grown up, they've become wonderful writers themselves and strong story deconstructors. They're always my first editors and approach my work with a sharp analytical eye and generous heart.

And Tash designed the original mood covers, pulling out the essence of each story and turning it into a compelling, artistic image. Her covers were the starting point for Holly Dunn's wonderful series of cover designs.

Thanks also to Sarah Beaudette, an award-winning writer, who took on the epic task of being my story editor. I appreciated her honesty and encouragement and know the books are much better for having had her on board.

I owe gratitude, too, to my writing teacher and mentor on this book, Kathryn Heyman, whose amazing eye for story structure and development was very useful. And to my secret writing group—you know who you are—who've had my back for almost a decade. Their skill and beta-ing of my work has made me lift my writing game.

Early drafts can be tough. Thanks to those who read the book in its raw stages—Dale Cash and Cornelia Vallis and their offspring! Your encouragement spurred me on.

And thanks to you, reader. In this world crammed with so many books, you tried mine and took this journey with Madison, Riley and me.

I hope you enjoyed reading it as much as I did writing it.

HISTORICAL NOTE

The Time Travel Chronicles is a YA science fiction series. However, because my characters travel to real places and periods in our time, it's also historical fiction.

Which bits are historical and which fiction?

I spent months reading widely about each period in the series before sitting down to write, generally filling an A4 pad and more with notes taken from a variety of sources. My aim was not to focus on the real-life characters and moments in history, but on the way ordinary people lived—the food, play, law and order and courting rituals. I wanted my readers to have an immersive experience, to feel as if they were walking along those dusty ancient streets.

I didn't nominate a particular year or location in *Secrets of the Nile*. This was to give myself maximum flexibility to tell the story. This has been my approach to history throughout the series—to set the scene in as gritty and realistic a way as I can, bringing to life as many true details (especially the gory ones) as I can find about each period, while allowing myself licence to move within the landscape and time period however best serves the story.

Let's face it, if I stuck too closely to reality, this would be a history book! And Madison, a girl, wouldn't have had any of these adventures in time. Throughout most of history, females were restricted to managing the home and family life. And that is NOT the book series I wanted to write.

BOOK 2 PREVIEW

THE TIME TRAVEL CHRONICLES

Fight like there's no tomorrow

REVENGE OF THE BLACK KNIGHT

PAULENE TURNER

CHAPTER 1

When my science teacher, Mr Johnson—Johnno as we students called him—asked me to explain Einstein's theory of special relativity in a nutshell, I thought he was joking.

First, he knows I'm no science nerd. And second, I was pretty sure that theory, which great scary-looking books had been written about, would not fit into any nutshell. Not unless it was a really, really big nut. He had to be kidding, right?

So, I answered: "Relativity? Well, Mr Einstein was *related* to Mrs Einstein through marriage. And was father to Edwin, Edwina and, err, Egbert. They were his closest *relative*-ities."

A few seconds' pause, then my class at Crows Nest High cracked up, hooting and howling—any excuse for a distraction from work. As usual, David Payne brayed like a donkey and pretended to fall off his chair. He always goes too far, that guy.

I am quite a funny girl, if I do say so myself. But even I couldn't believe I'd get such a big laugh at what was such an obvious and, if I'm honest, rather lame joke. It must have been the way I told it. Unfortunately, not everyone found me so amusing.

"Do you think this class is a joke, Madison?" Johnno asked, his lips pressed into a tense line. That shut everyone up. (Except Donkey Brain who *hee-haw*ed several more times into the silence before, finally, ceasing.)

"No, of course not, Mr Johnson," I answered.

Well, paint my face pink and call me a lobster! He was serious! He expected *me*, playful, non-sciency, drama-loving Madison Bryant, to summarise Einstein's theory? Even my mate, brain box Riley Sinclair, who'd won every science award in his age group and many beyond, would have trouble doing that.

"Okay, then," said Johnno, "what's your answer? I'm sure you have one as, no doubt, you worked diligently on it at home last night like you were asked to?"

It had been a homework assignment? I missed that. It must have been given while I was thinking about something else, which was pretty much any time after Johnno's "Good morning, class".

"What's my answer? Umm...?"

At this point, I would usually have confessed that I didn't have a clue. But I could see Johnno was in no mood for my brand of ignorance, charming though it might be. If I didn't say something along the right lines, I would have detention for sure. Maybe a whole week of it.

I rested my chin on my hands and narrowed my eyes, as if thinking deeply. In reality, I was watching what went on behind Johnno's back where *Operation Save Maddy* was underway.

First, Riley used sign language to send the answer to Chi. She's fluent in signing as she has a deaf brother. Chi muttered to Courtney, beside her, who extracted a mobile phone from her tightly twirled hair and, with the fastest digits in town, texted the answer to Lauren's class email. When the message hit her screen, Lauren enlarged the text and swivelled her laptop around so I could read it over Johnno's shoulder. All of this took about seven point five seconds.

"Err, well..." I stammered, "basically time and length are relative to speed."

"That's right, Madison." Mr Johnson seemed surprised.

I flashed Riley a grin of thanks.

Then came the kicker: "But do you know what it means?" my teacher asked. "Can you elaborate?"

Basically no and yes. No, I didn't have the slightest idea what it meant. But could I elaborate? Could I what? Improvised elaboration in extreme circumstances was my specialty.

"Well, as you know, that theory is one of science's most important discoveries," I began pompously. "It's called *Einstein's* theory. Because it was Mr Einstein who came up with it. And it's a *theory* of relativity because, although a lot of clever brains have examined it, it's still not proven beyond a reasonable doubt. And *special*...why? Well, if you have to ask that, you haven't been listening to Mr Johnson's fine lectures."

At this point, David spluttered into laughter again, setting off others around the class. Johnno looked irritated but it bought me more thinking time.

"So, let's see—" I counted off my answers on my fingers "—I've covered Einstein's...Theory...Special? Sorry, I missed out 'of', which means...belonging to...or deriving from."

Cackling turned to full-on jeering around the class. Johnno closed his eyes, as if in pain.

"That's enough, Maddy," Johnno said. "Riley, could you take it from there. Put us out of our misery."

I sat down, outwardly disappointed, inwardly delighted. Somehow, I had slithered out of that one. When it came to talking my way out of trouble, no-one could touch me. Except perhaps my gran, who was a gambler and taught me pretty much all I know.

Riley explained the complex science behind Einstein's theory to the class. I tried to tune in, but it was drier than a camel's top lip. Soon, the words blurred into one indistinct sound and I just focused on his face: his skin smooth and lightly tanned; his lips as red as a crunchy apple; his eyes dark blue and mysterious, like twilight. And the unruly golden locks. It was easy to see why so many girls and guys fancied him. Though not me, of course. We were just good friends. And when I got between him and those who went gaga over him—especially my best friend, Lauren—I was only trying to help him focus on science. For the benefit of all humankind. Not for any other reason.

Riley was still talking. Around the room, the kids had zoned out and struggled not to doze off. *Poor Riley.* He had so much to give, but no idea how to give it. Then it hit me. Maybe one day there'd be a career in this for me. Riley and super-smart people like him had all the knowledge; I had all the chat. I could *Help the Nerds with their Words.* Mmm, catchy!

"Madison, what are you looking so pleased about?" Mr Johnson stuck a pin in my happy balloon.

"Well, I was just enjoying Riley's explanation, sir," I said.

He tilted his head. "Really? So could you summarise it for us?"

"Ahhhh."

And then the buzzer went for lunch break. It zizzed the comatose kids back to life. They rocketed out of their chairs and crammed their books and devices into their bags. Most were halfway down the corridor before they'd fully woken up.

I did the slow not-my-fault shoulder shrug to Johnno then began packing up, pausing briefly to touch fists with my friends in thanks for getting me out of a tight spot. I was about to step through the doorway to freedom when Johnno called: "See me after school, Madison. You can give me the summary then."

What? That sucked. Now I'd be late for hockey training. Which meant I'd be benched during the game later this week. All that hard work being devious and I was on detention anyway!

ABOUT THE AUTHOR

Paulene Turner lives in Sydney, Australia, with her husband, twin daughters and twin pugs. A graduate of the Faber Academy, she writes novels, short stories and scripts for the stage and screen. Her short stories have appeared in magazines and anthologies in the UK, US and Australia. As well as writing short plays, she also directs them for Short and Sweet, Sydney. She has worked as a journalist in Sydney and London.

Secrets of the Nile is her first novel, with five more to come in The Time Travel Chronicles series.

If you wish to hear more about Paulene's writing, you can sign up to her mailing list at pauleneturnerwrites.com.